SAN DIEGO NOIR

San Diego Noir

EDITED BY Maryelizabeth Hart

This collection is comprised of works of fiction. All names, characters, places, and incidents are the product of the authors' imaginations.
Any resemblance to real events or persons, living or dead, is entirely
coincidental.

ALSO IN THE AKASHIC NOIR SERIES:

FORTHCOMING:

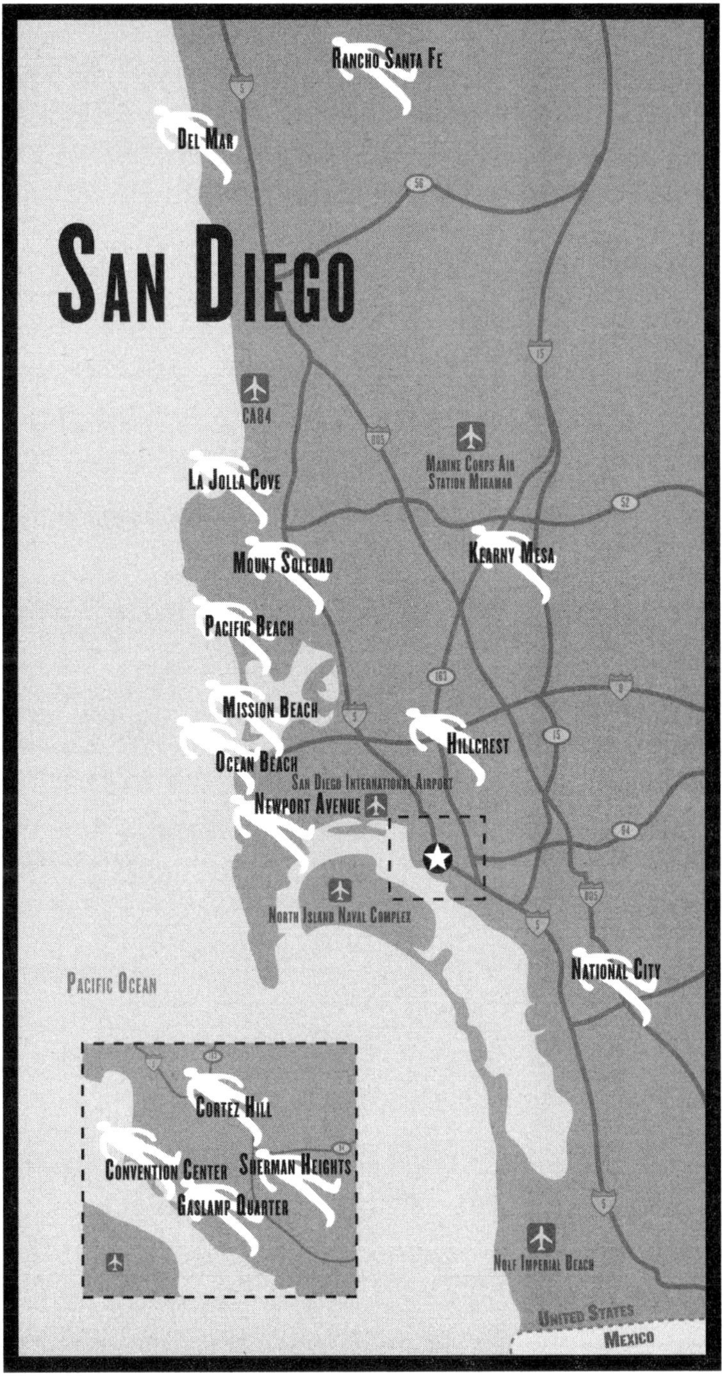

Rancho Santa Fe
Del Mar
San Diego
CA84
La Jolla Cove
Marine Corps Air Station Miramar
Mount Soledad
Kearny Mesa
Pacific Beach
Mission Beach
Hillcrest
Ocean Beach
San Diego International Airport
Newport Avenue
North Island Naval Complex
National City
Pacific Ocean
Cortez Hill
Convention Center
Sherman Heights
Gaslamp Quarter
Nolf Imperial Beach
United States
Mexico

TABLE OF CONTENTS

PART III: LIFE'S A BEACH

PART IV: BOUNDARIES & BORDERS

INTRODUCTION
"America's Finest City"

The southwesternmost metropolis in the contiguous United States, resting a mere forty feet above sea level, tends to garner positive national attention. San Diego is home to the world-famous San Diego Zoo, Balboa Park (with its history reaching back to the 1915–16 Panama-California Exposition), temperate climes, and a sunny reputation. It is also the home of shooter Brenda Ann "I Don't Like Mondays" Spencer, disgraced Congressman Randy "Duke" Cunningham, and San Diego County medical examiner–turned-killer Kristin Rossum.

Joseph Wambaugh chronicled crime crossing the border in 1984's *Lines and Shadows*, a saga about the challenges facing the Border Crime Task Force that continues today, even after the squad whose efforts it chronicled has been disbanded. My first strong sense of the city's noir undertones came in the late 1980s, when La Jolla socialite Betty Broderick fatally shot her ex-husband Dan and his new wife Linda Kolkena, after gaining entrance to her ex's new home with a key she'd taken from her daughter's purse. (The incident where she drove a vehicle into his home was separate.) When Mysterious Galaxy, the bookstore I co-own, opened its first location in Clairemont in 1994, the Clairemont Killer, Cleophus Prince Jr., had already been convicted of killing six women in the neighborhood—including a murder in the apartment complex my family briefly resided in.

San Diego has a strong military presence dating back to the establishment in the early 1800s of what is now Old Town Historical Park, along with army and naval intelligence divisions, the nation's first military flying school (remember *Top Gun?*), and active ports and support industries. San Diego was where Shawn Nelson stole an M60 Patton tank in May 1995 and drove it down the freeway until forcibly stopped by police. Downtown, once filled with quick entertainment for military men passing through, has risen to meet and exceed the community center dreams that Ray Bradbury and company conceived for Horton Plaza . . . although the locals still recall the Gaslamp Quarter's not-too-distant history as a haven for tattoo parlors and hookers.

The city is sometimes referred to as San Diego–Tijuana, a conurbation, with all its attendant border issues—illustrated in true noir fashion in Orson Welles's classic *Touch of Evil*, adapted from *Badge of Evil* by Whit Masterson. A ways up the coast from the border lies the grave of Raymond Chandler, who resided in the wealthy enclave of La Jolla from 1946 to 1959; that area masquerades as "Esmeralda" in *Playback*, his final Philip Marlowe novel. Robert B. Parker's Spenser visits Esmeralda in *Stardust*.

San Diego has been the setting for a number of television and film mysteries, including the unforgettable chase across the rooftops of the Hotel del Coronado in *The Stunt Man*; and has been the backdrop for investigations by the protagonists of *Simon & Simon*, *Veronica Mars*, and most recently *Terriers*. While the city can exist as a cohesive whole, drawn together to rally against fires, mudslides, or rival sports teams, like many places in the American West, it is a metropolis of a variety of individual neighborhoods whose boundaries have slowly grown into each other. The upper-crust concerns of Del Mar and its racetrack have little in common with the idiosyncratic habits of Ocean Beach residents. The working-class neighborhood of Kearny Mesa is only minimally impacted by the surrounding high-tech development areas like Sorrento Valley. And while some San Diegans welcome the annual influx of 150,000 attendees at the largest celebration of popular culture, Comic-Con International, others bemoan the invasion of aliens and superheroes.

Through the stories in this volume, readers can visit many of the popular local sites, as well as some prosaic areas that are more familiar to residents than tourists. The contributors cover a wide range of the diversity of this Pacific Rim city. Don Winslow, Astrid Bear, and Diane Clark include the town's military history in their stories. Ken Kuhlken, Debra Ginsberg, and Taffy Cannon weave tales that could perhaps occur in any city—but are colored with the particular scents and sounds of San Diego. The protagonists of the stories by T. Jefferson Parker, Jeffrey J. Mariotte, Martha C. Lawrence, and Cameron Pierce Hughes all make a living because of crime. Morgan Hunt, Gar Anthony Haywood, and Lisa Brackmann imbue local attractions with a new sensibility. Gabriel R. Barillas reminds us that for many residents, the town is defined by its connected freeways—freeways put to use by Luis Alberto Urrea's characters. And Maria Lima contributes something rare for the Akashic Noir Series, a cross-genre story set in the heart of the city's downtown.

I hope that reading this intriguing collection will result in you not just thinking of Shamu (the whale of SeaWorld fame), but maybe a shamus or two, when America's Finest City comes to mind.

Maryelizabeth Hart
San Diego, California
March 2011

PART I

WORKING STIFFS

VIC PRIMEVAL

BY T. JEFFERSON PARKER

Kearny Mesa

Y ou know how these things get started, Robbie. You see
her for the first time. Your heart skips and your fingers
buzz. Can't take your eyes off her. And when you look
at her she knows. No way to hide it. So you don't look. Use all
your strength to not look. But she still knows. And anybody else
around does too."

"I've had that feeling, Vic," I said.

We walked down the Embarcadero where the cruise ships
come and go. It was what passes for winter here in San Diego,
cool and crisp, and there was a hard clarity to the sunlight. Once
a week I met Vic at Higher Grounds coffee and we'd get expensive drinks and walk around the city. He was a huge guy,
a former professional wrestler. Vic Primeval was his show name
until they took his WWF license away for getting too physical in
his matches. He hurt some people. I spend a few minutes a week
with Vic because he thinks he owes me his life. And because he's
alone in the world and possibly insane.

"Anyway," said Vic, "her name is Farrel White and I want
you to meet her."

"Why?"

"Because I'm proud to have you as a friend. You're pretty
much all I got in that department."

"Are you showing us off, Vic? Our freak show past?"

He blushed. "No. But you do make me look good."

Vic was bouncing at Skin, an exotic dance club—strippers,

weak drinks, no cover with military ID. "I don't love that place," I said.

"Robbie, what don't you like about pretty women dancing almost naked?"

"The creeps who go there."

"Maybe you'll get lucky. You're lucky with the ladies."

"What do you know about my luck with ladies, Vic?"

"Come on, man. You've got luck. Whole world knows that."

More luck than I deserve, but is it good or bad? For instance, seven years ago Vic threw me out the window of the sixth floor of a hotel he'd set on fire—the Las Palmas in downtown San Diego. I was trying to save some lives and Vic was distraught at having had his World Wrestling Federation license revoked. This incident could be reasonably called bad luck.

You might have seen the video of me falling to what should have been my death. But I crashed through an awning before I hit the sidewalk and it saved my life. This luck was clearly good. I became briefly semifamous—The Falling Detective. The incident scrambled my brains a little but actually helped my career with the San Diego Police Department. In the video I look almost graceful as I fall. The world needs heroes, even if it's only a guy who blacks out in what he thinks are the last few seconds of his life.

"Just meet her, Robbie. Tonight she goes onstage at eight, so she'll get there around seven-thirty. I start at eight too. So we can wait for her out back, where the performers go in and out. You won't even have to set foot in the club. But if you want to, I can get you a friends-and-family discount. What else you got better to do?"

We stood in the rear employee-only lot in the winter dark. I watched the cars rushing down Highway 163. The music thumped away inside the club and when someone came through the employee door the music got louder and I saw colored shapes hovering in the air about midway between the door and me.

I've been seeing these colored objects since Vic threw me to that sidewalk. They're geometric, of varying colors, between one and four inches in length, width, depth. They float and bob. I can move them with a finger. Or with a strong exhalation, like blowing out birthday cake candles. They often accompany music, but sometimes they appear when someone is talking to me. The stronger the person's emotion, the larger and more vivid the objects are. They linger briefly then vanish.

In the months after my fall I came to understand these shapes derived not so much from the words spoken, but from the emotion behind them. Each shape and color denotes a different emotion. To me, the shapes are visual reminders of the fact that people don't always mean what they say. My condition is called synesthesia, from the Greek, and loosely translated it means "mixing of the senses." I belong to the San Diego Synesthesia Society and we meet once a month at the Seven Seas on Hotel Circle.

Farrel had a round, pretty face, dark eyes, and brown hair cut in bangs, and one dimple when she smiled. Her lips were small and red. Her handshake was soft. She was short even in high-heeled boots. She wore a long coat against the damp winter chill.

"Vic tells me you're a policeman. My daddy was a policeman. Center Springs, Arkansas. It's not on most maps."

"How long have you been here in San Diego?" I asked.

"Almost a year. I was waitressing but now I'm doing this. Better pay."

"How old are you?"

"I'm twenty-four years old." She had a way of holding your eyes with her own, a direct but uncritical stare. "Vic told me all about what happened. It's good that you've become a friend of his. We all of us need at least one good friend . . . Well, guys, I should be going. I'd ask you in and buy you a drink, but it's supposed to work the other way around."

I glanced at Vic and saw the adoration in his eyes. It lit up his face, made it smarter and softer and better. Farrel smiled at him and put her hand on his sleeve.

"It's okay, Vic."

"Just so good to see you, Farrel."

"Vic walks me in and out, every night. And any other of the dancers who want him to. You're a cop so you know there's always someone coming around places like this, making trouble for the girls. But not when Vic Primeval is in the barnyard."

"I don't really like that name," said Vic.

"I mean it in a good way."

"It means primitive."

"It's only a show name, Vic. Like, well, like for a dancer it would be Chastity or Desire."

I watched the inner conflict ruffle Vic's expression. Then his mind made some kind of override and the light came back to his eyes. He smiled and peered down at the ground.

A hard look came over Farrel's face as a black BMW 750i bounced through the open exit gate and into the employees-only lot. It rolled to a stop beside us. The driver's window went down.

"Yo. Sweetie. I been looking for you." He was thirty maybe and tricked out in style—sharp haircut, pricey-looking shirt and jacket. Slender face, a Jersey voice and delivery. He looked from Farrel to Vic, then at me. "What's your problem, fuckface?"

I swung open my jacket to give him a look at my .45.

He held up his hands like I should cuff him. "Christ. Farrel? You want I should run these meatballs off? They're nothing to do with me and you, baby."

"I want them to run *you* off. I told you, Sal. There isn't a you and me. No more. It's over. I'm gone."

"But you're not gone, baby. You're right here. So get in. Whatever you'll make in a month in there, I'll pay you that right out of my pocket. Right here and now."

"Get off this property," said Vic. "Or I'll drag you out of your cute little car and throw you over that fence."

Vic glanced at me and winced right after he said this. When he gets mad at things he throws them far. People too.

Sal clucked his tongue like a hayseed then smiled at Vic as if he was an amusing moron.

"No more us, Sal," said Farrel. "We're over."

"You still owe me eight thousand dollars, girl. Nothing's over till I get that back."

I saw black rhombuses wobbling in the air between us. Black rhombuses mean anger.

"I'll pay you back as soon as I can. You think I'm dancing in a place like this just for the fun of it all?"

"Move out of here," I said. "Do it now."

"Or you'll arrest me."

"Quickly. It'll cost you forty-eight long cheap hours or two expensive short ones. Your pick."

"I want what's mine," Sal said to Farrel. "I want what I paid for."

"Them's two different things."

"Maybe it is in that redneck slop hole you come from."

The window went up and the car swung around and out of the lot, the big tires leaving a rubbery low-speed squeal on the asphalt.

"I'm coming in for a while," I said.

I had a beer and watched Farrel and the other dancers do their shows. They were uninhibited and rhythmic to say the least. Some were pretty and some were plain. Some acted flirtatious and others lustful and others aloof. Farrel seemed almost shy and she never once looked at either me or Vic from what I could tell. She had a small attractive body. Vic stood in the back of the room, lost in the lush plum-colored curtains, his feet spread wide and arms crossed, stone still.

After an hour passed and Sal had not come back, I nodded a goodnight to Vic and went home.

* * *

Two days later Vic left a message for me and I met him outside the Convention Center. There was a reptile show in progress and many of the people were entering and leaving the building with constrictors around their necks and leashed iguanas in their arms and stacks of clear plastic food containers filled with brightly colored juvenile snakes.

"Look at this thing," he said. He reached into the pocket of his aloha shirt and pulled out a huge black scorpion. "They don't sting."

Vic Malic had enormous hands but that scorpion stretched from his thumb tip to the nail on his little finger. It looked like it could drill that stinger a half inch into you anytime it wanted. In his other hand was a clear plastic bag filled with crickets. They were white with dust of some kind. They hopped around as crickets do.

"Scorpion food?" I asked.

"Yeah. And they dust them with vitamins for thirty cents."

He looked down at the creature then slid it back into his shirt pocket. "That son of a bitch Sal is stalking Farrel. That was the third time I've seen him. He shows up everywhere she goes."

"Tell her to come fill out a report. We can't do anything until she does that."

"Doesn't trust cops."

"She seemed proud of her dad."

"I'm only telling you what she told me. Sal loaned her ten grand because she totaled her car with no insurance, and her baby had to have chemotherapy. Darling little baby. I saw it. Just darling but with cancer."

"That is a shame."

"Yeah, and he was all charm at first, Sal was. She kind of liked him. Started paying with favors, you know, but the way he had it figured was he'd get anything he wanted for two years and she'd still owe him half. Plus he likes it rough and he hit her.

Then he said he's got friends. He can introduce her to them, you know—they'd really like her. He's a Jersey wise guy, all connected up. Says he is. You heard him. He said he wants what's his and what he paid for."

I know who the mobbed-up locals are here in America's Finest City. Sal wasn't one of them. We've had our wise guys for decades, mostly connected to the L.A. outfits. There's a restaurant they go to. You get to know who they are. I wondered if Sal was just a visiting relative, getting some R&R in Southern California. Or maybe a new guy they brought in. Or if he was a made guy trying to muscle into new territory. If that was true there would be some kind of trouble.

I watched the scorpion wriggle around in the shirt pocket. The pocket had a hula girl and it looked like the pincers were growing out of her head.

"I'm gonna get that eight grand for her," said Vic.

"Where?"

"I got a start with the book sales."

Vic has been hand-selling copies of *Fall to Your Life!*, which he wrote and published himself. It's about how "the Robbie Brown-law event" seven years ago at the Las Palmas Hotel changed his life for the better. He does pretty well with it, mostly to tourists. I see him sometimes, down by the Star of India, or Horton Plaza, or there at the Amtrak station, looming over his little table with copies of the book and a change box. He wears his old Vic Primeval wrestling costume of faux animal skins—not fur, but the skins sewed together into a kind of bodysuit. It's terrifically ugly but the customers are drawn to it. To attract buyers, he also sets up an aging poster of me falling through the sky. He used to charge five bucks a copy for the book but a year ago it went up to ten. Once a month he still gives me a cut from each sale, which is twenty-five percent. I accept the money because it makes Vic feel virtuous, then turn it over to the downtown food pantry and ASPCA and various charities.

I did some quick calcs based on what Vic paid me in royalties for July—traditionally his best month due to tourists. My take was five hundred dollars, which meant that Vic pocketed fifteen hundred plus change for himself.

"It'll take you at least six months to get eight grand," I said. "Plus winter is coming on and you've got your own expenses to pay."

Vic brooded.

"Do you have any money saved up, Vic?"

"I can get the money."

"So she can give it to him? Don't give her anything. Have her file a complaint with us if he's such a badass. She can get a restraining order. You don't know her and you don't know him. Stay away, Vic. That's the best advice you'll get on this."

"What do you mean?"

"What about this doesn't scream setup?"

"A setup? Why set up a guy who doesn't have any money? She hasn't asked me for one nickel. She's the real thing, Robbie. That little baby. I don't have a world class brain, but my heart always sees true. Farrel passes the Vic Malic heart test."

"The best thing you can do is have her file a complaint."

"She won't. I already told her to. She said the cops can't do anything until they catch him doing something. What she's afraid is, it's gonna be too late when that happens."

Which is often true.

"But Robbie, what if you tell her? Coming from you, it would mean a lot more than from me."

The San Diego mob guys own and frequent a downtown restaurant called Napoli. It's an unflashy two-story brick affair not far at all from police headquarters. They have controlling interests in a couple of much swankier eateries here, but they do their hanging out at Napoli.

"Hey, it's Robbie Brownlaw," said Dom, the owner.

"Dom, I need a word."

"Then you get a word, Robbie. Come on back. How's San Diego's famous detective?"

He's a round-faced, chipper fellow, early sixties, grandson of one of San Diego's more vivid mob figures, Leo the Lion Gagnas. Leo and his L.A. partners ran this city's gambling and loan-sharking. Back in 1950, two men out of Youngstown tried to get in on the Gagnas rackets, and they both washed up in Glorietta Bay one morning with bullets in their heads. Leo and company opened Napoli back in '53. He was tight with Bebe Rebozo, who was a big Nixon fundraiser. Beginning in 1966 Leo did two years for tax evasion and that was it. He never saw the inside of a prison before or after.

We sat in his dark little office. There were no windows and it smelled heavily of cigar smoke and cologne. The bookshelves were stuffed with well-read paperback crime novels—plenty of Whit Masterson and Erle Stanley Gardner and Mickey Spillane. A floor safe sat in one corner and the walls were covered with framed photographs of Dom's ancestors and the people they entertained at Napoli—Sinatra, Joey Bishop, John Wayne, Nixon, Ted Williams.

I looked at the pictures. "Where's the new celebrities, Dom?"

He looked at the pictures too. "They don't come around here so much anymore. A time for everything, you know? It's good. Business is good. What do you need, Robbie?"

I told him about Sal—his alleged New Jersey outfit ties, his bad attitude and slick black Beamer, his fix on a young dancer at Skin named Farrel.

Dom nodded. "Yeah. I heard. My nephew, he's a manager at Skin. I got some friends checking this guy out."

"Ever had any trouble out of Jersey?"

"Never. Not any trouble at all, Robbie. Those days are long gone. You know that."

"What if he's what he says he is, trying to move in?"

"In on what?"

"On business, Dom."

"I don't know what you mean, *business*. But somebody blows into town and starts popping off about he's a made guy and he's mobbed up in Jersey and all that, well, there's fools and then there's fools, Robbie. Nobody I know talks like that. Know what I mean?"

"I wonder if he's got help."

"He better have help if he wants to shoot off his mouth. I'll let you know what I find out. And Robbie, you see this guy, tell him he's not making any friends around here. If he's what he says he is, then that's one thing. If he's not, then he's just pissing everybody off. Some doors you don't want to open. Tell him that. You might save him a little inconvenience. How's that pretty redhead wife of yours? Gina."

"We divorced seven years ago."

"I got divorced once. No, it was three times. You know why it's so expensive, don't you?"

"Because it's worth it."

"Yeah."

"You've told me that one before, Dom."

"And I was right, wasn't I?"

I met Farrel at Skin that night before she was set to perform. We sat at the bar and got good treatment from the bartenders. Dom's nephew, a spidery young man named Joey Morra, came by, said hello, told Farrel the customers were liking her. I took down Farrel's numbers and address and the name of her daughter and hometown and parents. And I also got everything she could tell me about Sal Tessola—where he lived and how they met, what he'd done for her and to her, the whole story. I told her she'd need all these things in order to write a good convincing complaint. We talked for a solid hour before she checked her watch.

"You going to stay and see me perform?"

"Not tonight."

"Didn't like it much, then?"

"You were good, Farrel."

She eyed me. "I don't want Vic trying to get me the money. I didn't ask him to. I asked him *not* to. He's not the brightest guy, Robbie. But he might be one of the most stubborn."

"You've got a point."

"How come you're not married? You must be about legal age."

"I was once."

"I'd a found a way to keep you."

"You're flattering me now."

"Why don't you flatter me back?"

"Center Springs took a loss when you packed it in."

She peered at me in that forthright and noncommittal way. "It sure did. And there's no power in heaven or earth strong enough to drag me back there."

I saw the black triangles of dread and the yellow triangles of fear hovering in the air between us.

I followed her from Skin. I'm not suspicious by nature but it helps me do my job. The night was close and damp and I stayed well behind. She drove an early-'90s Dodge that was slow and slumped to starboard and easy to follow.

She drove to a small tract home out in La Mesa east of downtown. I slowed and watched her pull into the driveway. I went past, circled the block, then came back and parked across the street, one house down.

The house was vintage '50s, one of hundreds built in La Mesa not long after World War II. Many of those navy men and women who'd served and seen San Diego came back looking for a place to live in this sunny and unhurried city.

A living room light was on and the drapes were drawn casually, with a good gap in the middle and another at one end. Someone moved across the living room then lamplight came from the back of the house through a bedroom window on the side I could see. A few minutes went by and I figured she was showering, so I got out and strolled down the sidewalk. Then I doubled back and cut across the little yard and stood under the canopy of a coral tree. I stepped up close to the living room window and looked through the middle gap.

The room was sparsely furnished in what looked like thrift-shop eclectic—a braided rug over the darkly stained wood floor, an American colonial coffee table, an orange-yellow-black plaid sofa with thin padding. There was a stack of black three-ring binders on the coffee table. Right in front of me was the back end of a TV, not a flat screen but one of the old ones with the big butts and masses of cords and coax cable sprouting everywhere.

I moved along the perimeter of the house and let myself through a creaking gate but no dogs barked and I soon came to a dark side window. The blinds were drawn but they were old and some were broken and several were bent. Through a hole I could make out a small bedroom. All it had was a chest of drawers and a stroller with a baby asleep in it, and I didn't have to look at that baby very long before I realized it was a doll.

Farrel walked past the room in what looked like a long white bathrobe and something on her head. I waited awhile then backed out across the neighbor's yard and walked to my car. I settled in behind the wheel and used the binoculars and I could see Farrel on the plaid sofa, hair up in a towel, both hands on a sixteen-ounce can of beer seated between her legs. She leaned forward and picked up one of the black binders, looked at it like she'd seen it a hundred times before, then set it down beside her. She seemed tired but peaceful with the TV light playing off her face.

Twenty minutes later a battered Mustang roared up and parked behind the Dodge and Sal got out. Gone were the sharp clothes and in their place were jeans and a fleece-lined denim jacket and a pair of shineless harness boots that clomped and slouched as he keyed open the front door and went through.

I glassed the gap in the living room curtains and Farrel's face rushed at me. She said something without looking at Sal. He stood before her, his back to me, and shrugged. He snatched the beer can from her and held it up for a long drink, then pushed it back between her legs and whipped off his coat. He wore a blue shirt with a local pizza parlor logo on it. This he pulled off as he walked into the back rooms.

He came out a few minutes later wearing jeans and a singlet, his hair wet and combed back. He was a lean young man, broad shouldered, tall. For the first time I realized he was handsome. He walked past Farrel into the kitchen and came back with a can of beer and sat down on the couch not too near and not too far from her. He squeezed her robe once where her knee would be then let his hand fall to the sofa.

They talked without looking at each other but I can't read lips. It looked like a "and how was your day" kind of conversation, or maybe something about the TV show that was on, which threw blue light upon them like fish underwater.

After a while they stopped talking, and a few minutes later Farrel lifted the remote and the blue light was gone and she had picked up one of the black binders from the pile at her end of the couch.

She opened it and read out loud. There was no writing or label or title on the cover.

She waved the binder at him and pointed at a page and read a line to him.

He repeated it. I was pretty sure.

She read it again and he repeated it. I was pretty sure again. They both laughed.

Then another line. They each said it, whatever it was. Sal stood over her then and aimed a finger at her face and said the line again. She stood and stripped the towel off her head and said something and they both laughed again.

He got up and brought two more big cans of beer from kitchen and he opened one for her and took her empty. He tossed the towel onto her lap and sat down close to her, put his bare feet up on the coffee table by the binders and scrunched down so his head was level with hers. She clicked the TV back on.

I waited for an hour. Another beer each. Not much talk. They both fell asleep sitting up, heads back on the sofa.

It was almost three-thirty in the morning when Farrel stood, rubbed the back of her neck, then tightened the robe sash. She walked deeper into the house and out of my sight.

A few minutes later Sal rose and hit the lights. In the TV glow I could see him stretch out full length on the couch and set one arm over his eyes and take a deep breath and let it slowly out.

Two mornings later, at about the same dark hour, I was at head-quarters writing a crime scene report. I'm an occasional insomniac and I choose to get paperwork done during those long, haunted times. Of course I listen to our dispatch radio, keeping half an ear on the hundreds of calls that come in every shift.

So when I heard the possible 187 at Skin nightclub I was out the door fast.

Two squad cars were already there and two more screamed into the parking lot as I got out of my car.

"The janitor called 911," said one of the uniforms. "I was first on scene and he let me in. There's a dead man back in the kitchen. I think it's one of the managers. I tried to check his pulse but couldn't reach that far. You'll see."

I asked the patrolmen to seal both the back and front entrances and start a sign-in log, always a good idea if you don't want your crime scene to spiral into chaos. You'd be surprised how many people will trample through and wreck evidence, many of them cops.

I walked in, past the bar and the tables and the stage, then into a small, poorly lit, grease-darkened kitchen. Another uniform stood near a walk-in freezer, talking with a young man wearing a light blue shirt with a name patch on it.

I saw the autoloader lying on the floor in front of me. Then the cop looked up and I followed his line of sight to the exposed ceiling. Overhead were big commercial blowers and vents and ducting and electrical conduit and hanging fluorescent tube light fixtures. A body hung jackknifed at the hips over a steel crossbeam. His arms dangled over one side and his legs over the other. If he'd landed just one inch higher or lower, he'd have simply slid off the beam to the floor. I walked around the gun and got directly under him and stared up into the face of Joey. It was an urgent shade of purple and his eyes were open.

"The safe in the office," said the uniform, pointing to the far back side of the kitchen.

The office door was open and I stepped in. There was a desk and a black leather couch and a small fridge and microwave, pictures of near-naked dancers on the walls, along with a Chargers calendar and Padres pendants.

There was also a big floor safe that was open but not empty. I squatted in front of it and saw the stacks of cash and some envelopes.

The officer and janitor stood in the office doorway.

"Why kill a man for his money then not take it?" asked the uniform. His name plate said *Peabody*.

"Maybe he freaked and ran," said the janitor, whose name patch said *Carlos*.

"Okay," said Peabody. "Then tell me how Joey got ten feet up in the air and hung over a beam. And don't tell me he did it to himself."

Carlos looked up at the body and shrugged but I had an opinion about that.

"What time do you start work?" I asked him.

"Two. That's when they close."

"Is Joey usually here?"

"One of the managers is always here. They count the money every third night. Then they take it to the bank."

"So tonight was bank night?"

"Was supposed to be."

I drove fast to Vic's hotel room downtown but he didn't answer the door. Back downstairs the night manager, speaking from behind a mesh-reinforced window, told me that Vic left around eight-thirty—seven hours ago—and had not returned.

I made Farrel's place eleven minutes later. There were no cars in the driveway but lights inside were on. I rang the bell and knocked then tried the door, which was unlocked. So I opened it and stepped in.

The living room looked exactly as it had two nights ago, except that the beer cans were gone and the pile of black binders had been reduced to just one. In the small back bedroom the stroller was still in place and the plastic doll was snugged down under the blanket just as it had been. I went into the master bedroom. The mattress was bare and the chest of drawers stood open and nearly empty. It looked like Farrel had stripped the bed and packed her clothes in a hurry. The bathroom was stripped too: no towels, nothing in the shower or the medicine chest or on the sink counter. The refrigerator had milk and pickles and that was all. The wastebasket under the sink had empty beer cans, an empty pretzel bag, various fast-food remnants swathed in ketchup, a receipt from a supermarket, and a wadded-up agreement from Rent-a-Dream car rentals down by the airport. Black Beamer 750i, of course.

Back in the living room I took the black binder from the coffee table and opened it to the first page:

THE SOPRANOS
Season Four/Episode Three

I flipped through the pages. Dialogue and brief descriptions. Four episodes in all.

Getting Sal's lines right, I thought.

Vic didn't show up for work for three straight nights. I stopped by Skin a couple of times a night, just in case he showed, and I knocked on his hotel room door twice a day or so. The manager hadn't seen him in four days. He told me Vic's rent was due on the first.

Of course Farrel had vanished too. I cruised her place in La Mesa but something about it just said she wasn't coming back, and she didn't.

On the fourth afternoon after the murder of Joey Morra, Vic called me on my cell phone. "Can you feed my scorpion? Give him six crickets. They're under the bathroom sink. The manager'll give you the key."

"Sure. But we need to talk, Vic—face to face."

"I didn't do it."

"Who else could throw Joey up there like that?"

Vic didn't answer.

"Dom and his people are looking for you, Vic. You won't get a trial with them. You'll just get your sentence, and it won't be lenient."

"I only took what she needed."

"And killed Joey."

"He pulled a gun, Robbie. I couldn't thinka what else to do. I bear-hugged and shook him. Like a reflex. Like when I threw you."

"I'll see you outside Higher Grounds in ten minutes."

"She met me at Rainwater's, Robbie. I walked into Rainwater's and there she was—that beautiful young woman, waiting there for me. You should have seen her face light up when I gave her the money. Out in the parking lot, I mean."

"I'll bet," I said. "Meet me outside Higher Grounds in ten minutes."

"Naw. I got a good safe place here. I'm going to just enjoy my-self for a couple more days, knowing I did a good thing for a good woman. My scorpion, I named him Rudy. Oh. Oh shit, Robbie."

Even coming from a satellite orbiting the earth in space, and through the miles of ether it took to travel to my ear, the sound of the shotgun blast was unmistakable. So was the second blast, and the third.

A few days later I flew to Little Rock and rented a car, then made the drive north and west to Center Springs. Farrel was right: it wasn't on the rental-car company driving map, but it made the navigation unit that came in the vehicle.

The Ozarks were steep and thickly forested and the Ar-kansas River looked unhurried. I could see thin wisps of wood stove fires burning in cabins down in the hollows and there was a smoky cast to the sky.

The gas station clerk said I'd find Farrel White's dad's place down the road a mile, just before Persimmon Holler. He said there was a batch of trailers up on the hillside and I'd see them from the road if I didn't drive too fast. Billy White had the wooden one with all the satellite dishes on top.

The road leading in was dirt and heavily rutted from last season's rain. I drove past travel trailers set up on cinder blocks. They were slouched and sun-dulled and some had decks and others just had more cinder blocks as steps. Dogs eyed me with-out bothering to sit up. There were cats and litter and a pile of engine blocks outside, looked like they'd been cast there by some huge child.

Billy answered my knock with a sudden yank on the door then studied me through the screen. He was mid-fifties and heavy, didn't look at all like his daughter. He wore a green-and-black plaid jacket buttoned all the way to the top.

"I'm a San Diego cop looking for your daughter. I thought she might have come home."

"Would you?"

"Would I what?"

"Come home to this from San Diego?"

"Well."

"She okay?"

"I think so."

"Come in."

The trailer was small and cramped and packed with old, overstuffed furniture.

"She in trouble?"

"Farrel and her boyfriend hustled a guy out of some money. But he had to take the money from someone else."

Billy handed me a beer and plopped into a vinyl recliner across from me. He had a round, impish face and a twinkle in his eyes. "That ain't her boyfriend. It's her brother."

"That never crossed my mind."

"Don't look nothing alike. But they've always been close. Folks liked to think too close, but it wasn't ever that way. Just close. They understood each other. They're both good kids. Their whole point in life was to get outta Center Springs and they done did it. I'm proud of them."

"What's his name?"

"Preston."

"Did they grow up in this trailer?"

"Hell no. We had a home over to Persimmon but it got sold off in the divorce. Hazel went to Little Rock with a tobacco products salesman. The whole story is every bit as dreary as it sounds."

"When did Farrel and Preston leave?"

"Couple of months ago. The plan was San Diego, then Hollywood. Pretty people with culture and money to spend. They were going to study TV, maybe go start up a show. San Diego was to practice up."

"The scripts."

"Got them from the library up at Fayetteville. Made copies of the ones they wanted. Over and over again. Memorizing those scripts and all them words. They went to the Salvation Army stores and bought up lots of old-time kinda clothes. They both did some stage plays at the junior college but they didn't much care for them. They liked the other kind of stories."

"What kind of stories?"

"Crime stories. Bad guys. Mafia. That was mainly Preston. Farrel, she can act like anything from the Queen of England to a weather girl and you can't tell she's acting."

"Have they called lately?"

"Been over a week."

"Where do you think they are?"

"Well, Center Springs is the only place I know they ain't. I don't expect to ever see them out this way."

I did the simple math and the not-so-simple math. Eight grand for two months of work. Farrel dancing for tips. Preston delivering pizza and working his end of the Vic hustle. Vic caught between Farrel's good acting and his own eager heart. And of course betrayed, finally and fatally, by his own bad temper.

I finished the beer and stood. "Two men died because of them. Eight thousand bucks is what they died for. So the next time you talk to Farrel and Preston, you tell them there's real blood on their hands. It's not make-believe blood. You tell her Vic was murdered for taking that eight thousand."

"I'll do that."

"Thanks for your time."

"I can come up with a couple a hundred. It's not much, but . . ."

I saw the orange triangles bouncing in the air between us. I thought about those triangles as I drove away. Orange triangles denote pity and sometimes even empathy. All this for Vic Primeval, as offered by a man he'd never met, from his vinyl chair in his slouching home in the Ozarks. Sometimes you find a little speck of good where you least expect it. A rough diamond down deep. And you realize that the blackness can't own you for more than one night at a time.

THE HOME FRONT

BY DIANE CLARK & ASTRID BEAR

Sherman Heights

The sailor sat in the wooden chair across from the desk, twisting his white cap. His hair was white-blond, his face tanned to walnut. He was young. They all were. San Diego was full of young sailors in their crisp blue uniforms.

"It's my sister. She came out to work for Consolidated. They trained her as a riveter. She was real good, just loved it. She shared a house with a bunch of girls but got tired of the noise and late nights, so she moved to a boardinghouse on K Street. About a week later, she didn't show up for work. No one's seen her since. I went to the police. They asked around some but couldn't find out anything. They said there's no law against someone going missing, but it's just not like her. Can you help?"

Mike McGowan had called that morning to say he had a case for me. "Sailor. Missing kid sister—probably ran off with a jarhead—let him off easy, okay, Laura? The boy's shipping out soon and wants to know what happened to her."

Ever since my husband Bill got called up by the navy and left me in charge of the agency, his friends in the police department had been pretty good about sending work my way. I liked the work, and when Bill came back, I was planning to tell him we needed to change the name to Taylor & Taylor Investigations.

I pulled open a drawer and took out a notebook. The pen was resting in a leather cup, along with some of Bill's chewed-up pencils. "Okay, Navy, let's get some details. What's your name?"

"I'm Joseph Przybilski. My sister's Magda, but she went by Mary once she came out here."

"Got a picture?"

He fished a photo out of his jumper pocket, a little crumpled at the corners. It showed a pretty, slight blonde, standing with a dour-looking old man and woman on the steps of an aggressively neat house. "That's her with our mama and papa—I took that picture on the day I left for the navy. They weren't too happy with me for going."

"I see that." I examined the girl's face. She looked eager, excited. "Your sister seems happy."

"She was excited for me to be leaving the farm, going off to see the world. She really wanted to get away too. We'd talked about it, and she'd already decided to leave as soon as she could. When Papa arranged to get some German POWs to work for him, she skedaddled out west. She never wanted to look another chicken in the eye again!"

"Can I keep this?"

He nodded.

"And when did she get here?"

"In May. She got taken on right away at Consolidated, and they put her on the PBY assembly line as soon as she finished her training. Flying boats."

"Mm-hmm."

"They had her working tail, cause she fits into small places." He grinned shyly. So young and cute. "Her last letter said she got to see the first flight of a plane she made. She was so proud!"

I could imagine that slim girl creeping into the cutaways and nooks in the rear of the fuselage, toting her rivet gun, snaking the air hose along and avoiding sharp edges and snags, then getting to work, the staccato *slap-choo* of the gun echoing in the tiny space. Tending chickens somehow didn't seem so bad compared to that, but I hadn't grown up with them.

"Any boyfriends?"

"Not that she told me about. There was a boy at home who was sweet on her during high school, but I don't think they stayed in touch."

I got the details of Mary's workplace and the address she'd moved to and told Przybilski I'd see what I could do. He gave me two dollars for my retainer and left.

I decided to check out where Mary had been living. I locked the office and walked downstairs to India Street. It was a typical San Diego September day, sunny and warm with a gentle breeze ruffling the bay. The water sparkled with heartless beauty. I caught a streetcar heading south, then transferred to a bus. I got off at Market and 20th.

I looked down 20th toward K Street. Three blocks away, I saw a red-roofed tower lording it over the small bungalows that made up the neighborhood. It was the Jesse Shepard House, a mansion built by rich men for an eccentric musician in the 1880s in the hopes of bringing culture to their dusty town. With a start, I realized that it had been converted into the boarding house that Mary had moved to. It was a jumble of architectural features and finishes punctuated by stained-glass windows. Wrought-iron panels topped a low concrete fence that rose up from the sidewalk. The whole effect was of a cut-and-pasted Victorian Sears catalog.

As I came closer, it was clear that this grand building, once the pride of San Diego, had been thoroughly humbled by the needs of wartime. The white paint had cracked and peeled into loose flakes. Blackout curtains framed the panels of stained glass. Wide windows showed the edge-on shadows of partitions. Formerly spacious rooms had been roughly subdivided.

I crossed the street to a corner market and bought a soda.

"Pretty fancy building over there," I commented to the clerk, an older woman with her gray hair in a tidy bun.

"Just a shame what they've done to it since the Lynches died. I know people need places to live, what with the housing shortage and all, but it's too bad they had to turn that fine old place into a boarding house. Can I open that for you?" she asked, gesturing to the bottle.

"Sure!" I took a sip of the fizzy cold Coke and leaned against a vegetable bin. "So they've got a lot of folks living there now?"

"They put up so many partitions to make rooms, they must have twenty people staying there. All girls, they don't take men. Each girl gets her own personal cracker box. They mostly work at the aircraft factories."

"Must be a nice bit of extra business for you, with so many girls around."

"Well, they're gone all day and they hardly cook, but we make sandwiches to sell for their lunch pails, so we're doing okay. Sometimes a few girls will get together and buy some stew meat and vegetables to make dinner on the weekend, but the owners are pretty stingy with kitchen privileges. It's almost like they don't want them to have a good time when they get a chance."

I pulled Mary's picture out of my handbag. "I think a friend of mine might have been staying there—have you seen her?"

The woman peered at the photo. "I couldn't say. Some of those girls come and go so fast, I just can't keep track. There's a group of them that've been there for a while, but sometimes I'll no sooner see one than she's gone. With all the girls coming to take jobs at the plants, those rooms don't stay vacant but hardly a day."

I finished my Coke and put the bottle in the return rack. Another customer came. Her eyes shifted to him, narrowed, and she shook her head slightly at him. I took the opportunity to wave goodbye and head back down the street.

A group of Mexican boys, pachucos, were leaning against the wall of the next building. Their wide-lapeled zoot suits were elegantly draped but frayed at the edges. Their dark eyes gave me the once-over. One let out a piercing wolf whistle, another made a remark in rapid-fire Spanish. They all laughed, with a bit of a nasty edge to it. I sped up my stride and grabbed my purse more tightly with suddenly sweaty hands.

I mentally turned over questions to ask the landlords. In the shadow of the big house's tower, I mounted the ornate steps and paused before a sign: *Room for Rent*.

What if I did more than just ask questions? Bill always said that it was important to get first-hand information and really understand the scene of a possible crime. And what could be more first hand than living there?

A prickle of worry started in my stomach as I thought about this, followed by excitement. I damped both feelings down as I smoothed my skirt and finished walking up the front steps.

I knocked at the elaborately milled door. Almost immediately a tall, wiry woman opened it. Her black hair parted in the middle and coiled into a smooth knot resting on the nape of her neck. Her hands were large and strong-looking, with a man's knobby fingers and closely trimmed nails. No polish. I swallowed. "The sign said you have a room for rent?"

She pursed her lips and looked me over with an appraising eye. "We might." I felt like a cut of meat in a butcher's window. "We only rent to girls with good jobs—respectable girls, factory jobs."

I thought fast. "I'm starting tomorrow morning at Consolidated."

"Doing what?"

Might as well pick up where Mary left off. "I'm working on PBYs. Riveting."

"Let me get you an application. Come on into the office and you can fill it out. I'm Mrs. Smith. My husband and I own the place, and we live right here, so we don't allow any funny business. No parties, no men." She glared significantly at me.

"I'm very quiet."

"Quiet is good."

We walked across the wide foyer and through a dining room

that smelled of stale coffee. She pushed open a swinging door and led me into a large kitchen. One corner was dominated by a huge rolltop desk. Mrs. Smith pulled a pad of rental applications out of a cubby, peeled one off, and pushed it toward me. "Have a seat. Fill this out."

She sat in the heavy rolling chair at the desk and crossed her legs. The black crepe of her dress lay obedient over her knobby knees.

I sat on a flimsy dining chair at a small deal table by the side of the desk and started on the form, facts and history all made up. I figured by the time any address or reference checking was done, I'd be long gone.

Done. I handed her the form. She pulled a pair of gold-rimmed glasses out of a brown clamshell case and snapped it shut with a clack. She peered over my peerless work of fiction.

"You're from Iowa?" she asked. "We get a lot of girls from the Midwest—must be nice to get away from that heat."

I nodded, trying to look both respectable and quiet. Mrs. Smith glanced at the ring on my left hand.

"Married?"

I almost nodded again, but inspiration struck. "My husband was killed at Guadalcanal. I couldn't take being alone in our house back there, so I came out here to help with the war effort. It's hard being away from my family and everyone I know, but at least I feel that I'm helping get back at those Japs for killing my Bill." Thinking of my real Bill possibly being killed brought me to real tears, and I dabbed my eyes with my handkerchief.

"So you're all alone?" Mrs. Smith's eyes softened a bit. "Well, the room's yours then. That'll be five dollars for the first week, plus another five-dollar deposit—refundable if you leave it in good shape."

I fished my change purse out of my handbag and handed over two fives. The two-dollar retainer I'd gotten from Joseph Przybilski didn't cover this at all—too bad I didn't really have a job at Consolidated to pay for it.

The back door opened and a burly man with wide fat shoulders and heavy bare arms, wearing a T-shirt and khaki pants, came in. Through the doorway, I saw the handles of garden tools lined up on the back porch. He was sweaty, with dirty hands—the odor of dirt and perspiration followed him in.

He tipped his chin at her, gave me a curious glance, then took the straw hat off the back of his head and hung it on a hook by the door. He went to the sink and began to wash up.

"George," said Mrs. Smith, "come meet Laura Taylor, our newest tenant. She'll be in number 14. Mrs. Taylor, this is my husband, Mr. Smith."

"How do you do," I said.

He took a clean white huck cloth towel from the swinging chrome rack by the sink and wiped his hands thoroughly, then came over to shake. "Pleased to make your acquaintance," he rumbled. His hand was lumpy from hoeing and mowing and brown from working in the sun. He continued to look me over closely. Again, I felt like a piece of meat.

"George takes care of everything outside, and I handle all the inside work," Mrs. Smith explained. "It's a perfect partnership."

Mr. Smith nodded. "I like the outdoors. Restful. But always something to do." They exchanged a look that said things I couldn't fathom.

"I'll be running along now," I said, and thought that running might be a very good idea. "I'll be back with my suitcase later."

"Later, then," replied Mrs. Smith. Mr. Smith nodded. They both saw me to the door and stood on the porch as I walked down the steps and along 20th to the bus stop at Market Street.

Back at the office, I smiled as I opened the safe. The combination was our anniversary: 6-16-37. "That way, I'll never forget it," Bill had said, and it worked.

This year, knowing he was going to ship out soon, we'd taken a trip to Mexico for the day. We'd strolled the streets of Tijuana and enjoyed the mariachi music pouring from the clubs. Bill had convinced me to pose for a picture with a donkey painted to look like a zebra. In the mercado, Bill had fallen deep into discussion with the owner of a leather goods shop while I browsed the tailored jackets. He'd had a small package under one arm as we left, and didn't unwrap it until we got home. It was a sewn leather bag filled with lead shot and attached to a sling—a sap, quiet and lethal.

"It's too hard to get ammo for the gun now, with the war on, but if you're going to take cases, I want you to have some protection," he'd said, and we practiced various moves as he showed me how to use it. Now, I took the sap out of the safe and slipped it into the bottom of my handbag. Then I packed a small suitcase and went downstairs to wait for the streetcar.

The house loomed up against the deep blue sky. A dragon-like gargoyle snarled down at me from the top of the tallest tower. Like the house, he was painted white, with great green eyes and sharp wooden teeth.

I shivered despite the evening's warmth as I hauled my suitcase up the old stairs. I found the bell-pull and gave it a tug. The pachucos watched me from their post down the street.

The massive door swung wide with an eerie silence. Mrs. Smith frowned down at me.

"There you are. This way." She hooked a thumb at me as a signal to follow her into the dark maw of the house. I followed, though every ounce of me suddenly wanted to run like hell. I had a job to do. I owed it to Bill. I owed it to the agency.

We crossed the wide entryway and climbed the paneled stairwell as it turned and twisted to the third floor. The hall was barely lit by dim wall sconces. Cheaply constructed partitions bisected the original rooms. "Toilet's in the basement, sink for washing up is down there too. You've got your own soap?"

I nodded.

"What, speak up!"

"Yes'm," I replied meekly, thinking this was getting off to a bad start with her.

She said sternly, "Better keep it with you. Those girls are like a pack of crows, steal anything not nailed down."

Mrs. Smith tilted her head and eyed me with a half-smile, looking a bit like a crow herself, as she unbolted a flimsy plywood door and ushered me into a tiny room. There was hardly room for the metal chair and the skinny bed. It had a thin mattress made of ticking material with a flat pillow and a tired crocheted afghan for a blanket. She pulled the blackout curtains closed and clicked on an old lamp with a low-wattage bulb. An old orange crate set up sideways served as a bureau.

After she left, closing the door softly behind her, I almost collapsed. I just managed to hold back tears. It was nearly nighttime, dark and shadowy. There was no bolt on the inside of the door, so I put my suitcase up against it, then tiptoed up to the window. I lifted the edge of the curtain and saw 20th Street in the failing dusk. The little grocery store was closing up for the evening. A man stood at the door, looked furtively around, and then knocked softly. The door opened a crack and he slipped in. A few people strolled in the dimness and the pachucos headed toward Market Street in a tight little pack.

I pulled the curtain back some more. I could just see part of the rear garden below, a miniscule flash of day lilies and geraniums. A palm tree rustled in the breeze off the bay.

I moved the chair over to the window, turned off the light, and fully opened the curtains to look down at the city. The waterfront and warehouse districts were graded squares of deep gray and black. The only illumination came from a dim layer of stars trying to twinkle through the evening fog on the bay.

Strangely, I felt removed, almost peaceful. I don't know how long I stared out at the view, but sometime later, when the street had become completely black and I couldn't imagine anyone moving out there, I dropped the curtain and turned back to the tiny cubicle. I made up the bed as best I could and, without undressing, lay back.

A fluting, wailing noise, distant and awful, set my hair on end. I rushed to the door and pulled it open. I heard it again, coming from down the hall. I rushed toward the sound and began thumping on another of those plywood doors.

"Are you all right in there?" I asked breathlessly.

A swallowed scream. A scraping noise. The door opened. A wild-eyed young lady farsightedly peered out at me. "Who're you?" she whispered, skinny hands flying to the rollers that held her hair. "I'm a mess!" she mumbled.

"You were screaming," I said. "Is everything all right?"

"It's the dreams, the bad ones. I'm so sorry to have disturbed you. You won't tell Mrs. Smith, will you? I can't get another place, and I got to keep my job!"

"Don't worry, I won't snitch you out." I paused, then added, "What's the matter?"

"It's ever since Mary left."

"Mary?" I kept my face blank. My heartbeat raced.

"Had the room on the end. Real good-looker. But she up and left. Didn't even say goodbye. I seen Mrs. Smith cleaning out her things real early in the morning and hauling 'em out the back door in a gunny sack. She didn't see me, but I saw her all right. I tell you, I got scared and then the dreams started."

"I'm Laura, what's your name?"

"Nancy Bell, from Dayton, Ohio. Pleased to meet ya."

"Are you okay now?"

She nodded. "Don't mind me. I've gotta get some sleep— that alarm sure goes off early. Say, thanks for checking on me. That was swell of you. Really."

"Sure thing, Nancy. Sleep tight."

As I climbed back into my bed, after barricading myself in

again, I vowed to have a thorough look around the house and the yard in the daylight.

I slept fitfully, and dreamed of the dragon I'd seen at the top of the tower growing huge, breaking into my window and attacking me.

When I woke, I lay in bed a few minutes listening to the mourning doves. I could hear the clatter of the other girls getting ready for the day. I had to get up with them so that I looked like just another factory worker. I pulled on my dungarees and plaid shirt, laced up my sturdy shoes, and went downstairs to use the bathroom. Nancy was there, splashing water on her face.

"Hey, sorry I bothered you last night. Listen, lemme buy you a cuppa coffee to make up for it," she said.

"That sounds great—meet you out front in ten minutes?" Perfect! That would give us a chance to talk away from Mrs. Smith. I wouldn't put it past her to listen at doors.

Ready for the day, our hair tucked into bright bandannas, Nancy and I walked to the corner grocery and bought thick meatloaf sandwiches and apples for our lunches. The woman I'd talked with the day before took our money. "Are you living around here now?" she asked.

"Yep, I lucked into a room at the Shepard House," I said, with more gusto than I really felt.

"Welcome to the neighborhood. I'm Mrs. Giordano. The mister's off working at the tuna cannery, so I'm here all the time. We live right upstairs here, so if you need something after I've put out the *Closed* sign, just come knocking at the side door. But not too late, now."

"Well, that's real nice! I'm Laura Taylor, pleased to meet you." We shook hands.

Mrs. Giordano leaned forward and gave me a meaningful look. "I've got some extra ration coupons for sale if you're interested. Meat, sugar, even gas . . . Just don't spend them here, if you catch my drift."

"Err, no thanks," I said. Those "extra coupons" would be counterfeit, and I wanted nothing to do with them. There was a lot of money changing hands in that racket, and I knew that organized crime was involved. Could Mary have threatened to report the Giordanos and they or their supplier decided that she was too dangerous to their operation? Mrs. Giordano turned back to the deli counter. A shaft of sunlight hit the knives hanging in a rack over her head, and her face was reflected in the broad blade of a cleaver, distorted into a brutal mask.

Nancy and I grabbed our lunches and headed downtown. We found a little café just off Horton Plaza. It was called The Bomber. It had a red ceramic tile front wall and sported, over its door, a huge painted cutout of a B-24.

Nancy and I squeezed in at the counter between clumps of sailors who looked like they'd been out all night. The mugs were thick and heavy and the coffee was hot. Not much more was needed for two factory girls after a restless night.

"So you knew Mary?" I asked.

"Not real well, she'd hardly been there a week before she left, and I've been busy with my beau, so we only visited a bit in the hall. But it's weird the way she just left like that, and not taking her stuff. We'd talked about maybe going on a double date— my Fred's got a cousin who was looking to meet a cute girl. But then . . . she wasn't there anymore." Nancy shuddered. "Gives me the willies."

I hesitated, then decided to take her into my confidence. Having someone on my side in that house seemed like a good idea. I explained, and her eyes got wide.

"You're a private dick? Holy cow, I never woulda guessed! But . . . what do you think happened to Mary?"

"It looks suspicious to me. The whole neighborhood's pretty creepy! Black-market coupons, those Mexican boys, the Smiths—what's next, white slavers?" We both laughed nervously. "I think my first step is to poke around the house and see if I can find out anything. Is there ever a time when the Smiths aren't there?"

"Gosh, I'm not sure. I did hear Mrs. Smith talk about going out to pick some avocados today, maybe he'll go with her." Nancy glanced at her watch. "I gotta run, shift starts in fifteen minutes! See ya!" I saw her cross Horton Plaza in the bright sunshine, startled pigeons wheeling overhead.

I went to the office and changed clothes—a wide-brimmed hat and quiet brown dress seemed less conspicuous than my bright shirt and bandanna—and made my way back to the boarding house. I positioned myself to the side of a hedge of jade plant and peeked around it now and then to keep an eye on the house.

After a long two hours, while I repeatedly looked at my watch and sighed to give the impression of waiting for someone who was late, I saw the Smiths get into their car and slowly drive away. Everyone drove slowly those days, when they drove at all. Between the gas rationing and the impossibility of finding new tires, cars were used very cautiously. I missed being able to race down the Coast Highway from Del Mar, just for the joy of it. With Bill at the wheel of the Ford roadster, we'd laughed like maniacs and come home windburned and happy.

I quickly crossed the street and let myself into the too large, too quiet house. The Smiths had kept the back parlor for themselves and used part of the adjoining old-fashioned kitchen for an office. I started there, rifling through the letters and files in the rolltop desk. Nothing unusual there. I picked open the center drawer and found the ledger book where Mrs. Smith had recorded my deposit and first week's rent. The records began in 1942, after the Smiths bought the property and converted it to a rooming house. Her careful Spencerian script noted dates, amounts, and names. Each week, each girl's payment would be recorded, and the room number she was paying for noted. Now and then a box in a separate column would be filled in with the word *moved*, and then that room number would show up with a new name, usually in the next week. Sometimes *moved* was written in red. I flipped to the previous month. Mary Przybilski was there—five-dollar deposit, five dollars for the first week, then the notation *moved*. In red.

I felt a chill. I found the other girls' names with the red final entry and jotted them down. Then I put the ledger back in the drawer and locked it again. My heart was pounding. Red entries in a ledger didn't mean anything—did they? I pulled open a bulky file drawer and found the folder of rental applications with mine on top, as the newest resident. There was a tiny notation in pencil at the bottom, a *Y*. Did that mean, *Yes, rent a room to her?* The next application was for Betty Andrews, a leggy blonde I'd said hi to on the stairs that morning. At the bottom of her application, a tiny *N*. Betty's application listed her parents as references and they lived in nearby Lemon Grove. Then, Mary's application. Her parents were listed as references, but they were in Iowa, and there was a *Y* on the bottom of her form. I thumbed through more of the file, finding *N* after *N*, then about six months back another *Y*. It was for Bessie Jones, originally from Oklahoma—and her name in the ledger had ended with a red *moved*.

I paged back through the rental applications looking for the other girls on my list. Three . . . four . . . So far all of them had no local ties and *Y*s on their forms. My hand trembled as I searched for the sixth.

Just as I found her application I heard a car door slam and then Mrs. Smith's grating voice: "Just wait there. I'll go through and open the back door so you can bring in that box direct to the kitchen."

Her firm tread on the front steps sounded like pistol shots. *Bam! Bam!* I gulped and stuffed the folder back in the drawer. *Bam!* I gave the drawer a good shove and got it mostly closed. *Bam!* I ran for the back door, and peeked out its small window. I could see the nose of the Smiths' car. *Bam!* I slipped outside and frantically searched for someplace to hide. There was a huge gardenia bush by the back steps and I scrambled behind it. The heady smell of the flowers was overwhelming.

Mrs. Smith popped out of the back door like a giant cuckoo. "Would you believe it? Unlocked! One of those stupid girls must have stuck her nose out for some fresh air." Mr. Smith, biceps bulging, carried a wooden box piled high with avocados into the kitchen. The door closed.

I stayed frozen in place for just a couple of minutes to make sure neither of them came out again. I crept out the side garden gate and walked briskly away down 19th Street.

I pulled the bourbon out of Bill's desk drawer at the office and poured two fingers into a tumbler. Then I added a third. The bite of the tan fire on my dry tongue was bracing. I had chided Bill for his now-and-then habit of a drink during working hours, but now I completely understood.

What next? So far I knew that Mary had left her clothes and other items behind and had gone without saying goodbye to anyone. Mrs. Smith had been awfully fast on the mark to get rid of her stuff, cleaning out her room shortly after she left. The red notations in the ledger matched up with girls who seemed to have no local ties and had also moved away from the house. The town was full of workers from the Midwest who'd left small-town life for good jobs at the aircraft factories.

Like Mary.

I pulled the list of names from my handbag and started making phone calls. After working my way through the personnel departments of all the factories with my story of checking employment references on a group of girls who wanted to rent a house together, I learned that they had all left their jobs with no notice, just didn't show up one day.

Just like Mary.

Then I called the coroner's office. Ten minutes later, saying goodbye and promising a home-cooked meal for Bill's buddy there, I hung up and looked at the list again. None of them had shown up as bodies. It was as if they'd vanished into thin air.

Just like Mary.

I had a pretty fair idea that something was afoot in that old place, but I had no proof. All the girls with Ys on their paperwork had disappeared. Except for me. Was I next on this filthy list? Was I slated to die just because I seemed to be alone in a strange town? I slammed the glass down so hard that the pencils lifted and resettled in their holder, and the phone jumped off the hook.

That's it, I decided, and reached for the phone to call Mike McGowan at the police station. I knew the number by heart—FRanklin 1101. Bill had had me commit it to memory before he left. "If you're ever in over your head, doll," he'd said with a clownish half-grimace, "you call Mike, got that?" I'd laughed, shaking my head, and quivered my bare shoulders in mock fear. He'd just looked at me and given me a big kiss hot enough to melt the North Pole.

We were in love, and he was going away. The next morning he took a cab to the navy base, got on his ship, and I hadn't seen him or heard from him since.

I started to dial—and then hung up. What would Mike say to me, half in pity? No habeas corpus, no crime. Bill wouldn't go running to the cops, not before he had proof. I knew what I had to do—go back to the house and find something concrete.

I sighed as I changed out of my dress and back into my Rosie the Riveter dungarees.

Downstairs on India Street, the day was just winding down. People were heading toward the Waterfront Bar to have some beers. Sailors three and four together were laughing and talking too loud. The driving beat of "String of Pearls" pulsed from a radio. A newsie announced, "Allies take Salerno! Get yer late edition here!" I bought one and tucked it under my arm.

The iron monger rode down the street in his old buggy with the run-down nag, calling, "Rags, iron, any old iron!" Mr. Papadopoulos from the Greek café came running out of the house with an armful of rusty Model T parts.

A streetcar jangled up the tracks and I ran to catch it. "That'll be a nickel, lady."

I pulled out my coin purse. "Transfer, please," I said.

"Okay, Rosie."

I read the headlines while holding on to a canvas strap as the car swayed and bounced. One man, seeing my amateurish clinging, vacated his seat and with a patriotic salute waved me to it. I smiled and settled in to read the paper.

That night, before I allowed myself to lie down on the narrow bed, I again pushed the suitcase against the door. My mind sparked with thoughts, like men flicking cigarettes in a dark room. I tossed and turned, and as the first hints of dawn came through the edges of the blackout curtains, I dropped into a leaden sleep.

I had breakfast with Nancy in the musty dining room—three cups of coffee and a heel of bread with a scraping of margarine on it. We were the last ones at the table and Mrs. Smith was looking at us balefully. As soon as we began to slide our chairs away from the table she pounced on it like a vulture and began to clear it off.

"Come with me," said Nancy, leading me to a back door and down a short flight of steps to the backyard. The yard was still in full summer dress, even thought it was September. A profusion of datura and morning glory tumbled over the back fence. Arches and paths ran around rosebushes heavy with nodding blooms; day lilies, carnations, and lobelia grew out of cracks, and paths of wood chips and slate stones wound round lush lawns.

"Oh, Nancy, this is beautiful! A secret garden! It's like being in another world." My previous trip through the garden had been too brief and panicked to notice much. I twirled around and around, enchanted and bewitched by all the flowers and vines. The scent of jasmine and roses and blooming cacti filled the air and swaying grasses danced with towering blue delphiniums. Bright orange canna lilies stood tall.

Nancy stepped under a bower of bougainvillea and grape vines and came out with a battered cardboard box. I ran up to see a tiny brown puppy with black spots on his back and big floppy ears.

"I got him yesterday. He's part beagle and part lab. And he's all mine." She pulled out a greasy paper bag containing pieces of last night's dinner and this morning's bread and fed it to the puppy, who whimpered and then chowed down like he was starving. "His name's Spot! Here, you take him and I'll put on his leash," she said.

He was soft, warm, and wiggly as I held him. I looked skeptically at the length of cord she was attaching to his collar. When she was done, I put Spot down and he ran in circles around her, tangling her feet with the rope. She tried to step out of it, tripped, and sprawled on the ground. The little dog took off and we tried to catch him. He thought it was a game and kept on running, then stopped abruptly, sitting, tongue out. He caught a new smell, lifted and twisted his head, ears swinging, and suddenly took off again.

"Oh no! If Mrs. Smith catches me with Spot, I'm ruined," wailed Nancy. "It's just I'm so lonely here and the beggar boy said his papa was gonna drown the whelp, so I had to take him."

I was scanning the yard, looking for the little dog, dreading discovery by the landlady, when I saw him digging busily in a pile of dirt in the far corner. I trotted over there and scooped him up, then looked at where he'd been digging. For a small dog, he'd pawed pretty deep into the dirt pile. I saw something white and angular sticking out. A horrible idea formed in my head, but I didn't want Nancy involved. I knelt down and swept dirt over the object.

"Here he is, safe and sound," I said, and handed Spot back to her. "Let's get going, we don't want to be late for work."

Nancy stashed Spot in his box and we ran for the bus.

I spent the day pacing back and forth in the office, working up my courage. I had to go back and see if my suspicions were true. The white thing in the dirt looked like a bone, and not a soup bone, either. I was terribly afraid that I'd found Mary, dead in the backyard.

I taped several layers of newspaper onto the lens of a flashlight and took it into the closet to see how well it worked. It gave off a sickly light, just barely enough to see by, and I hoped not enough to violate the dim-out regulations—or be noticed by the Smiths.

Five o'clock found me back on the bus, heading up the hill to 20th Street. I was so nervous that I could barely hold up my end of a conversation, but the other girls had enough silly chatter that no one noticed. I got ready for bed like everyone else, but then changed back into my dungarees and shirt and lay silently on the bed waiting for the darkness to be complete. The sap was in my back pocket, and I could feel it pressing into my behind. By eleven o'clock it was pitch black out and I couldn't hear anyone moving in the house. It was time for me to get to work.

I grabbed my shoes and carried them as I slid my feet slowly over the wooden floor. The door opened with a tiny noise, and I paused there for several minutes until I was sure I hadn't woken anyone. I crept down the stairs, staying close to the wall to keep the steps from creaking as I gently lowered my weight onto them. I glided through the kitchen and eased myself out the back door.

The garden was fragrant in the night, and the air was cool. A car ghosted past with only its running lights on. I sat in the damp grass and slipped on my shoes, then walked back to the corner and felt my way over to the dirt pile. I turned on the flashlight and laid it in the dirt angled downward. I found the hollow I'd partly filled in and began digging. The dirt was sandy and moist in my hands. I carefully brushed it sideways until I saw the bone.

A dainty triangle of bone, a fingertip, still attached to the next joint by tendons. As I excavated further, I saw shards of flesh clinging to the bones. The smell of decay was overpowering. I felt sick to my stomach and lurched off to one side and threw up.

I brushed the dirt back over the remains of the small hand, picked up my flashlight, switched it off, and walked gingerly through the blackness toward the side gate. Now I had evidence— proof that at least one of the girls who had "moved" was really murdered. I couldn't wait to hear what Mike McGowan thought of my find.

As I reached out for the gate latch, something snuffed in the shadows. I turned, not so much startled as expecting to feel Nancy's puppy brush up against me. But there was nothing.

"Bitch," the darkness said. What seemed to be a large bush to the side of the path reached out and grabbed me from behind. A cloth-draped hand clamped over my mouth, a thick, strong arm reached around and pinned my arms to my body. I smelled the sickly sweet odor of chloroform and tried to hold my breath. The combination of the burn of vomit in my throat and chloroform in my nose made me gag. Fury and panic took over—and somewhere, a cold reminder of one of Bill's lessons in self-defense.

Stomp on the instep. Go for the crotch, the eyes. Spin inside the arms.

I tried to spin but the man was too strong. His arm was thick and hairy. The chloroform was closing me down. With the last of my conscious strength, I kicked up my leg, then stomped his bare foot with the heel of my shoe. He made a noise like a startled pig. I finally managed to whirl around as the man's grip loosened. Then with a clenched fist I hit him below the stomach. My knuckles met flab and then bone, and I grabbed below the bone and twisted as hard as I could through the thick pants.

Now my attacker actually squealed. "Shit!" he gasped, curling over. Mr. Smith's voice, definitely. And it smelled like him. I pushed him away, grabbed the sap from my pocket, and swung it wildly. It was too dark to see more than vague outlines. The sap didn't connect. I took a step back and turned my head, following a faint movement. A shadow the size of a truck coming back to hurt me. I swung again. The sap came down with a wet crunch on Smith's clutching hand. He drew back and squealed again, so much like a pig. I zeroed in on his head and swung again. He fell with a heavy thump, like so much dead meat.

The back door swung open and Mrs. Smith peered out. "George? George!" she called. "Are you all right?"

I ran for the gate and fled down the street. There was a tiny sliver of light in the upstairs window at the corner grocery. As instructed, I pounded on the side door. The window raised with a high squeak of old wood on wood and Mrs. Giordano peered out. "Now look here," she called, "this is far too late!"

"Do you have a phone? I have to call the police! Let me in," I begged.

"What's this about? Who's there? Laura, is it?" Her gray hair hung down in a long braid as she leaned out the window, and I wished it were long enough to clamber up, like Rapunzel's.

"It's an emergency, let me in! Someone's going to kill me."

"Well, we'll have none of that—this is a *nice* neighborhood! The mister'll be right down." I could hear her yell something in Italian to her husband, then his heavy steps on the side stairs. The door opened and I dashed in past him. I hoped I wasn't leaping from the frying pan into the fire. Mr. Giordano was short and round. He wore a sleeveless T-shirt and suspenderless twill workpants that exposed a great deal of pale, hairy belly.

"Come in, missy, what's the trouble?" he asked, and I felt like crawling into his big arms for protection.

"I . . . I just need to use the phone. And maybe wait for the police." I began to shake. Mr. Giordano shooed me upstairs into the apartment. Mrs. Giordano put the kettle on while I used the phone. She looked at the curtained window and the darkness behind it while the tea water boiled. "They should just try it," she muttered, holding up the biggest butcher knife I'd ever seen. "Let them try it!"

"Watch that thing," her husband said.

I gave a deposition about what I'd seen and a judge issued a search warrant for the house and yard. Then I headed back to the office. Now I had to wait and see if it was Mary's body I'd found—and if there were any others there. The police brought in a team of men to shovel deep into the lush garden. They found the body in the dirt pile right away and arrested the Smiths on suspicion of murder. They kept on digging—in the dirt pile, in the lush garden beds, under the bower where Nancy had hidden Spot. The final count was six.

Six lost women. Six human beings, like me, like the girl next door, like all the rootless, hopeful young women in this goddamned country, this goddamned world.

Goddamn Bill for not telling me how bad it could get. Goddamn me for my happy little smart-girl moxie.

Mike McGowan called me with the news. "Good work, Laura. You really uncovered a can of worms. Bill would be proud."

Bill could sleep at night after this kind of thing.

"You were lucky to get away in one piece," Mike went on.

"A little luck," I said, my stomach taking a twist. Mike knew about the sap, which wasn't strictly legal. We both knew that if I hadn't had it, I would have ended up in the garden as number seven. "Any idea what the Smiths were up to?"

"Well, it seems they were taking a novel approach to war profiteering. Girls who disappear don't take their room deposits. Or their purses. They had a tidy sum tucked away."

"That's awful! Those poor girls."

"It's not a pretty world out there, Laura. So, you going to call Przybilski first or do you want us to do it? He'll have to come down and see if he can ID his sister's body. Not that there's much recognizable to ID with. We'll probably need dental records."

"I'll call him, Mike. Thanks." I rang off and stared at the phone. Then I called the navy base and left a message for Przybilski to come see me.

I rehearsed a hundred different ways of breaking the news. Przybilski showed up later that afternoon. There was no easy way, so I told him straight out.

"I'm so sorry, but I think your sister's dead."

"What! What happened?"

I explained. He sat and hung his head as he turned his cap around in circles, his hands sliding over the stitched brim with a tiny rasping noise. I offered to come down to the coroner's office with him, but he said he'd go by himself. I gave him back the picture of Mary and he stared sadly at the bright face of his sister. "I guess that's it, then."

"One more thing." I felt like a rat, a war profiteer myself, but this was a business, after all. "Here's my bill." I slid the invoice across the desk.

"I don't get paid again till the end of the month. But I'll be back with it."

"Okay, Navy, I trust you." We shook hands and he walked out into the sunny afternoon. The bay was still sparkling.

GOLD SHIELD BLUES

BY JEFFREY J. MARIOTTE

Mount Soledad

Mount Soledad was a cushy gig.

Mostly, it was a matter of driving around in a company car with a light bar on top and the Gold Shield Security logo emblazoned across the doors. Occasionally, I had to interrupt drag-racing teenagers, and even more occasionally respond to a dispatch call, which more often than not turned out to be raccoons or feral cats, rather than genuine intruders. What security companies never tell their customers is that most actual break-ins take place in lower-middle-class and poor neighborhoods, where the loss of property can do real damage to a family's shaky financial status. The rich have fences and walls and alarms, buttressed by decent police response times and private security companies like Gold Shield. The bad guys know that, and since your high-class cat burglars are mostly fictional, most real-life burglars don't bother trying to hit the mansions of the rich.

So when I got a call from dispatch, one overly warm August night, sending me to a house on Via Capri—a reported intruder—I wasn't too worried about what I'd find when I got there. I knew the place from the outside, high up on the hill, facing west-northwest for the primo ocean view. An eight-foot masonry wall, spiked on top, surrounded the property, and a cobblestone drive led through double wrought-iron gates before sweeping up to the house.

When I arrived, less than five minutes after taking the call (my strobes slicing the darkness into ribbons of tinted black), the gates were closed. I pulled up to the call box mounted on a post, and pressed a button. In a moment, a crackly voice responded. I identified myself and was buzzed in. The gates parted with a slow majesty, and I drove through into a lushly landscaped estate full of mature trees and what looked like enough lawn to graze cattle on.

It was hardly unique in that. Some of the priciest real estate in La Jolla—itself one of the most expensive enclaves in the United States—was on Mount Soledad. Dr. Seuss had lived here; I sometimes saw his widow out and about in their Caddy with the GRINCH license plate.

Every light in the place was burning, showing me a three-story Tuscan-style home, all vast slabs of stucco in a dark mustard color with turrets and red-tile roof and all the extras. I parked between the house and a fountain that looked like it belonged on a postcard from Rome. By the time I was out of the car, flashlight in hand, a front door opened that two Los Angeles Lakers could have passed through, one standing on the other's shoulders.

A man stood in the doorway. He was probably in his late sixties, trim, with neat gray hair, wearing a white shirt with the sleeves rolled back over his forearms, dress pants, and leather slippers. Well put together, the way wealthy men often are; plenty of time playing tennis or golf helping keep them in shape. I couldn't tell if his tan had come from the sun or a spray, but it was rich and even. I had checked the dispatch report as I made my way down the driveway, and the homeowner's name was Terrance Paulson.

"Are you Mr. Paulson?" I asked.

"That's right."

"I'll need to see some ID, please. We had a prowler report for this residence."

"I look like a prowler to you?"

"No sir. But I need to make sure. If you're really Mr. Paulson, you wouldn't want me to take any shortcuts, would you?"

"No, that's true." He fished around in his pocket and came up with a slim leather wallet. I had never understood why the richest people didn't have the fattest wallets, but his looked like the addition of even a single dollar bill would stretch it out of shape. He slid a driver's license from it and handed it over. The picture matched the face, and the name matched what I'd been given. "I'm Terry Paulson, as you can see."

"Very good, sir." I handed back the license.

"And you are . . . ?"

"Mike Rogers," I said. "The police have been alerted and they're on the way. Do you know if the prowler is still on the property, Mr. Paulson?"

"Call me Terry, Mike. I don't know if it was really a prowler, in retrospect. My wife heard a noise. She thought it was a prowler. I didn't see anything but thought it was safest to trigger the alarm."

"That's the best thing to do. Let us take a look for you. Where did she hear it?"

"She can tell you best herself." He stepped back through the door, into a foyer that appeared to be floored with fine marble. A staircase curled up from there. "Sharon!" he called.

She came out of a side door, wearing a shy look and not a lot else. When I saw her I forgot why I was there, forgot everything for a few seconds. I had never seen a woman like her, except on a movie screen, or a computer one. She had plump lips, a slightly olive complexion, and smoky gray eyes. Long dark hair framed her face in ringlets and then curled off the tops of breasts that were high and round and barely contained by a low-cut, silky blue nightgown that more than hinted at the rest of her impressive curves. A ring glinted off the little toe of her left foot. She could have bracketed my thirty-one years by five in either direction.

"Hello," she said, and her voice was low and frank and warm and not at all shy. "I'm sorry I got you out here. It's probably nothing."

"Don't worry about that, it's what I'm here for," I replied. "If it's okay, I'll look around just the same. Where did you think you heard something?"

She flashed a smile, showing me a couple of front teeth that should have seen braces but hadn't. Somehow the imperfection made her all the more stunning. "In the back," she said. Barefoot, she stepped outside, onto the cobblestones. "That's nice. Cool. Come, I'll show you."

She padded softly past me. I glanced at Terry Paulson, who indicated with a nod of his head that I should follow his wife. I did, happily, trying not to stare at the round ass swishing back and forth under the thin layer of silk.

She showed me the area where she thought she'd heard something, between the pool house and the tennis court. I stayed for a few minutes, waved the flashlight around. When the cops arrived, they took over, but they didn't see anything either.

Finally, I had to get back to my patrol. The company had installed GPS units in all the cars, which had not only cut back on unauthorized excursions to Tijuana and Ocean Beach, but also allowed them to enforce a time constraint. If we spent more than fifteen minutes at any given address we had to account for it in writing. Before I left, I tried to find Terry Paulson, but he was in back with the cops. Instead, I found Sharon, or she found me as I was heading for the car.

"Mike," she said.

"Oh good, there you are." I had a business card in my hand already, and I held it out to her. "This is my card. I put my cell number on the back. Sometimes it's quicker to just call me directly, rather than go through dispatch, because I'm on duty in the area most nights."

"Thank you, Mike. Thanks for coming over, too. I feel so much better."

"Like you said, it was probably nothing, maybe an animal passing through. But you don't want to take chances. If you hear or see anything unusual, just call."

She took the card, letting her hand linger on my fingers for a long moment. She held my gaze with hers for a few seconds, showed me those two crooked teeth again, then turned and walked back into the house. Once again, memory fled. It wasn't until the huge front door closed that I remembered I was leaving.

I heard from her two nights later. My cell phone rang and when I answered it there was a voice on the other end, barely audible, as if calling from somewhere in outer space.

"Mike?"

"Yeah?" It took a few seconds to place her. "Mrs. Paulson, is that you? Is everything okay?"

"No. Yes. I mean . . . Mike, can you meet me?"

The car's digital clock blasted *11:18* at me. "I can be there in five minutes. Should I call the police?"

"No," she said, more firmly this time. "Not here, Mike. You know the cross?"

"On the hill?"

"That's right."

"Sure."

"Meet me there," she said. "Give me fifteen minutes."

"Fifteen minutes," I echoed, but she was already gone.

The cross was at the top of the mountain. Parking surrounded it, and walking paths, mostly used by tourists and lovers who looked out at the nearly 360-degree view and made out in the dark. Everyone who had been there more than once knew to dim their lights when they pulled into the little circle. People fought about the cross all the time, since it's on public land. One side considered it an inappropriate display of religion, the other insisted that its value is historical, not specifically religious, and it should be left alone. A few years earlier someone had decided to get around the controversy by converting it into a war memorial honoring anyone whose family ponied up the money to buy a plaque. When I was up there, I barely saw the cross, because it was in the center of the circle and the view was on the outside.

I made it there in ten minutes. She was five minutes late. That left me plenty of time to wonder about what she wanted, why she hadn't wanted me to come to the house. Time to wonder, and fantasize.

When she emerged from a black Lexus IS F10, I didn't wonder anymore. I didn't do anything but stare.

She was fully dressed this time, in a blue tank top and faded jeans that clung to her thighs like a sheen of perspiration. Her hair was loose, like before, and if anything she looked even sexier. More relaxed.

I was glad one of us was relaxed, because I was buzzing. On fire.

"Hello, Mike," she said.

"What . . . what can I do for you, Mrs. Paulson?"

"Please, Mike. Sharon."

"Okay, Sharon. What did you need to see me for?"

She shot me a *you're kidding* look. "What do you see when you look at me, Mike? Be honest."

I couldn't be completely honest. "A very beautiful woman. Wealthy, happily married—"

She stopped me with an arched eyebrow and a waggled finger. "Don't. Mike, don't patronize me, please."

"What?"

"Tell me what you *see*."

"I see probably the most amazing woman I've ever encountered. Are you really real?"

"I don't come from money, if that's what you mean. Everything I've got is what I was born with. You like it?"

"It's impressive. You're impressive. Your husband is a lucky guy."

"He gets what he wants, I get what I want. It's a trade-off, but it works for us."

"What do you mean?" I didn't know why I felt so stupid around her, but apparently it wasn't going away.

She came closer, enveloping me in a musky scent that made the fine hairs on the back of my neck stand up. It was feral and rich at the same time, and I didn't want to exhale and let it go. She took my hand and walked me away from the cars, toward one of the overlooks.

The air was alive with a brittle clarity. I could see the lights of Del Mar and beyond, up the coast. Looking back the other way, while waiting for Sharon, I had seen SeaWorld and downtown San Diego and Mexico past that. Closer in was the working-class community of Clairemont, and below us La Jolla glittered, then dropped off to black at the coastline.

"Like I said, I don't come from money. I need it, though, and do what I need to do to get it. My mom's not well, and my little brother . . . he's got MS, we don't know how long he'll live but while he does he needs special care, special equipment. Terry's generous. But he doesn't give me everything I need."

"Like what?"

"What do you think? I'm a young woman, Mike. I have needs. Terry is kind, he's gentle, but . . ." She let the sentence trail off. By now even I had figured out where she was going, but I wasn't going to let her not lead the way. I stayed quiet, and she picked up where she'd left off. "Viagra's great, but at a certain point, the world's finest chef could prepare his finest meal, and a man who'd just eaten a three-pound steak wouldn't touch it. Availability and appetite are two different things. I'm lucky if he wants it once a week."

"I'm sorry," I said. It was stupid, but I was at a loss for words. "I'm sure you could get—"

"There are plenty of guys I could get. The question is, which one do I want?"

She pushed me down on a bench and stood in front of me, hands on my shoulders, leaning in, letting her breasts brush my face. "See, I have a *much* bigger appetite than Terry does. I'm just about always hungry." She ran her hands down my chest, lowering herself to her knees in front of me, and clawed at my zipper. I sat on the bench, hands pressed against the cool stone, feeling her heat on me and my response to it, and at the same time feeling like a trout that had just bit into a nightcrawler only to find a barbed hook hidden inside.

Hooked, I was. That meeting by the cross was only the first. I had never known a woman anything like Sharon. Her appetite, as she'd said, was enormous, and it wasn't surprising that she was too much for Terry to handle. As she'd said, he didn't seem to mind. After a couple more meetings on top of the mountain, in the dark, she started inviting me to the house. Every now and then we saw Terry, usually as she led me by the hand toward a spare bedroom. He'd give us a knowing smile and a nod, and now and then a few friendly words. I wasn't sure how a man with such a fiery animal of a wife could be so utterly nonpossessive, but I wasn't about to question it. Sometimes we'd hear him moving around, and once I saw someone at the window as I was driving away, watching from behind a sheer curtain—someone who didn't look like him in that instant's glance, but who must have been.

Sharon exhausted me. When I was away from her I couldn't think of anything but her. When I was with her I didn't think at all. I just was. There was no intellectual engagement; we barely spoke, beyond the necessary words: *Faster, slower, here, like that, there, don't stop.* I tried to keep our meetings outside working hours, but when she called, I came. Sometimes I left the company car someplace and drove my own over to the house, then made up a story about why I had been parked for so long.

I started to think I was in over my head when I got my third reprimand at work. My supervisor wasn't buying my stories anymore, and I was on the verge of being fired. I shouldn't have cared—private security was a game for kids, anyway, or ex-cops trying to stretch their pensions, and unlike most of my coworkers I wasn't in it for the power that a badge and a steel-clad flashlight offered. I liked the solitude, the freedom to chart my own course through the night, to drive the quiet streets and watch the houses, the ocean down below, the stars wheeling overhead.

But I was only fooling myself if I thought I didn't need the job. Sharon had her financial demands, and I had my own—an apartment two blocks from the water in Mission Beach, alimony from an early, stupid marriage, car payments, a TV that was too big for the apartment and had cost more than I could afford. People needed money to get by, and I was no exception.

In high school I had been a jock, an outfielder who could snag a ball that had wings on it, then sail it to first base or third or home without breaking a sweat. I had been so good that it took awhile to understand that I just wasn't quite good enough to win any scholarships, and without that I couldn't afford college. Since then, I'd been a guy that things happened to. My wife had proposed to me, and I'd gone along with it. She had decided the marriage was over, and I'd accepted that too. I fell into low-paying jobs, like the one at Gold Shield. I had pretty much given up thinking I would ever have anything like real money, or real love, or any real excitement.

Sharon was something else that happened to me, not anything I had set out to claim, to conquer. And as much as I hated to consider it, I knew I'd have to stop seeing her before I lost my paycheck. One more time, I told myself, and then one more time, and one more time after that.

When I was away from her I was resolute. Then when she called, I was putty.

On a mid-October night, with the first hint of autumn crispness in the air, she called again. "Mike," she said, "I need you to come over. Right now." Her voice was different, her words terse, clipped.

"On the way," I answered. The night had been quiet so far,

one alarm that had gone off without any evident cause, home-owners not there. I'd had it shut off and decided to make regular swings past the place throughout the evening, just in case.

But I could be gone for the hour or so it would take to see Sharon. Anyway, she didn't sound amorous, she sounded upset.

When I got there, the house was dark. I buzzed myself in—I had long since been given the gate code—and parked in my usual spot beside the fountain. I got out of the car, listened to a breeze rustling through the leaves of a banana tree, then ducked back in for the flashlight. I started to wish I'd been as-signed a gun. Something wasn't right; the place was never this quiet.

I tapped on the big door with the end of the flashlight. "Sha-ron?" No answer, so I leaned on the handle, pushed the door open a few inches. They never set the alarm these days, not with me coming around so often. "Terry? Sharon?"

No sound came from inside. I clicked on the flashlight and went in. The house looked like it always did, but there was a sense of emptiness to it that was new. Usually I was with at least one of them, and the other was close by.

I scanned the downstairs quickly. Nothing seemed out of place, so I went up. I hadn't turned on any lights, even though it made me feel vaguely criminal—I told myself I didn't want to advertise to the neighbors that anyone was in the house, even though I knew the nearest neighbors could barely see a corner of the top floor. The flashlight was plenty bright, and using it I picked my way down the hall to the bedroom we always used. Empty. I turned the other way down the wide corridor, to the room she'd told me she shared with Terry. That door had always been closed during my visits, one aspect of their life together off limits to me.

It was open now.

Even before I reached it, the stink hit me. Blood and shit, unmistakable, mixed with other odors I couldn't identify. Her name fell from my lips. My left hand went to my nose and mouth, covering them, and sucking in shallow gasps, I went in.

She was on the bed, her head dangling off the near side, her arms splayed out, legs flung toward the far edge. A spray of blood flecked with gray painted the ceiling, and more of it streamed down the bed covering, puddling thick and black on the lush carpet under my feet. My stomach gave a quick flip and I swallowed hard, afraid I was going to lose the fish tacos I had bought for dinner down in Pacific Beach.

"Sharon?" I said, sobbing the word.

But it wasn't her, and I knew it almost at once. This woman had a hole in the middle of her forehead, just between the eyebrows. But she also had gray streaks in auburn hair and wide green eyes staring at me, and she was at least fifteen years older than Sharon. Attractive, or she had been before the bullet, and relatively fit, but thicker and less voluptuous.

I stared at her, uncomprehending, just as stupid as I had been while in Sharon's bed, in her arms, clutched between her thighs. I was still standing there, unable to move, my gullet spasming, when the door creaked behind me.

"I see you've met Sharon," Terry Paulson said.

I spun around, shined the light at him. She stood behind him, glorious as ever. "But . . . if that's Sharon . . ."

"It is," Terry said. "Meet Lacie."

"I don't understand."

"That, my friend, is self-evident. Come on, let's go to the kitchen and talk this over, shall we?"

I let them lead me back downstairs. Lights were on now and the house felt more like it usually did, except there was a dead woman upstairs and I was utterly lost.

We sat at their big rustic wooden dining table, and Terry filled me in. Sharon—no, Lacie—sat close to him, occasionally stroking his arm, smoothing his hair. She made no effort to touch me, and I was too afraid to try reaching out to her.

"Here's the deal," Terry said. "I have this big house, this terrific life, right? Or I did, until I lost a bundle in the meltdown. Since then, things have been getting tight. We were in serious debt—another month or two or five, and we would have lost all this. Sharon wouldn't have wanted that. She has never been particularly healthy, and worse these last couple of years, sick all the time. We had major insurance policies on each other, of course, and I kept thinking I'd be able to collect on hers in time to save everything. But although she was close to dying, she wouldn't actually die. She was in pain, absolutely miserable, really, but she kept hanging on. Lacie and I, well . . . we couldn't wait."

"So you killed her?"

"You still don't get it, do you? *You* killed her."

"What the fuck do you mean by that?" I slammed my palm against the table, making it jump.

"You've been having an affair with her for months. There's plenty of documentation of that. Phone records, saved texts, surveillance video showing you coming to the house at all hours. I bet if we subpoenaed the GPS records of your company car, they'd back that up."

"But . . . not with *her*. Not the real Sharon."

"Phone records and texts don't divulge that kind of detail. So you've been having an affair with a married woman. Tonight, she called you. You came over. I guess you fought or something, and . . . well, you just snapped."

"But that's not what happened!" I said.

He smiled, and the jam I had put myself in started to become clear.

"It doesn't have to be what happened," he continued. "But it might have been, and we can prove that version if we have to. There's video of you coming in here tonight. There's her phone call—her last phone call, to your cell. That's your company car outside."

I stared at them, my gaze shifting from one impassive face to the other. "What kind of sap do you think I am?"

"How many kinds do there have to be?" Lacie asked, throwing me the kind of smile that a day ago would have caused a stirring at my groin instead of nausea in my gut. "We only needed one. It was down to you or the pool service guy, and I liked you better."

Terry picked up where he had left off. "Or it could go this way. Lacie has an apartment, down by the Cove. We were all there tonight, the three of us. A kinky little threesome. Some man-on-man action, along with both of us on Lacie."

"I don't—"

"I don't either," Terry said. "That's why it's beautiful. A man in my position, with my reputation, would never make up something like that just for an alibi. It's too embarrassing. So everybody will believe it. I'm still important enough in this town to keep it quiet, but the people who need a story—a few detectives, a prosecutor or two—we'll give them a story they'd never imagine was a lie."

"You killed her." I was slow, but I wasn't impenetrable after all. "You fucking killed her for the insurance money!"

"I guess you weren't with him for his brains," Terry said.

"Not hardly," Lacie agreed. "To be fair, that wasn't what he saw in me, either." She squeezed her arms together, popping her breasts out. "It's all about the jugs, isn't it, Mike?"

I scraped my chair back, stood up fast enough to knock it over with a loud crash. I picked it up, then realized I had put my fingerprints on it. They were all over the house. I'd never be able to wipe them all. "You make me sick!" I said. "Both of you!"

"We're not particularly interested in your opinion of us, Mike," Terry said. "You were meant to serve a purpose. You've served it. Now, you either go to prison for Sharon's murder, or you alibi us and we alibi you. Sharon goes into the unsolved files, and everybody's happy."

"Not everybody. Not me. I didn't kill anybody."

"You stay out of jail. We'll help you out financially, of course. Say, fifty thousand when the insurance check clears. Another fifty in three years, if you've kept up your end of the bargain. Not life-changing money, but a pretty nice little bonus."

I buried my face in my hands, paced the kitchen, scratched my head, my arms. Everything itched. How could I have been so stupid? I wondered. Then I looked at Lacie, and remembered.

She had been straight with me in the beginning. She'd told me she did what she needed to do to get money. What made me think that fucking me was any different from fucking Terry?

And that face I'd seen in the window one day, behind a sheer curtain. That had been Sharon, who had known, even then, that something was happening around her. She could have called out, could have told somebody. Was she a willing accomplice in all this? Knowing she wouldn't die but couldn't really live, wanting to let Terry get the big paycheck?

That was what I told myself when I finally agreed to Terry's plan. I kept telling myself that through the investigation, the hours and hours of interrogation. When it was over, when it didn't look like I was being fired because of suspicion, charges never leveled against me, Gold Shield cut me loose. The fifty grand came in handy then, and I was barely able to stretch it for the three years until the next fifty.

When he brought me that second fifty, a surprisingly small bundle in a reusable Ralph's grocery bag, Terry looked worn out. His face was blotchy and lined, his hair unkempt. Dark half-moons drooped from his eyes like a crying woman's mascara. We had become something resembling friends over the past three years, meeting at bars every now and then, or at the Cove, watching the seals play, talking about our lives. Mostly me talking, him listening; many of my friends had drifted away after the murder, losing my job. I didn't have people I could talk to who really understood what I'd been through, except him.

But not this time.

He sat in my living room, on a Goodwill couch, slouched forward with his arms on his knees, doing almost all the talking. "I never should have married her," he said. "That's when it all started to go wrong."

I'd seen the wedding in the newspaper. His wife in the grave just over a year, some had clucked about it but he'd said life goes on, it's what Sharon would have wanted for him. A detective named Givens had stopped by the next day, asked what I thought about it. I told him they deserved each other, and left it at that.

"Wrong how?"

"She's a captivating woman, don't get me wrong. Well, you know that already, don't you? But she's only interested in one thing, really. When it comes down to it, it's always been the money for her."

"I thought that's what you wanted."

"She gets under your skin."

"Tell me."

"But no matter what she says, whatever we do, I always know it's the money she's doing it for."

"Life sucks," I said.

"I'm worried, Mike. She made me sign a prenup, but it's all in her favor. If I die, she's a rich woman."

"I guess you've been investing more wisely."

"I've made some good plays, I don't mind saying. That insurance money saved my ass."

"And now she wants to kill your ass."

"That's what I think. We've got to kill her first, Mike. It's the only way out."

"We?"

"I've still got the goods on you. I could bury you with one phone call. Not just Sharon's murder, but the ongoing blackmail."

"Blackmail?"

He kicked the grocery bag. "You think there aren't records of these big withdrawals?"

"If I'm being accused of blackmail, I might as well ask for more."

"You'll have it, don't worry. Help me get loose of Lacie, and you'll have plenty."

"No," I said. "Absolutely not."

"Seems to me like you really don't have much choice."

She called me two days later, on an unseasonably gloomy autumn afternoon when the sun had ducked behind a gray haze and wouldn't show itself again. When I recognized her voice, I almost called her Sharon, but I caught myself in time.

"Meet me," she said. "At the cross."

"When?"

"Now. Soon as you can."

I was home in Mission Beach, so it took awhile to get up there. When I arrived, she was sitting on the bench, our bench. We were above much of the haze there, but it sat all around us like a thick, fuzzy blanket, blocking out the world below. Sounds of traffic on the 5 and 52 freeways wafted gently up. The parking area was deserted. I zipped up my leather jacket and approached her, half expecting her to pull a gun.

"You came." She wore a considerably more expensive leather coat, and leather gloves with fur linings. Her jeans were expensive too. She was still beautiful, would always be beautiful, but she was more finished than she had been in the old days, before she was Mrs. Terrance Paulson. She'd even had her teeth fixed.

"Did you think I wouldn't?"

"I didn't know."

"You've always known."

She reached up, took my hand, pulled me onto the bench

beside her, the outer edges of our thighs touching. I could smell her. That, at least, hadn't changed.

"He's going to kill me," she began.

A chill ran though me, as if my clothes had suddenly dissolved and I was sitting naked on this fog-enshrouded mountain. "What makes you think that?"

"The way he looks at me. I can tell." She gave a single dry chuckle. "I've seen it before, right?"

"I guess."

"So I know."

"What are you going to do about it? You can't exactly go to the cops."

"What am I going to do?" She put her hand on my leg, rested her head on my shoulder. Two fingernails began tracing up my thigh. "You mean, what are *we* going to do?"

"We?"

"Of course."

"Hold on, Lacie."

"What?" she said. She had shifted again, so her mouth was close to my ear, her voice a low purr. Her breasts pressed against my arm, and those fingers kept tracking north. "It's always been you and me, Mike. Always. I just . . . I just had to bide my time. Until it was safe."

"Safe? You call that safe? You're talking about killing your husband."

"Safer than letting him kill me. And don't worry, if he goes, I inherit everything. And then there's his life insurance—I'm the beneficiary on that too."

"Some people just don't learn," I said.

Her lips grazed my cheek. Her fingers found home.

I was right. I was the only one of the three of us who hadn't taken part in a murder, and yet I was lunging for that nightcrawler, the one with the hook inside, the barbs that would jab into my cheek and draw me along. Some people just don't learn.

When it came to lures and hooks, hers were better than Terry's, and they always would be. But if Terry was murdered, the cops would take an especially close look, given Sharon's fate. They might even reopen that case. And I didn't know what Terry had done with the goods he had on me, when they might show up.

I pulled myself away. The effort was almost more than I could make. "Listen, Lacie, I . . . I have to go."

"So soon? You just got here." She twirled some hair around her right index finger, then lowered the finger slowly, letting it glide across the swell of her breast. "We're all alone."

"I know. But we'll have plenty of time for that, right?"

Lacie smiled. "Yes. All the time we need."

"Then there's no rush."

"No rush."

"I'll call you," I said. I turned and made for my car as fast as I could, afraid I'd change my mind, go back to her, throw her down on that cold stone bench and take her right there.

Take her. Funny how a simple phrase can have multiple meanings.

I got in the car and turned the key, listening to the engine start, the radio come on.

During the next few days, I'd have to kill someone, or help do it.

Between now and then, I had a lot of thinking to do.

They wanted to turn me from a fake murderer into a real one. I was willing to go along with that. What I didn't want was to be left out in the cold when it was over.

The time had finally come, I thought, to look out for myself. Time to chart my own course again, to pick my path through the unbroken darkness. I knew what Terry had to offer, and what Lacie did.

I looked back once, in the rearview, and saw Lacie sitting on our bench, arms wrapped around herself to fend off the cold, and I wondered which one I would choose.

KEY WITNESS

BY MARTHA C. LAWRENCE

La Jolla Cove

The beach was nearly empty. I checked my air hose and regulator—twice—before diving into the surf. The early-morning skies over La Jolla Cove were clear and blue but beneath the sparkling surface the tides were restless and the water murky. On the plus side, a tropical storm brewing up from Mexico had warmed the ocean by a degree or two. On the down side, the storm had churned up a lot of debris. Visibility near shore wasn't great; fifteen feet at best.

The ocean can be murderous. Ask any life insurance agent who writes policies for scuba divers. But gliding nearly naked underwater is as close as I've come to free flight, and the irresistible sensuality of it overrides my usual caution about such things. Admittedly, it was stupid to dive alone that June morning. No excuses there. I rationalized that my dive partner would be arriving any minute. I promised myself I wouldn't go out too far.

Swimming through the shallow water, I pushed past rocky ledges filled with lobsters, shrimp, crabs, and abalone. Divers here can look but cannot touch; the cove is an ecological preserve. Visibility improved the farther out I swam. Tempted by schools of small bass and bright orange garibaldi, I covered a few hundred yards.

I hesitated when I reached the swirling masses of feather-boa kelp that spanned the outer edge of the cove. The dense plants made me feel claustrophobic. Kicking hard, I shot through the kelp forest and the bottom dropped away to thirty feet.

That's where I saw Wendy, though I didn't know her name at the time.

Her long, blond hair undulated with the tide. Looking down at her, I couldn't see her face. For one hopeful moment I thought she might be a mermaid, unencumbered as she was by scuba gear. But mermaids don't wear bikinis, and they don't have ghostly white legs. Her arms stretched in front of her as though reaching for some treasure at the bottom of the sea. Moving closer, I saw the dull glint of metal at her wrists. She wasn't reaching for anything; she was handcuffed to a heavy chain that was anchored to the ocean floor.

It was terribly quiet. I remembered to breathe, and soon heard the reassuring sound of oxygen rushing through my air hose, followed by my own carbon dioxide bubbling toward the surface.

I knew from the woman's rigid form that she was past saving. I swam around her body and looked into a face so likeable that it broke my heart. She hadn't been in the water for long. Her skin was smooth and unblemished, except for some redness where her wrists chafed against the handcuffs. Her mouth was open to the sea that filled her lungs. Her wide green eyes seemed to be staring at a small leather pouch on a thin leather strap that floated loosely around her neck.

Feeling an urgent need for fresh air, I followed the chain up to the surface, where it attached to a buoy floating about three hundred yards from shore. Treading water, I removed my mouthpiece and took several grateful breaths.

A crowd had gathered on the beach to watch the activity offshore. Coast Guard officers in small boats had been posted around the crime scene to keep swimmers away as divers searched for evidence.

"What time did you find the body?" Carlos Rico, one of the officers who'd responded to my 911 call, had been interviewing me for some time. We'd already covered this question. My answer didn't change.

"Sometime between seven-ten and seven-fifteen."

"You seem pretty sure about that."

I shrugged. "Occupational habit. I'm an investigator."

He made a note on his report. "Private?"

"Yeah." I fished a business card out of the backpack I'd retrieved from my truck and handed it over. The type read, *Elizabeth Chase, Psychic Investigator.* Rico studied the card for a moment before attaching it to his clipboard. If he thought there was anything peculiar about my title, he didn't let on.

"You say you got here about ten minutes to seven and went in the water a few minutes after seven. Can anyone confirm that?"

I looked around to see if I recognized anyone on the beach, someone who might have seen me go into the water.

"Not really. My dive partner was supposed to meet me here, but I guess she couldn't make it this morning." Shivering in my damp bathing suit, I watched Rico print my statement word for word. The sudden blaring of car horns and screeching of brakes made us both look up.

The uncommon sight of police and emergency vehicles in the posh La Jolla neighborhood had caused a nasty traffic jam on Coast Boulevard, the road that snakes along the shoreline. Residents in the high-rise condominiums facing the ocean had come out onto their balconies to see what the ruckus was all about. Some of them looked cranky. They'd plunked down several million dollars for their homes. Klieg lights and crime scene looky-loos were not the view they'd bargained for.

The Motorola on Rico's hip spit out a static-filled message. I only caught part of it, something about moving the body. I felt a sudden stab of protectiveness toward the dead woman, as if my discovering her somehow made me responsible for her too.

"Where are they taking her?" I asked.

"The lifeguard station in Quivera Basin."

That made sense. Quivera was a fairly remote location at the mouth of Mission Bay. Far from the beach-going masses, it would be a good place to examine and identify the body.

Rico's female partner, an officer several years his senior, took over the questioning. By the time we were done, my bathing suit was dry. She took one last look at my business card.

"Is this information up-to-date?" she asked.

"Yes, ma'am."

"Okay, you're free to go. A case investigator will be in touch with you soon."

Heading back to my truck, I had the uneasy feeling that comes over me when I sense I'm being stared at. I looked up at the condominiums clinging to the cliff. If someone was peering down at me, I couldn't tell. The reflected sunlight in the windows of the ocean-facing condos made them impenetrable as one-way mirrors.

Later that afternoon, the case detective rang my doorbell as I was working in my home office. I checked him out in the CCTV monitor above my desk, the one that's fed by a hidden security camera and microphone on my front porch. His thick silver hair, dark eyebrows, and sharp features were reminiscent of Sean Connery, but his wrinkle-free pants and unfashionable jacket screamed undercover detective. He was whistling a haunting rendition of "Stairway to Heaven" and looking vaguely bored. Like any good investigator, he hadn't called in advance to announce his visit. I closed the file I was working on and went to the door.

"You Elizabeth Chase?" He was holding the business card I'd given to the patrol cop that morning.

"Yeah, and you're Detective . . ." I drew the word out, waiting for him to fill in the blank.

"Baxter." He looked at me with a face that made me want to confess, even though I hadn't done a damn thing wrong. I wondered how many years he'd been perfecting that trick.

I led him into my office, where he did a quick survey of the room. His eyes scanned my P.I. certificate and my doctoral diploma—a PhD in parapsychology from Stanford—and lingered on a framed letter from San Diego's chief of police. The letter was a commendation for a kidnap case I'd cracked last fall.

"Your business card says you're a psychic," he said as he continued to read the framed letter.

"For lack of a better word."

"You don't like that word?" he asked.

"Hate it. Every time I hear it, I see embarrassing images of scam artists and phony hotline counselors. Don't you?"

He was staring directly at my face now, studying me through narrowed eyes.

"They say you're the real thing."

"I am. I don't tell people what they want to hear. And when I draw a blank, I don't make stuff up."

"If that's true, I'm eager to hear what happened to the woman in the cove." He stepped closer to get a better look at the books on my shelves. He was slightly shorter than me but exuded an easy confidence. No Napoleon complex here.

"Afraid it's not that simple," I said.

"Yeah, I didn't think so. How do you work the psychic angle?"

"It's more accurate to say that it works me. I don't control my psychic experiences, I just receive them. If I don't receive anything, I'm as clueless as the next Joe."

He arched a thick black brow. "You can't summon visions at will, like they do on TV?"

"Receive, yes. Summon, no. Most of the time I have to investigate the methodical way, like everybody else. I can tell you how I found the body."

"Okay."

I repeated for Baxter everything I'd told the patrol cops earlier that morning. He sat in my guest chair and took notes on a small spiral pad. When I was done, he read the notes silently to himself as he chewed on the top of his pen.

"Anything else you know about this?" he asked.

"I know that the victim's name was Wendy Woskowicz. She was a college dropout with a history of mental illness. She hadn't had a permanent address for at least three years. Lived in an '82 Dodge van with a pet pig named Tiny. Let's see . . . she had a rap sheet of sorts . . . misdemeanor drunk-in-public and animal-control violations, mostly. Guess she and her pet pig had a habit of disturbing the peace."

"You get all that in a psychic vision?"

"No. I made a few calls and searched a few websites."

Baxter smiled as he pulled a box of Altoids from his pocket. I declined the mint he offered. He slipped one of the white tablets into his mouth and sucked thoughtfully for a few moments.

"So you've been digging," he said.

"I wanted to know who she was."

"Just remember you're a witness here, not an investigator."

"Witness. Got it." I smiled at him and meant it. I liked the warmth I saw in his eyes. If I had to put money on it, I'd bet Baxter was a decent guy. Cynical, but decent.

"I have to tell you," he said, "that I think the psychic thing is bull crap. I've never met a medium who told me a damn thing that wasn't an educated guess."

"I know what you mean. The real thing is pretty rare. Can I ask you a question?"

"Sure."

"What was in that little pouch around the victim's neck?"

He crunched down on his mint and shook his head. "You're the psychic. You should be telling me."

"I told you, I can't summon my powers at will. What was in there?"

He got up to go. "Sorry, we're not releasing that information."

I still can't fully explain what happened the next morning. My Himalayan, Whitman, was napping on a sunny windowsill when something—a feline nightmare, perhaps—startled him from a sound sleep. He bolted from his perch and knocked a potted plant to the floor, where it shattered on the hard tile. As I was vacuuming up the soil, I heard a loud clattering in the machine that let me know I'd sucked up something metallic. I turned off the vacuum and gave it a vigorous shake to loosen the offending article.

A tiny key bounced onto the floor. From its round, hollow shaft and single notch, I recognized it as the key to a handcuff. Immediately I thought: *This is from Wendy.*

Before getting carried away, I looked for a logical explanation. After all, I did own a pair of handcuffs. I went to the closet and opened the box in which they were stored. The handcuffs were there, complete with the accompanying pair of keys. Wherever it had come from, the key in the vacuum cleaner wasn't mine.

A candle and incense burner on a cabinet in my upstairs bedroom serves as my humble altar. I walked upstairs, placed the mystery key by the candle, and studied it for several minutes. I was wondering if I might be witnessing a case of telekinesis—mind over matter—similar to an incident from the crash of Alaska Airlines Flight 261 in January 2000. The daughter of one of the crash victims had made a pact with her father: the one who died first would send a signal that all was well on the other side. After the plane went down in the Pacific, fishermen found Bob Williams's red-and-gold Masons ring on debris they pulled from the ocean. That the ring was recovered at all seemed miraculous. The fishermen returned the ring to the victim's daughter, who felt certain it was a signal from her deceased father.

Could this handcuff key be a message from Wendy Woskowicz? Lighting the candle, I said a prayer for her.

* * *

I fully expected to hear back from Detective Baxter, and prepared to be called up for duty as a witness in the Wendy Woskowicz murder case. But that's not what happened. Instead, the next morning's paper reported that police were considering the possibility of suicide. The idea struck me as ludicrous.

This time it was my turn to drop in unannounced on Baxter, who worked at SDPD headquarters downtown. Having done a lot of business there over the years, I was on a first-name basis with the receptionist. She didn't hesitate to give me a building pass—a plastic name tag on a cord that I draped around my neck.

I found Baxter talking on the phone in his eighth-floor office. When he hung up I said: "What's this about suicide? You guys honestly thinking of ruling it that way?"

He ran a hand through his thick silver hair. "Not thinking about it. We already have. How'd you get up here?"

I flashed my pass at him. "May I ask why suicide?"

"Several reasons. One, the victim left a suicide note. Two, she had a history of depression. Three, the autopsy found a whopping 2.1 alcohol level in her bloodstream. Four, the day before she died, she gave her pet pig to her brother and asked him to take care of it. These are the things a person does before committing suicide."

I took a minute to add it all up. "I'm sorry, I just can't see a woman handcuffing herself underwater," I said.

"That's because you're not mentally ill." He kept a straight face but his eyes were laughing. "You're weird, maybe, but not certifiable." He motioned me to sit. "Where'd you get that building pass?" he asked as I lowered myself into a nearby chair.

"Oh, this?" I glanced down at the pass around my neck. "I cast a spell and materialized it out of thin air. Since when does a history of psychiatric problems automatically mean a person committed suicide?"

"We're looking at her overall state of mind. It wasn't just depression. She was losing a battle with alcoholism too."

"But I can't imagine—"

"Of course you can't. It's impossible for you or me to imagine doing what she did. But when someone has an extreme death wish, even horrifying suicide methods start to look good. The way they see it, life's a lot more painful than the brief suffering they'll go through as they die."

"Why am I not convinced?"

"Look, if she'd been tied down there with a rope, that would concern me. Tying yourself up is pretty hard to do. But it's easy to handcuff yourself."

"That's weak, Baxter."

"There were no bruises on her body. No signs of a struggle. And no one in the area saw anything unusual."

"Of course they didn't. The newspaper reported her time of death between four-thirty and five that morning. Not a whole lot of people up at that hour. Plus, it's barely light out." I thought back to the redness I'd seen on her wrists. "What about the lacerations under her handcuffs? Don't they indicate a struggle?"

"Sad to say, but it's likely she changed her mind after it was too late."

I chewed on that for a while. "Where would a woman living out of her van get handcuffs?"

He shrugged. "Anywhere. They weren't police quality. More like cheap imitations from a small manufacturer. Maybe she found them at a porn shop, who knows."

He really was convinced, so much so that it was almost convincing me.

"So, about that leather pouch around her neck," I said.

"What about it?"

"Did you find a handcuff key inside?"

I'd hit a nerve, because Baxter froze. "So you looked in the pouch when you were down there," he said.

"No. As I said to the cops at the scene, I didn't touch a thing."

A smug smile crossed his face. "Okay. So you made a good educated guess."

I decided not to tell him about the key that turned up in my vacuum cleaner. It was too hard to explain on too many levels. Not to mention that if the key in my house matched the key to the cuffs at the murder scene, I'd have some impossible explaining to do.

For the umpteenth time, my mind replayed the moment I discovered Wendy's body. "Sicko," I muttered.

Baxter's brows shot up. "You talkin' to me?"

"No. I'm talking about the person who locked Wendy Woskowicz to that chain and then put the key in the pouch around her neck, taunting her with it."

"Creepy scenario, but I don't think that's what happened. I think she used the key to get the handcuffs open. She put a cuff on one wrist and put the key in the pouch. Then she swam out there, dove down, and locked the other cuff to the chain."

"Pretty amazing feat for a woman with a 2.1 blood alcohol level."

"An alcoholic is used to functioning at those levels. I'm telling you, if someone had chained her down there against her will, we'd be seeing some sign of a struggle."

I imagined how a killer—or killers—might have done it. "Suppose they got her drunk and talked her into a sunrise scuba dive. They took her out, showed her the buoy chain, and before she knew what was happening, they handcuffed her to it. Then put the key in the pouch around her neck, just to torment her."

"Yeah, okay. So where's her scuba gear?" Baxter asked.

"They cut it from her body and left her there without oxygen."

"Without putting a scratch on her," he said sarcastically.

"She was drunk. The deed was done by the time she caught on."

Baxter sighed and looked at his watch. I took the hint and got up to leave. "One more question," I said at the door. "Isn't it pretty standard to get two keys with a pair of handcuffs?"

"Yeah."

"If one key was in the pouch around her neck, where do you think the other key is?"

"Moot question, Chase. The case is closed."

I did my best to push Wendy Woskowicz from my mind and tend to my own work. I was doing an investigation for a high-tech manufacturer, tracking down a disgruntled employee who'd erased the company's hard drives. The company directors were eager to find the former systems analyst they now called Hell Boy, since his tantrum had caused a $3 million loss in revenue.

But Wendy Woskowicz wouldn't go away. Granted, she didn't come to me as a specter in the night, rattling her chains. But every morning I'd see the handcuff key on my dresser and churn with the feeling that her case wasn't settled. I began to obsess about her suicide note. What had she written? I wanted to read her words for myself, if for no other reason than to come to peace about her death.

I shelled out ten bucks for a copy of the police report on Wendy's drowning. Her brother, Joseph Woskowicz, was listed as next of kin. He lived in Normal Heights, a mixed neighborhood north of downtown.

The house was a 1920s bungalow, refurbished and neatly landscaped. Like a crafty telemarketer, I picked dinnertime to ring Mr. Woskowicz's bell. A wholesome-looking man in his mid-thirties answered the door. He wore the classic white-collar uniform: khakis and a button-down shirt. With his conservative demeanor and haircut, he bore only the faintest resemblance to his late sister. The resemblance was there, though, in his wide green eyes.

"Joe Woskowicz?"

"Yes?"

"My name's Elizabeth Chase. Sorry to disturb you at home. I'm the woman who found your sister in La Jolla Cove."

His eyes got even wider. His mouth opened, but no words came out.

"I was wondering if I could talk to you for a few minutes," I said.

He came out of his daze. "Sure. Come on in."

He led me into a small but pleasant sitting room—hardwood floors polished to a bright shine—and offered me the comfort of a large leather armchair.

"Please, have a seat." He lowered himself into the chair facing mine. "It must have been pretty traumatic, finding her that way."

"That's what I wanted to talk to you about. I know the police have closed the case, but I'm having a hard time getting my own closure."

"Me too, but it's only been a week. It'll take time. For both of us."

"Are you convinced she killed herself?" I watched him closely. He'd passed his interview with the police department, but he hadn't passed mine.

"Yeah, I guess. Wendy wasn't a well person. Even as a kid she was difficult." His shoulders sagged. "She really went downhill after she dropped out of college. Started living on the street. Or the beach, to be more accurate."

"When was that?"

"About three years ago. I did everything I could for her. Psychologists, psychiatrists, rehabs. Tried to find her jobs, support groups, you name it. A year ago, I pulled away. I had to, for my own sanity."

The guy's torment was palpable. He sounded like a man struggling to convince himself that he wasn't somehow at fault for his sister's death. Or like a man who was flat-out guilty.

"So you believe she killed herself," I said, rephrasing my earlier question.

"I guess so. I mean, she had a hard life."

He paused and looked away, a stoic expression on his face. But the emotions roiling inside him were broadcasting loud and clear to my solar plexus. Beneath Joe's guilt, I sensed a mother lode of unexpressed grief.

"The police said all the evidence pointed to suicide," he said at last.

Living on the street—or in Wendy's case, the beach—carried certain risks, particularly for a substance abuser.

"Any possibility she got into trouble over a drug debt?" I asked.

"No. Wendy refused to put drugs in her system, including antidepressants. The irony is, if she'd been open to drugs, she'd probably be alive today."

"So I take it there was a lot of despair in the note she left."

"Note?"

"Detective Baxter told me she left a suicide note."

"Oh, that. It wasn't a note, really. More like a diary entry." He went into the back of the house and came out with a dog-eared journal. He flipped through the pages and handed the open book to me. "This is it," he said.

The entry was written in a slanting, uneven hand:

I guess the years and escapades have finally done me in. I'm sorry I'm letting so many people down. People who love me. But I don't love myself anymore, so what's the use? Going down, down, down . . .

"*Down, down, down,*" I read.

"That's the part the police picked up on," he said.

"She doesn't come right out and say she's killing herself, though."

"Not in so many words, but—"

We were interrupted by a banging noise coming from the back of the house.

"That's Tiny," he said. "She wants in."

I followed Joe into the kitchen. Outside, an enormous gray pig on tiny cloven hooves stared through the sliding glass door, impatiently switching her tail. This was no pot-bellied piglet. Tiny weighed a hundred pounds if she weighed an ounce. Much of her mass hung in flabby folds from her neck and belly. She jammed her flat, round snout against the glass and kicked the door with a foreleg.

Bang.

"All right, all right, just a second." Joe slid the door open. With surprising grace, the pig trotted right up to me. She plopped her fat bottom on the floor like a dog and looked longingly into my face.

"She wants to be petted," he said.

"I see." I scratched Tiny's ears and she blinked thoughtfully. Scientists say that pigs are the fourth smartest creature on the planet, behind humans, apes, and dolphins. This pig had more going on behind her eyes than a lot of people I knew. "What a charmer," I said.

"Isn't she? I think having to give up Tiny was the final straw for Wendy. This pig was her soul mate."

"Did she have to give Tiny up? I thought she left the pig with you voluntarily, because she was planning to take her life. Tying up loose ends and all."

"Not exactly. People were complaining to the city about Tiny. Wendy was forced to give her to me."

That put a slightly different spin on the matter.

"Did she ever mention who was making the complaints?" I asked.

"No. I don't think she ever knew who made them."

* * *

Watch enough TV and you'll think that murder motives must be dark and deep. Hang out with cops and you'll discover that many murders are utterly stupid, with motives so lame officers are ashamed to write them into their reports. The man who killed his brother fighting over whether the angel or the star went on top of the Christmas tree is a classic example. The guy who shoots the neighbor whose dog won't stop barking is commonplace. With that in mind, the following morning I went to the city's code compliance department to see who had made the complaints against Tiny.

Reports filed with the animal control department are available to the public. Unfortunately, the names, addresses, and phone numbers of those who complain are confidential information. I got around that by asking to see the inspector in charge, Helen Drood. A grim-faced woman, Ms. Drood didn't strike me as an animal lover, or a lover of much of anything. I explained that I was an investigator working with Detective Baxter on the Woskowicz case—it was almost the truth—and that I was looking into complaints made about the victim's pet pig.

"Woskowicz. That's the woman who drowned in La Jolla Cove, right?" She said it almost cheerfully.

"Yeah. Do you know if Ms. Woskowicz ever received copies of those complaints?"

"Yes, eventually she did. Ordinarily, we send a copy of the letter to the complainant and mail the original to the party being accused of a code violation. But in the Woskowicz case, we didn't have a deliverable address."

"Because she lived in her van."

"That's correct. A compliance officer had to go down to the beach and deliver the complaints to her there."

"Would you have a record confirming that?" I asked.

"It should be in the computer. How do you spell that last name?"

I spelled out Wendy's last name and Helen Drood punched

the letters on her keyboard. The document popped up and I craned my neck to get a good look at the monitor. As she scrolled through the complaints, the same name and address kept appearing in the field for the complainant: *Thomas Gunn, 1717 Coast Boulevard, Apt. 303.*

"Yes, we got confirmed delivery on all those complaints. March 22, April 6, and May 15."

I jotted down the dates, as well as the address I'd seen on her monitor. "Thanks. That's all we needed to know."

Seventeen-seventeen Coast Boulevard turned out to be one of the ocean-facing condos overlooking the cove where Wendy had died. I took the stairs to the third-floor landing and knocked on the door marked *303*. A frail man with sparse gray hair and pouches under his eyes opened up. The hand he used to grip the door was a study in rampant liver spots. He stared at me harshly without bothering to utter a greeting.

"Hello." I smiled, doing my best to appear upbeat and efficient. "I'm following up on some complaints you made to the animal control department."

He looked at me like I was a pile of smoldering excrement and started to close the door.

"Excuse me, sir—"

"I didn't make any complaints." The door slammed in my face.

I knocked again. When he didn't answer, I spoke through the closed door. "Sir, I'm just trying to clear up a few details. Were you living in this residence in March, April, and May of this year?"

There was no sound from the other side of the door. Maybe he was hard of hearing.

"Listen," I shouted, "I just need to confirm that in March of this year you—"

The door flew open. He glared at me, his eyes like poison

darts. "It's none of your damn business, but I've lived here since 1969."

"And you're Mr. Gunn?"

"Who?" He glowered and waved me off as if to swat away the stench of me. "Go on, get out of here."

I heard footsteps coming up the stairs and turned to see a bare-chested man step onto the landing. His longish sandy hair and baggy shorts gave him a youthful look but the face that eyed me warily had seen at least forty summers without sunscreen.

"Is there a problem up here?" he said.

"Not at all," I said reassuringly. "I was just asking Mr. Gunn—"

"My name's not Gunn!" the old man yelled. "And yes, there's a problem. This woman won't leave me alone."

The aging beach boy looked at me suspiciously. He had the deeply tanned, muscled torso of a surfer and would have been model material but for the lines on his face and his over-large, beaklike nose.

I explained, "I was just following up on some complaints this gentleman made to the animal control depart—"

"I did not make any complaints!" Color was rising in the old man's crepey face and the beach boy-man stepped protectively toward him.

"He says he didn't make any complaints. Who'd you say you were?"

"Animal control," I muttered, slipping past him and heading down the stairs. "Never mind. I must have the wrong address."

So much for that theory. Even if the old man in 303 had been the one making complaints about Wendy's pig, he was pushing ninety and as weak as papier-mâché. Thomas Gunn or whatever his name was could no sooner have chained Wendy underwater than he could have bench-pressed an SUV.

I walked across Coast Boulevard to my parked truck. All along I'd felt that Wendy had been murdered. Now doubts were creeping in. Maybe she had committed suicide. Hadn't that *down, down, down* bit in her journal described her imminent death with chilling accuracy? Then again, she might have been talking about her mental state.

I looked back at the condominium. Shining with the reflected light of the midmorning sun, its windows now reminded me of mirrored sunglasses. The eyes behind the glass could see me, but I could not see them.

I had one last theory to test.

I got my beach towel out of my truck and walked down the stairs that led from the top of the cliff to the cove below. Dozens of sunbathers and swimmers lined the beach and bobbed in the water. Lots of swimming buddies today. I staked out a spot with my towel and stripped down to the bathing suit I wore underneath my clothes.

Three hundred yards from shore, the buoy floated in the water, marking the spot where Wendy had lost her life. How hard was it to swim from the beach to the buoy? Could an inebriated woman have pulled it off?

I waded into the surf, feeling at once free and handicapped without my mask, tank, and flippers. I fought through a strong set of waves, keeping my eye on the buoy. When I reached the deep water beyond the breakers, I knew I was swimming over the kelp forest. I felt no claustrophobia floating above the dense plants, but not being able to see what was teeming beneath my belly gave me a new kind of creeps.

There were no other swimmers this far out, but I wasn't entirely alone. North of me, a couple of kayaks sliced through the water. A bit further in, a group of surfers straddled their boards, waiting for the next big wave. Peering back at shore, I had a postcard view. The lush La Jolla hills rose into a brilliant blue sky. Fat brown seals sunned themselves on a rocky cliff that jutted into the sea.

The swim to the buoy had looked daunting from shore but I'd been gliding along at an easy crawl and was already nearing my destination. I turned over and relaxed with a few backstrokes.

Something under the water skimmed my ankle. I winced and pulled away. A seal? I tried to see what it might be, but the surface of the water was a choppy expanse of reflected sunlight.

"Hey!" I called out, hoping to catch the ear of the nearest surfer. But when I looked for him, he was disappearing toward shore on a breaking wave.

Quit freaking out, I told myself. The buoy floated a dozen or so yards farther out to sea. I'd covered enough distance to convince myself that even a drunk woman could have made the swim. I turned around and started back toward shore.

I heard a splash behind me. I turned to see a gloved hand come up from below and clamp around my ankle. I gasped and kicked hard with my free leg. A hand caught that ankle too, and started to pull me under.

I jerked my legs, trying desperately to kick free. The hands around my ankles wouldn't let go. Splashing furiously with my arms, I tried to keep my head above the water. But I wasn't strong enough to resist the downward pull. I took a last gulp of air before my head slipped beneath the surface.

The underwater world was murky, but even without a mask I could see by the oxygen tank strapped to his back that my assailant was a scuba diver. Firmly gripping my ankles, he pulled me toward the bottom. I fought hard, yet he had the advantages of flippers and superior strength. The sound of my pounding heart thudded in my ears.

I twisted toward the diver, grabbing at his face. My fingers caught his regulator and I pulled as hard as I could. I felt the breathing apparatus come loose and kept pulling. His mask came off with the mouthpiece, and I recognized the sandy-haired man with the oversized nose. He grabbed for his mouthpiece, letting go of my ankles.

Free at last, I shot upward. My lungs were on the verge of exploding as I broke through the surface. I had time to let out one hoarse cry for help before I felt his hands on my ankles again. I gulped for air. The last thing I saw before going back under was the bright blue California sky.

Down, down, down. I grabbed for his regulator again. He was ready for me and ducked out of reach. The exertion left me oxygen starved. The urge to inhale was overwhelming. I didn't know how much longer I could fight the instinct to breathe. I saw stars and blotches of gray. It occurred to me that I was probably going to die.

But as suddenly as he'd attacked, my assailant let go and darted away. Willing myself upward, I saw why. A neon yellow kayak floated directly overhead. I broke the surface gasping and sputtering. The kayaker grabbed my arms and pulled me across the bow.

"You okay?"

The brown-faced boy who helped me up couldn't have been a day over eighteen. I nodded my head, too breathless and dizzy to speak.

I spent much of that afternoon in the hospital, where I was treated for shock and kept under observation as police asked seemingly infinite questions. Finally, my father—who happens to be a doctor—insisted on my discharge and brought me home. Friends and family had gathered at my house to show their support. I finally convinced them all to go, telling everyone that what I really needed was sleep. Dad left reluctantly, reminding me that my assailant was still out there somewhere. I reminded him that I had a state-of-the-art security system—and a nine-millimeter Glock.

Still, I admit my heart jumped later that night when the motion light went on and the closed-circuit television showed a man coming up my walk.

It was Baxter.

"What's up?" I asked when I opened the door.

"We arrested the guy who tried to drown you," Baxter replied. "I thought you'd like to know."

Feeling a rush of relief, I motioned him inside, eager to hear about it. "Where'd you find him?"

"Picked him up a couple miles north of the cove, at Torrey Pines State Beach. He's being held downtown. The DA's office will be getting in touch with you after he's charged."

"Attempted murder?" I asked.

Baxter nodded. "That too. We arrested him for the murder of Wendy Woskowicz."

This came as a surprise. "On what evidence?"

"Plenty," said Baxter. "The guy's name is Gunner Thomas. We figure he's the one who filed complaints under the alias Thomas Gunn."

"As in tommy gun. Cute," I said dryly.

"The old man you visited at the condo was his grandfather. We got a warrant and found scuba gear on the back porch. Get this: the straps were cut and we found long blond hair strands caught in the mask. From initial tests we're pretty sure they came from Wendy Woskowicz." Baxter's eyes were shining. It was the first time I'd seen him genuinely happy.

"You think the evidence will hold up in court?" I asked.

"It should. Technically, Wendy's hair DNA is the strongest thing we got. But we found something on Thomas that's even more damning, from a jury's point of view."

"What's that?"

"We found a key that opens those funky handcuffs he used on Wendy. It's an exact match of the key we found in the pouch around her neck."

"So both keys are accounted for now."

"Yes," Baxter replied.

I felt a little let down. This meant the key I'd picked up in my vacuum cleaner hadn't been sent from Wendy after all.

His expression turned solemn. "You're lucky that kayaker came along when he did and bailed you out."

"I thanked him a hundred times, believe me," I said.

"I thought you were psychic. Thomas had outstanding warrants, one for assault with a deadly weapon. Didn't you sense he was trouble?"

I hadn't. Thomas had done such a good job of making me feel like an asshole for harassing the old man that I'd failed to notice what an asshole *he* was. I thought about standing on the beach and the sense I'd had of being watched through the opaque windows of the condo.

"I missed my cues," I said. "So let me get this straight. Thomas killed Wendy because of her pig?"

"He killed her because he's a sick son of a bitch. Now that we've made an arrest, all kinds of beach people are coming forward and describing his angry rants about the way 'immigrants' and 'indigents' are bringing down the neighborhood."

"Now they speak up." I wasn't surprised. People have all kinds of reasons for staying silent about the suspicious behavior they see. They don't want to get involved. They worry they'll be wrong. They worry they'll pay for talking.

"You were right about one thing," Baxter said to me.

"What's that?"

"The missing handcuff key. I blew you off about it, but it's going to be an important piece of evidence. How'd you know?"

To tell, or not to tell?

"My vacuum cleaner picked up a handcuff key the day after Wendy's drowning. This sounds stupid, but I honestly thought it was a message from her."

"I don't know about a message," Baxter said, "but it is a pretty weird coincidence. The important thing is, Gunner Thomas is going down, and it's because of you." He started for the door. "It's late. I'll let you get some rest."

I thanked him and waved from the door as he pulled out of

the driveway. Walking back to the family room, I imagined the suntanned boy-man sitting in a prison cell downtown.

Thomas, I thought, *you are one sick son of a bitch.*

With that, the tears came. Thomas had attacked me and nearly snuffed out my life. He'd forced a brutal death on Wendy. I wished I could rage at the ruthless bastard, but the best I could do was cry. Better than numbness, I thought. At least I was alive and feeling something. When my tears were exhausted, I turned off the lights and trudged upstairs, feeling the full weight of the day in every step.

Before collapsing into bed, I went to my altar to light some fragrance and a candle, small gestures of thanks for my deliverance. I found a book of matches by the incense burner and fired up a stick of sweet Nag Champa. I moved the flame slowly to the candle and froze. Something wasn't right.

Wait a minute.

The handcuff key was missing. I searched every inch of the bureau top, but it wasn't there. I got on my knees and scoured the floor. No key. I turned on the overhead light and searched again. Nada. I widened my search. Zip.

Standing in the center of the room, I asked out loud: "Did you take the key?"

There was no answer, of course. But I swear I could hear Wendy, in her silent way, telling me that I could stop looking now.

PART II

NEIGHBORHOOD WATCH

THE NEW GIRL

BY DEBRA GINSBERG

Cortez Hill

I suppose most people have some trouble with their neighbors at some point or other. It isn't possible to get along all the time, after all, especially not with strangers with whom you live cheek by jowl. People have such peculiar habits and inclinations—so evident when there are common alleys and kitchen windows without shades. Still, my policy has always been live and let live as long as nobody gets hurt. But sometimes the definition of "hurt" becomes a little murky. And sometimes people are just plain rude. There is no excuse for rudeness. It almost always leads to trouble.

Our particular trouble began last summer—in June, to be exact. The jacarandas were in fresh bloom and it was beginning to get warm. Not too warm, mind you. San Diego never really reaches a full boil until late August and into September. We're always lulled into a false sense of security by then because the weather's been so pleasant; warm enough to complain about all the tourists glutting the beaches but not hot enough to consider joining them there. And then, every year, there are two or three scorching weeks in the late summer and we all start falling apart like melting ice-cream sandwiches. By the time those bone-dry, fire-starting Santa Ana winds blow through here in October, we can't even remember what it was like to grumble about the marine layer making things too gloomy. But last June was lovely—bright, sunny, and sparkling— the kind of climate that makes you happy to be alive. And we were, Sheila and I. Until the dogs were installed in the condo next door.

I have nothing against dogs. I have nothing against animals of any kind, except rats (for which I am sure I can be forgiven) and panda bears (for which I most assuredly cannot). And actually, it isn't that I harbor any sort of deep-seated hatred toward panda bears—I merely think we spend too much of our animal-protection resources on these rather lame and maladaptive creatures simply because they are cute. The San Diego Zoo is so enamored with its "guest" panda bears, in fact, that it has installed a "panda cam" whose feed you can watch on the Internet twenty-four hours a day. Ridiculous.

Again, I am not an animal hater. I neither own nor eat animals, which, I think, actually makes me an animal *lover* of sorts. But I cannot stand a yipping, yapping dog. Two yipping, yapping dogs constitute sheer torture. So when our next door neighbor, Vida, brought home those wretched little toy dogs last June, Sheila and I knew there were going to be issues. Well, *I* knew there were going to be issues—it didn't bother Sheila until later. They were miniature terriers of some kind, or perhaps a mix. Yes, definitely a mix and not a good one. The few glimpses I caught of them (they were confined almost exclusively to the house; I have no idea when Vida walked them because I never saw it) weren't particularly pleasing—grayish, brownish, not very clean. But the problem wasn't their appearance, it was the nearly incessant barking that started the very minute she brought those animals into her home.

Now, you'd think such small dogs would be impossible to hear, especially downtown where we live. You see, all of downtown is pretty much directly in the flight path of planes coming in and out of Lindbergh Field. One can practically see the passengers inside them (who are doubtless horrified to be hovering so close to the ground) as they make their descent into America's Finest City. There has been endless discussion about moving the airport to a more "suitable" location (although Tijuana was suggested as well, which, although less than twenty miles from here, is anything but suitable), but nothing has come of it. Who is going to approve putting an airport in their backyard? So here we are, occupying some of the priciest real estate in the country (recession be damned!) and watching the dirty undersides of 747s as they roar above our heads.

When we first moved in, Sheila and I used to live in fear that one of them would accidentally dump that royal blue toilet ice in our backyard on the way in—and that was not a totally unfounded fear. It's not like it hasn't happened before. In California. But we got over that (mostly) and also managed somehow to integrate the sound into our lives. When an airplane went over our heads we just spoke a little louder without even noticing it. This is why we *did* hear the dogs. Also, at a certain point, the planes stopped flying for the night. The dogs were ceaseless.

"I think I should go talk to her," I told Sheila one night over dinner.

Sheila picked at her asparagus and gave me an impatient look. Her hair was tied back with a yellow ribbon and she seemed tired. "Talk to who? About what?"

"Vida." I gestured toward the other condo. "About those dogs."

"Are you sure her name is Vida?"

"What's that got to do with it, Sheila?"

"I just don't remember her introducing herself as Vida. I think you might have made that name up." I didn't dignify the comment with a response. She sighed. "Anyway, what about the dogs?"

"They bark *all the time*. It doesn't bother you?"

Sheila shrugged. "Not really."

"Well, I haven't been able to sleep at night."

"I don't think your insomnia is caused by the dogs," Sheila said.

"Well, I'm going to talk to her."

"I wish you wouldn't."

Sheila hated making waves of any kind, which was admirable on one level, but also, frankly, sometimes a little annoying. I understood that she didn't want any kind of ugly scene with our neighbor, but I had to say something. The dogs were driving me mad. And I would have—I had even planned which words to use—if not for the fact that on the very afternoon I had chosen to go next door, Vida brought home a human guest and, well, I just couldn't.

I was at my kitchen window when I saw them pull up in front of our condos. Residents are not allowed to park here. Because of space constraints and the desire to maintain property values, we are all assigned single parking spaces in a covered lot around the back of our buildings. So right away I knew she was up to something. Then I saw the blue "handicapped" tag hanging off her rearview mirror and was even more intrigued.

Vida got out first. She was smiling and looked almost deranged with happiness. The flowery muumuu she was wearing only added to that slightly nutty look. I don't know which sadistic designer first came up with the idea of the muumuu but he (for it really has to be a "he," no self-respecting woman would ever design such a garment) deserves a special place in fashion hell. Vida is not a heavy woman, but the muumuu, festooned with bright, badly painted hibiscus flowers, made her look like she weighed three hundred pounds.

She walked around to the passenger side of her car and, after a bit of effort which I couldn't see because it was obscured by Vida's sail of a dress, helped another woman out. The "new girl," as I immediately began thinking of her, was small, blond, and very pretty. She was also an amputee—and a recent one by the look of it. Her left leg ended at the knee and was bandaged in what appeared to be a haphazard manner. The dressing didn't look all that clean, either, and there were bloodstains at the bottom.

New Girl put her arm around Vida's shoulder and with much awkwardness they hopped and dragged their way up the driveway to Vida's condo. They had no crutches and no wheelchair. It was altogether most peculiar—as if they had both come directly from the scene of an accident. Needless to say, I couldn't go over there at that moment and complain about the dogs. It would have been rude.

We didn't see either one of them for a few days after that, though they were clearly at home. The lights were on and there was plenty of noise. There were the dogs, of course, yapping and squealing as if their miserable doggy lives depended on it, but there were other sounds as well. I'd never heard music coming from Vida's place before, but soon after New Girl's arrival, we were treated to the sound of thrashing guitars on a daily basis. Apparently, New Girl was very fond of death metal and loved to listen to it near an open window. We also heard construction— hammering, drilling, and several suspicious crashes. It wasn't until I saw Vida hauling canvases and easels up her driveway that I realized she—they—must have been building some kind of art studio in there.

"What do you think they're up to next door?" I asked Sheila one evening.

"I suppose they're just living like the rest of us," Sheila answered. She was sitting under a thin blanket on the couch watching *Law & Order*, a show she'd recently become addicted to, and she didn't even raise her eyes from the screen to talk to me.

"There's something going on over there," I said.

"Are you back on the dogs again?" she asked.

"Well, I was never *off* the dogs. They haven't stopped barking yet, have they? But no, that's not what I meant, Sheila."

"I wish you'd lighten up."

"I don't know what you mean by that."

"There are other things that you could better focus your attention on." She pulled the blanket tight around her shoulders. "Things even closer to home than our neighbors."

I wasn't following her line of reasoning so I walked over to her to ask her to explain. But before I could do that I thought of something else. "You know the guest star did it, right?" I said, and pointed to the TV. "The more famous the guest star, the likelier it is that person committed the crime."

Sheila looked up at me for the first time. The TV light on her face made it appear as if she was angry. "Way to ruin it," she said. "Thanks."

About a week later, I saw Vida and New Girl emerge from the house to take a walk. New Girl had crutches now, though they seemed kind of old and beaten up. Not the nice new crutches you'd expect a recent amputee to have been given. But maybe that was it—maybe she couldn't afford new crutches. I had no idea what Vida did for a living. Neither she nor New Girl ever seemed to work. Then again, many people around here don't seem to work and still find ways of making money. I couldn't see if New Girl's leg was still bandaged because she was wearing long shorts that came down below the knee. The two of them were laughing and carrying on as if they didn't have a care in the world. Vida was wearing another one of those hideous muumuus—daffodils, it looked like—and flip-flops. New Girl was splattered with paint of many hues and wore a pink tennis shoe on her remaining foot. Her hair wasn't blond anymore— she'd dyed it an awful burnt umber color—but she was still very pretty. Prettier, maybe, than the first time I'd seen her. I wanted to go out there then and say hello, introduce myself to New Girl, and inquire after the dogs in a civilized manner, but by the time I thought of the proper words to use they'd disappeared around the corner and the moment was lost. I regretted that missed opportunity soon afterward because the next interaction I had with our neighbors was very unpleasant indeed.

We had come to the thick of July when the windows were open all the time and the air had turned quite warm and still. Sound carried even farther than usual. The nights were heavy and not always comfortable. Vida's place was an assault to the senses—the smell of turpentine and some kind of smoke, the death metal, the inconvenience of her car which was now regularly parked in the driveway. But all of those things might have been forgivable if not for the dogs. The dogs were making me insane.

One morning, so bleary from lack of sleep that I forgot to put a filter in the coffeemaker thus causing an overflow of wet grounds and undrinkable coffee, I finally reached my limit and marched next door without even thinking about what I would say when I got there. It was a very short walk, but I was in a sweat by the time I got there. I knocked once and heard the dogs go mad. Each yip felt like a knife driven through my skull. I waited a few seconds and then knocked harder. Pounded, actually.

Finally, the door opened. I'd expected Vida wearing another one of her muumuus. I feel sure I would have handled the situation better if Vida had answered the door. But it was New Girl and, save for her crutches, she was completely naked. The shock of it was a bit much and for a moment I lost my manners and just stared at her. I made a few observations in that moment. For one, she was tattoo-free, which, I have to tell you, is quite a rarity these days. Second, she had new wooden crutches, topped with cute yellow terry cloth ducks where she rested them under her arms. And then, because I had to lower my gaze, I couldn't help but see that her stump was smooth and looked like it had healed well.

"What?" she said by way of greeting.

I tried to remember if I'd heard her speak before and if I had, whether her voice had sounded this deep and harsh.

"I'm your neighbor—"

"I know who you are. What do you want?"

"Those dogs," I said, pointing in the general area of her hip, behind which the canines in question were racing back and forth, yipping as they went, "are keeping me awake."

For a moment New Girl looked nonplussed as if she had no idea what I was talking about. As if, in fact, she didn't even know the dogs to which I was referring. But her expression changed again and she scowled. Really, the picture of rudeness. Just then a plane roared past overhead. American Airlines, I could tell by its silvery flash. I thought again about that rank blue ice and shuddered. New Girl followed its path with her eyes and then turned them back to me.

"How can you possibly hear anything with *that* going on all the time?" she said.

"That doesn't happen all the time," I told her. "The dogs never stop."

"You're one of *them*, aren't you?" Her scowl had turned into a sneer.

"What, someone who likes to sleep? Yes, I am. But I can't sleep because those dogs bark all night. Doesn't it bother you?"

"You know," she said, "you should mind your own business." And then she slammed the door in my face. I'd never had that happen before and it startled me so badly that I stood there for a full minute before turning around and walking home.

"I think maybe I should call the Humane Society," I told Sheila that night. She was sitting at the kitchen table, nursing a glass of wine.

"Why?"

"I just don't think it's right for dogs to bark like that. Maybe they're being mistreated."

Sheila sighed and took a long drink from the glass. I hadn't told her about seeing New Girl naked, though I'd implied that she'd been rude to me.

"I can't do this anymore," Sheila said.

"Can't do what?"

And that's when she told me she was leaving.

I tried to convince Sheila to stay but she'd already made up her mind by the time I pleaded my case. I blamed the dogs. The dogs had made me crazy and therefore impossible to live with. But Sheila just shook her head. "You really don't get it, do you?" she asked me. It took her a few weeks to gather and pack her things. I let her take whatever she wanted in the end. Not that there was much. The funny thing about those weeks was that I hardly noticed the dogs barking. I'm sure they kept up as always, but for once I had more pressing things on my mind.

I saw New Girl only once more in the flesh; in late August, the very hottest part of the summer. She was standing alone in the driveway looking up at Vida's condo, her hands hanging down at her sides. She was wearing a shiny green bikini top and a very short black skirt. She was leaning on one crutch, its terry duck smashed into her armpit, and I could see both of her legs. She'd been fitted with a prosthesis, I noticed. From my kitchen-window perspective, it appeared quite lifelike. I couldn't understand why she looked so sad.

Sometime after that (days or weeks, I can't remember now), they all left—Vida, New Girl, *and* the dogs. My ears were ringing from the silence. It was so bad I even went to the doctor, thinking I might have developed tinnitus. I wondered if they'd gone on vacation or if the move was permanent. I wondered how long the condo would stay empty before it could be considered abandoned. And I wondered why they'd taken the dogs. It just didn't seem in character.

I got a partial answer at least a few days later when I took my trash out to the dumpster in the alley I share with my neighbors. There, propped against the side, were New Girl's wooden crutches, yellow ducks still attached. Next to those was a large canvas with a life-size portrait of New Girl—as nude as I had seen her and leaning on those very same crutches. The painting was surprisingly sophisticated and beautiful. The colors were bold and bright—blues, reds, and pinks—and contained a great deal of life and light. I was unprepared for how emotional it made me feel. I hadn't liked New Girl at all, it was true, but it made me sad to see her abandoned this way.

Without even thinking about it, I picked up the painting and carried it home. I left it near the front door at first, as if I was going to take it out again, but then after a few hours I brought it into the living room. The next day I hung it up next to the TV so that I could see it all the time, even when I was watching a show. I'm not sure and I'll never know because there were no witnesses, but I think I may have, from time to time, conversed with it—with *her*—when I was feeling particularly lonely.

Vida came back alone right after Labor Day, and for a few weeks that was how she stayed. But just last week she brought another girl home. This one looks like a thicker, coarser version of New Girl, but she's also blond. And she's also missing the bottom half of her left leg. I saw them getting out of the car—Vida in jeans and a sweatshirt proclaiming *Hecho en Mexico* (the summer of muumuus is over, I guess) and the new New Girl draped in one of those woven blankets you can get for ten bucks in Tijuana. I saw the crutches—the beaten-up ones—and the bandages and the awkward journey up the driveway. The girl said something to Vida as they got close to the door but her words were drowned in the howl of a passing airplane.

Yes, I suppose all of us have trouble with our neighbors from time to time. And, yes, there is something very strange going on next door. But I am now convinced that New Girl was right—I should mind my own business.

After all, the dogs are gone and Sheila is never coming back.

INSTANT KARMA

BY TAFFY CANNON

Rancho Santa Fe

So okay, it's a sin to kill a mockingbird. We're all clear on that one. But what about a vulture?

Laverne Patterson probably doesn't consider herself a bird of prey whose specialty is hanging around waiting for something to die before ripping into the carcass. And in fact the analogy is imperfect; there's no creature in nature quite like this woman. At least I hope there isn't.

But it's close enough. And time is short.

A lot's been written and sung about what it's like to have nothing to lose, much of it poignant and evocative. Most of those authors and songwriters still had plenty to lose, however, hadn't even come close to hitting that sweet spot yet.

I have.

Bull's-eye.

My name is Tina and I am going to die very shortly. I know, that's a little too Twelve-Step cute for the announcement, but it happens to be true and there's not a damned thing I can do about it. As these things go, I'm fortunate that I'm not going the way some other people I knew already have. I'm still pretty lucid, retain control of my bodily functions, and have the bittersweet satisfaction of knowing that I did everything right and so did my medical team.

It just happens that mine is one of those rare and relentless orphan diseases for which there isn't yet the whisper of a cure.

I am single, childless, and without siblings. My parents were killed in a plane crash while I was in college, leaving me a settlement that seemed sufficient to last a lifetime if I were careful, to allow me choices I might not otherwise have had. No need to conserve now, and not too many choices, either. I'm just glad I took some really cool trips in my early twenties, because I don't have the energy for that kind of bucket list now, though I did buy a hot black Porsche after the diagnosis.

I hated the endless unctuous sympathy when my parents died so I made an early decision not to share my diagnosis with coworkers, or with folks I thought of as friends who were actually acquaintances. My symptoms were never obvious and I telecommuted a lot anyway, so it was easy to hide all the medical appointments. I've gradually circled the wagons till there's nobody inside but me and my cat, and I have arranged for her perpetual care when I go. Some charities will also be very happily surprised.

Nobody's going to miss me all that much, however, which is sad if you think about it, so I choose not to.

Once you make the acknowledgment that you're about to die, a form of letting go occurs that is far more grand and terrifying than skydiving or bull riding or walking a tightrope over burning coals. After that, an equally grand and terrifying window opens that most folks don't ever have the blessing or misfortune to see.

Final possibilities.

You might call it justice. Or liberty. Or merely opportunity.

Whatever it is, it's how I happened to be planning to murder a woman I have never met.

I certainly didn't think this would be my life when I was twenty-nine. As a teen and college student, I anticipated an interesting career, maybe a husband, possibly a child, certainly a bright and burning future. I got the first one, and for a while I also had the last, and maybe it's just as well that the two in the middle never came to pass.

Because not long ago, I sat across the desk in a generic doctor's office in an anonymous three-story medical building across from Scripps Hospital in Encinitas, getting a death sentence.

It wasn't put in those terms, of course, and I was given to believe initially that there was a great deal more hope than actually turned out to be the case, once I pulled myself back together after a few days of hysteria and started doing my own research. I'm a researcher by trade, a writer and editor of web content, and it didn't take long to discover exactly what the doctor had failed to mention.

It was very, very bad. As in invariably fatal. Palliative measures could extend my life a bit, of course. There was even an upcoming protocol for an experimental drug that I could and did apply for, but that was on the East Coast and only accepting a handful of patients. Also, I'd probably be dead before it began.

The diagnostic process had been going on for so long by then that I was ready for a definitive prognosis, even a bad one. Or so I thought until it happened.

I'd endured what felt like hundreds of needle pricks and biopsies and humiliating procedures. I'd been poked, X-rayed, lasered, MRI'd, biopsied, ultrasounded—everything but dunked in a vat of water to see if I swam or drowned, the way they used to test witches in the Massachusetts Colony.

Sometimes I think it would have been easier if we'd just started with dunking, except that as a native San Diegan, I've been in the water all my life and could certainly swim, which would have declared me guilty. Or, in this case, afflicted. Whereas a decision by drowning would have meant that my body actually wasn't in its final hours, not even close, and that I didn't need to die at all.

This is way beyond catch-22.

Instant Karma came about because of a dreadful illness contracted by my high school friend Molly Donovan, a young woman whose talents and gifts would have been really depressing and intimidating if she hadn't been such a genuinely nice person.

Molly died two years ago of a brain tumor. A glioblastoma multiforme, the baddest of the bad in a family of outlaw cells I have always found particularly horrifying. Brain tumors are terrorists who attack your centers of insight and reason, who fly straight into the control tower supporting your motor skills, who reprogram the axis of your body's global communication systems. And glioblastomas do it really, really fast.

Molly was a lawyer on the fast track at a small but powerful Los Angeles firm that specialized in environmental law and had won a couple of significant cases for the good guys. But being on the fast track meant she was a workaholic with no personal life, and when her health blew up on her, she moved back home, spending her final months in the pool house at her parents' Rancho Santa Fe estate. I was living just down the coast in Pacific Beach and it felt entirely natural to devote a lot of time to somebody who had once been a good friend.

Also scary as hell. But we became close again, closer than we'd ever been, and had some fine times in those last few months despite everything. I learned a lot about dying with style from her.

I just I hadn't intended to put it into effect quite so quickly.

Like so many great ideas, ours was born by accident.

Ever the overachiever, Molly had found herself a support group of other young adults facing terrifying diagnoses, facilitated by a La Jolla psychologist with a breathtaking coastal view from her sixth-floor offices. The only glitch was that Molly couldn't drive because she had the occasional grand mal seizure. So I served as chauffeur and while the group met, I waited in the coffee shop on the ground floor with my netbook and my latte.

Early on, a few of them broke off and continued to hang out when the sessions ended, and I was easily absorbed into that group. The common denominator, beyond age and mortality, was a very black sense of humor.

The default clubhouse became Molly's place, which offered privacy and space and a reasonably central location. One clear fall evening, with breezes off the ocean, glittering stars, and the occasional cry of a night bird or coyote, five of us sat on the patio outside her pool house. We might have been alone in the universe, nestled in this private little valley with its scents of eucalyptus, night-blooming jasmine, and money. Molly's parents were probably home, but their Spanish-style hacienda was enormous and whatever wing they might have been occupying at the moment, we couldn't see or hear them. The housekeeper's lights were out over the garage, and as for neighbors, the property had been landscaped decades ago to assure that nobody else would ever be visible from Casa Donovan. Yes, that's what it said on the sign by the locked gate down at the road. Multicultural to the max.

Ours was a pretty motley crew. Kenny Peters, an accountant with a rare and raging form of lymphoma. Adam Hillinger, a born salesman with multiple melanomas and an inability to go more than five minutes without sneaking a peek at his phone. Katherine Connelly, a third grade teacher and terrible exception to the rule that breast cancer doesn't strike the young. Molly. And me, the token healthy person, at least for the time being.

Kenny picked up the lament he had apparently brought to group earlier, excoriating the insurance company jackasses who had restructured their formulary and denied him the incredibly expensive chemo that appeared to be his best—and possibly only—hope. Kenny always struck me as pragmatic to the point of fatalism, a man whose chest might be increasingly sunken but whose tone remained mild-mannered and calm. However, he and his employer had been paying premiums to this insurance company for his entire career and he was well and truly pissed.

"I want to line those malevolent morons up against a wall

and shoot every last one of them," he announced. Kenny wasn't eating or drinking anything because the outdated chemo regimen that his insurance *did* permit had given him a charming blend of nausea, bloat, and hair loss. Food issues were one reason we didn't meet in restaurants. Those gangbangers and military dudes who go for the cue-ball look would covet Kenny's slick pate, if they could only skip the part where their internal organs were consumed by rogue cells and random poisons.

"There'd just be more bureaucrats lining up to take their place," Katherine responded mildly. "Like one of those video games where you kill three aliens and another twelve rise from the dust. A kind of bureaucratic whack-a-mole. Shooting won't stop them."

My mind hurtled off in related directions: heads lopped off hydras, *The Sorcerer's Apprentice*, plants that die at the center and send out a hundred pups or runners at the same time.

Metastasizing cancer cells.

"It would stop some of them," Kenny said.

It was tough to argue that one and nobody did.

"No reason to limit it to Western Health," Adam put in suddenly. He was "between fumigations," as he liked to put it, and had stopped on his way over to get a giant drink featuring caramel, chocolate, cinnamon, pumpkin, a whiff of decaf, and a mountain of whipped cream. He was on a lot of steroids just then and hungry all the time.

"Good point," Kenny agreed. "My wife was watching *Butch Cassidy and the Sundance Kid* the other night and I have to say I liked that ending. Going out in a blaze of glory."

"You mean having Western Health machine-gun you?" Molly asked. She had lost a lot of weight and was wearing a wig, now that radiation had zapped away much of her gorgeous blond hair, taking her energy along with it. "What's the point of that?"

"Well, it works better if I'm the one doing the shooting," Kenny admitted. "But either one would call a lot of attention to the power they abuse. Still. And it would make me feel better, at least for a minute or two. I'm probably going to be dead in six months anyway."

"Think positive," Adam the salesman told him, in a touchy feely, support-group tone that made me want to barf and sob at the same time.

"Wiping out Western Health would be very positive," Kenny insisted.

"Then why not go all the way and really clean house?" Adam asked idly. "Instant karma. I bet every one of us has a list of people who've given us trouble. My grandpa always said, 'Don't get mad, get even.'"

I had to admit I could see the appeal, particularly now that I was a firsthand witness to some of the insurance quandaries and medical horror stories I'd only read about before. But there were some potential problems.

"Mass murder is frowned on," I reminded them. "Also, I don't know you guys all that well, but I don't think anybody here is a professional hit man or even has military experience. I bet I'm not the only one who's never fired a gun. I don't even like it when my cat kills a mouse."

"But I bet you like having the mouse gone," Adam said. "That's the trouble with liberals. You want results with no personal involvement. Or guilt."

"It's got nothing to do with liberalism," I argued, though in fact he had a point. Both about Gwendolyn's mousing and my desire to avoid guilt. I've always felt guilty about pretty much everything and the only good element of that is that I'm not Jewish, which I suspected would tip the scales so heavily I wouldn't be able to get out of bed.

"Still, Tina has a point," Kenny said. "Murder is kind of extreme and I doubt any of us would be very good at it."

"Who knows till you give it a whirl?" Katherine asked. "What are they going to do? Give us the death penalty?"

* * *

The five of us kept hanging out at Molly's pool house after support group meetings as fall moved on and the days grew shorter.

Frequently the concept of instant karma arose, the proactive idea of punishing people now for this life's moral transgressions, rather than forcing them to wait for an upcoming life in which to suffer. For those among us uncertain about the concept of an afterlife, punishment for its own sake felt both comfortable and sufficient.

The flavor of these conversations varied with the participants; folks with serious illnesses are not always socially available, being prone to all manner of problems related to treatment side effects and opportunistic infections, not to mention the actual deadly disease. And face it, most of the time they're not feeling at their best to start with. It was hardly surprising, then, that the focus was almost always on players from the health care industry. This was a group of really sick people, with health care at the core of their current lives.

Katherine, the deceptively prim elementary school teacher, knew a surprisingly versatile catalog of dirty automotive tricks.

"I have brothers who love cars," she explained with a shrug, "and I guess I picked it up from them."

Picked it up seriously, it would seem, since she drove a red 1968 Mustang convertible, and drove it with panache. I'd followed her in and out of Rancho Santa Fe on dark winding roads several times on nights we gathered at Molly's, watching her whip around the curves.

"It mostly depends on whether you want to hurt the driver or the car," she went on. "If it's the car, then it's easy enough. There's all kinds of things you can do. Sugar in the gas tank, nails in the tires, a couple of cans of that gunk that expands and gets hard down around the gas pedal. Shove a potato into the exhaust pipe."

"Remind me to stay on your good side," Kenny said.

Molly, a champion shopper during her L.A. legal days—"It was the only social life I had," she told me once—liked the idea of ordering things in people's names. Like a few dozen magazine subscriptions from blow-in cards, the kind that say, *Bill Me Later*. Subscriptions to *Hustler* and *Bootylicious* delivered to the home address, or maybe to a neighbor's address, somebody who'd bring by the mailman's mistake, with a clothespin on her nose.

"Nice one," I said. "Or how about this? Mr. Big's secretary opens the box and an inflatable lady pops open ready for action, like a lifeboat. Or even better, the kid in the mail room opens it and everybody gets to see and hear about it as he carries it down the halls."

"You could go devious too," Molly suggested. "Send something that's allegedly a gift from somebody else. Like, oh, say, some really high-end sex toys delivered at a sanctimonious holy-roller church to the holier-than-thou preacher. As a thank-you gift for marital counseling from"—she hesitated for a moment—"some tight-ass lady who sings soprano in the choir. Labeled *Open immediately* when you know the guy is out of town for a week."

Adam laughed so hard that he choked at that one. "Let's not forget the Internet," he said, "and everybody's best friend, Photoshop. Start with a cold cybertrail that dead-ends in Eastern Slobbovia, and you could put together websites that would cause lots of problems for people. Eternal problems, since of course the Internet is forever. Blogs full of intimate revelations and confessions. Political stuff that's the polar opposite of what the person really believes. Horrible financial information offered as 'insider tips' from somebody who ought to know better and will definitely get in trouble with the SEC for it."

That got accountant Kenny's attention. "If you were willing to take your time about it and make a nonrefundable financial investment," he said slowly, "there are all kinds of ways you can cause trouble for somebody down the road. Get enough personal information to set up dummy accounts that would appear to be direct conflicts of interest, for instance. It would be a little complex and require a bit of research, naturally."

"But for somebody with your skill set," Molly noted, "no particular problem."

"I hate to think I'm becoming a cliché," Molly said at one point, "but I believe this is giving me reason to live."

It was all terribly hypothetical, of course. But since it *was* hypothetical, people kept bringing up not-so-hypothetical names. Objects of Attention, we called them. OoAs.

The woman who got the huge bonus from Western Health because she had cancelled coverage for the most insureds who had "lied" on their applications. The cancellations usually occurred right when the customers most needed assistance, and the purported lies often involved a forgotten yeast infection or ingrown toenail.

The health care executives who tried to enlist the aid of doctors in ferreting out similar application omissions so they could cancel coverage. Proactivity 101: Watch the Hippocratic Oath Circle the Drain. We were willing to bet that idea was a nonstarter, though, most doctors being unable to handle the paperwork they were already supposed to produce.

The bozos in San Diego County—elected officials for the most part—who managed to keep medical marijuana unavailable to those entitled to receive it for fifteen *years* after it was approved in a statewide vote. This wasn't a problem for Molly or these guys, since the young can always find private suppliers, but it hardly seemed fair to the general public, older people who might not have the savvy or resources to get up to L.A. or Orange County.

But then Katherine pointed out that those San Diego obstructionists also had support from the feds. So we rolled in everybody else attached to this mean-spirited daisy chain—a wretched and misguided mishmash of government lawyers, elected officials, antidrug zealots with personal agendas, and the horses they rode in on.

And some Objects of Attention were more personal.

Like the employer who laid off Sheryl Masterson in a way that she lost her medical benefits through some cockeyed application of the law which maybe wasn't even legal. This was a long time ago, when I was in high school, and Sheryl was a good friend of my mother's. She lost her job and her insurance and her husband was already long gone. So she toughed it out through increasingly serious symptoms until by the time she finally saw a doctor, her ovarian cancer had cobwebbed throughout her entire abdomen.

Sheryl died rather quickly after her diagnosis, in terrible pain. I wished I knew the names of the doctors who refused to give her enough morphine for fear that she'd become addicted, so I could add them to the OoA list. Her former employer, who advertised his carpet cleaning service county-wide, would be easy enough to find.

On a more immediate and prosaic note, Katherine nominated a jerk at her pharmacy who bellowed information about her prescriptions and possible unsavory side effects to her entire zip code, even as she begged him to stop.

Making these lists was like eating M&Ms, or chips and salsa. Satisfying, simple, and tough to stop.

"Do you think," Molly inquired mildly when we were together again a week later, "that perhaps we've taken this far enough?"

When we had all arrived earlier and settled around the fire ring on her patio, Molly pulled out and fiddled with her iPod. Moments later John Lennon warned from speakers hanging in nearby trees that instant karma was gonna get us, putting one and all in a relatively jolly mood. For once everyone was present and even feeling reasonably good.

At least until a group discussion of execution methods devolved to a detailed description of the Torture Museum up at Medieval Times in Orange County, a place that so creeped me out in seventh grade I couldn't sleep for a week. Torture unto death was what Molly referred to with her question about boundaries.

"You mean you're not gonna let us kill all these people, counselor?" Kenny asked.

"Afraid not," she answered.

Adam grinned. "Then can we just mess them up a bit?"

Three days later, Katherine had a bad reaction to a new drug and died.

Her funeral was every bit as horrible as you'd expect, with sobbing third-graders whose parents should have known better and shocked cronies of her parents and her grandmother who kept wailing, "It should have been me," until pretty much everyone agreed.

Molly went into a funk and stopped even going to the support group for a couple of weeks. She didn't want me to take her anywhere, thank you very much, and said that she didn't need anything and would be in touch if she did, as if I were some annoying telemarketer.

I pretended not to be terribly hurt and went about my business, working long hours and trying to remember the old Molly I knew in high school, the one whose bikini was always the sexiest, whose laugh the most infectious, whose mind the keenest. The brilliant girl whose vibrant energy made it clear that she was going to live forever.

Big. Fat. Lie.

I don't want you to think that I was unfeeling back then, that what's happening to me now is my own karmic payback for being too blasé or smart-ass around four people whose lives were slipping away by the minute. I gave up wearing mascara altogether for that year, and the one that followed, when the slightest thing could trigger a memory of Molly or one of the others. And when

Molly banished me that fall—which is what it felt like, banishment, no two ways about it—it broke my heart.

Molly texted me Thanksgiving week and asked if I could come by Tuesday night after work. The pool house door was opened by a pleasant-looking Filipina caregiver wearing floral-patterned scrubs, a new and alarming addition. Molly introduced us, then shooed the woman up to her parents' house and promised to call when we were finished.

I was shocked at how much her appearance had deteriorated. She slumped in a wheelchair in baggy sweats. The expensive blond wig which had been styled before her treatment began, to perfectly match her sophisticated hairstyle, now looked absurdly out of place atop her pallid, steroid-swollen face.

"I'm sorry I've been rude," she began, and I tried to cut her off but she waved a hand to stop me. It was something she'd been working up, I realized, and I let her go on. It was a wonderful summation, a sad reminder that a world full of crummy lawyers was about to lose a really first-rate one. When she finished the apology she asked if I would do her a favor.

"Anything," I said, and meant it.

"I knew I could count on you. It's just too weird to tell my parents. And my brother is on Planet Frank, pretending that I've got a bad cold." Her parents had always been fairly cool, as reactionary billionaires went. Her brother Frank was mega-intelligent but socially inept, a physicist up at the Jet Propulsion Lab in Pasadena.

"Let me guess. You want me to have your love child." She laughed. "No? Okay, then. You must want to revive the Instant Karma project."

Her smile was weak as she shook her head. "Too late for me on that, though I suppose it's never too late for justice. No, Tina, this is a lot simpler." She explained that when she was first diagnosed, after a grand mal seizure in the shoe department of Nordstrom at the Grove, she worried endlessly about loss of control. Once her diagnosis was firm and irrevocable, she decided that she wanted power over when and how she would die.

"But I'm a coward. And I didn't want to do anything that would make a horrible memory for my parents, or whoever found me. So much for guns and knives. I kind of liked the idea of jumping off a skyscraper, or out of a plane, but I figured by the time I was ready, that wouldn't be practical." She waved a hand at the wheelchair. "As it isn't. Anyway, one night I had an incredibly vivid dream.

"I was in some kind of medieval court, like one of those period movies where everybody's dressed in forty yards of satin. Mine was deep blue. We were speaking a language I'd never heard that sounded like chipmunks. Then, suddenly, huge doors swung open and warriors swarmed in, wearing ragged animal furs and carrying swords and shields. Everybody was screaming and slashing swords, but in the midst of it all I was totally calm. I looked into my lap and saw my hand, wearing an ornate ring with a huge ruby. Just as one of the warriors was about to pounce on me, I raised my hand to my mouth, unclasped the ruby, and swallowed a golden liquid."

Quite a dream, that. Mine tend to be about getting lost in parking lots, or being unable to find the right color pen on my way to the final exam for the course I didn't know I was taking.

"I woke up then," she continued, "and went on eBay and found a poison ring. They're big in Goth culture, in case you didn't know, so it's not as crazy as it sounds. I actually bought a couple, so I could pick the one I liked best once I had them all."

"The opal!"

Molly never wore jewelry when she was younger, was one of the few women my age I've ever known without a single piercing. I remembered noticing the ring as we sat around the fire ring outside her pool house after Halloween group session, and how she laughed it off as something she'd had forever. I looked at her hands now and her fingers were bare again.

She nodded. "The opal. And I got myself some potassium cyanide and I made my own poison pills, just like those guys in the spy movies who always have a fake tooth in their mouth in case they're captured. It was almost comic, actually. I mean the stuff *is* poison, and it's designed to kill as quickly as possible. So I had to keep from spilling anything or getting it on my skin while I was working. All I could think was that if I screwed this up, I'd be dead even sooner, and my final act on earth would be a failure."

Only Molly could think of the creation of poison pills in those terms.

"How many billable hours did it take?" I asked.

She chuckled. "You got me, Tina. Always could. Altogether, counting the online shopping and death pill construction, about four and a half, but that's cause I was taking my time. Perfectionism is a burden."

This from the Torrey Pines valedictorian, the Stanford National Merit Scholar, the Boalt Hall law review editor.

"So this is really the last loose end," she said. "I've signed all the powers of attorney and health care directives and financial papers, and my affairs, as they say, are in order. Donating organs, I'm sorry to say, isn't an option. My parents have sworn that they won't haul me to a hospital and that I can die right here, in hospice, with all the painkillers I want. I'm past pride about pretty much everything, and it will be easier for my parents that way. Between you and me, I'm ready to cry uncle and go into hospice. My head hurts and the drugs will be better."

"I'm sorry," I told her simply. "However I can help . . ."

She smiled and there was a spark of the old Molly again, looking up triumphantly after racing through the AP Physics exam. "You can take care of the damned poison rings. I don't want my parents to find that stuff after I'm dead or for anybody to accidentally get into the cyanide. What I had in mind, if you're willing, is for you to make it all disappear. Take it away and dispose of it for me, please."

I hesitated for a moment and she misunderstood.

"Listen, if this is too much—"

"Not at all," I said. "But you need to promise me something. You won't cut me off again. This is awful, Molly, but it tore me apart when you made me go away."

We both cried a bit then, and a few tissues later she told me where she'd hidden the rings and the poison, in a pretty little oval cloisonné box in her swimsuit drawer. I retrieved the innocuous-looking pink-and-gold box and found the opal and three other rather bulky rings nestled inside on black velvet, each holding a lethal gelcap. A miniature version of the cloisonné box beside them held a dozen more capsules.

"I used up what I had," she said with a shrug. "It's not something you can just toss into the stew with the leftover vegetables."

We never talked about it again, and the whole episode was so crazy that I just took the box home and pushed it to the back of the top shelf in my bedroom closet. I worked really hard and stopped by Molly's every couple of days and at Christmas I brought her new music by her favorite artists. By then she was in bed all the time and heavily medicated, and I wasn't always sure she knew I was there.

Every now and then I'd think about her poison rings, and once or twice I even got down the cloisonné box. But I never opened it.

Molly died on the last day of January. That was two years ago, and now it's coming into spring again, in a year where I won't reach Christmas. Maybe not even the Fourth of July.

So here we are.

I'm inches away from being reunited with Molly and Katherine and Kenny and my parents, if there's an afterlife, and inches away from oblivion if there isn't. I've gradually lost energy, as the doctors said I would, on medication that sufficiently masks my symptoms so that I sometimes forget for a few minutes just what's happening inside my body. I stopped working a few weeks ago, but I'm an information junkie and still spend a lot of my waking time online, just like I always did.

So I was onto the story immediately when it broke on the web midway through last Monday morning. Laverne Patterson had been named executive vice president of Western Health. The very same Laverne Patterson we used to rail about on Molly's patio. The woman who got that big fat bonus for cancelling health coverage for people who faithfully paid their premiums until they got sick, when Laverne started digging and discovered their applications didn't mention having had chicken pox in kindergarten.

Whereupon she gleefully booted them out the Western Health door.

It turned out that Western Health hadn't gotten rid of her at all, they'd simply shipped her off to Houston for a while to rehabilitate her in the finance office, given her a couple of quiet promotions, and a few months back slipped her once again into the San Diego home office. Now she would be number two in the whole damn company, and the damage she could do from that position was terrifying.

I'd been moping around, feeling bored and out of sorts, unwilling to start anything I couldn't finish, which in my case meant not ordering dinner until after lunch was concluded. Suddenly I felt a spurt of energy, a sense of mission, a belief that I could do one last thing before checking out of the Hotel California.

I could revive Instant Karma and take out Laverne Patterson.

I decided to be fair about things, to give her the benefit of the doubt that she had so merrily denied to others. Maybe she led a secret life of saintliness, cleansed lepers on the weekends and rocked babies in the neonatal unit on her lunch hour. Maybe her charitable donations exceeded tax-deductible levels and she offered a triple-tithe to her church. Maybe I was so caught up in my own pity party that I was prepared to punish somebody who, like any good Nazi, was simply doing her job.

Okay, I couldn't be entirely objective.

But though I searched diligently, I didn't find anything to mitigate my belief that she was a thoroughly despicable person, someone who would continue to fight the afflicted under the guide of reasonable care, a woman without whom this would be a better world.

It was absurdly easy to find out all about her personal life, mostly from information available online to anybody with a little interest and tenacity. Add in the tricks I knew from my years as a researcher, and some passwords to databases that I still remembered, and a picture emerged that made me quite comfortable with the decision I realized I had already made.

Laverne Patterson lived in a gated community in La Jolla. Her husband had taken early retirement for health reasons, picking up a whopping pension from his city manager job in a Los Angeles bedroom community. He now seemed to divide his time among managing his investments, sailing his thirty-two-foot boat, and playing golf. He had remained in La Jolla while Laverne was exiled to Houston, and didn't sound like the kind of guy who'd miss her very much, although he was quick with the platitudes when interviewed for business magazine profiles. Their photographs together always looked forced, even when they both wore their most practiced smiles.

She was an attractive woman, a snappy dresser who used a personal trainer but admitted to a weakness for Nirvana Chocolates. She belonged to a ton of civic and business organizations, drove a Lexus, and said she'd love to learn to fly if only she had the time. Her favorite vacation spot was Hawaii where she liked to take long walks on the beach. She was sorry that her earlier bonus had been misconstrued, though she still maintained that honesty was always important and that she had never acted with malice.

Clueless and mean, my favorite combination.

I could do this, I realized. I could actually kill this woman.

Well, maybe not put my hands around her throat and strangle her, or bludgeon her with a broken oxygen tank. I was always a little squeamish, to tell the truth, and that kind of in-close work would have been tough for me even when I had my full strength. But I could orchestrate her death. I just needed to figure out a way.

And then two factoids jumped together in my mind, just how it used to happen when I was writing web content for a nonprofit fundraiser, trying to find a way to up the ante with the same hopelessly dull information. It was so incredibly trite that I just couldn't resist.

He was diabetic. She loved Nirvana Chocolates.

I would send her a box of candy, delivered to the house, and there'd be no danger that he'd nip into it before she had her chance. I'd have it gift wrapped, anyhow. Pay cash, bring it home and shoot some potassium cyanide into each deep, rich chocolate truffle. Rewrap and send it by a shipping service to her home.

With a card saying, *Thanks for everything. I.K.*

And so that's what I did.

There were some comic moments working with the cyanide gelcaps and the truffles, and I was glad I'd bought three times as many as I thought I'd need. I wore gloves, of course, both to protect me from the poison and to avoid fingerprints, though I was fairly certain mine were in no database that could come back to haunt me. And because on one level it was all rather silly, I did wear one of the poison rings, a clunky silver number, for dramatic effect.

It's harder to inject poison into dense chocolate than you

might think, a matter of physics, really, and I had to do some experimenting with truffle reconstruction to make it work. At one point a failed venture rolled clear across the floor, dangerously close to the bathroom door where Gwendolyn was howling her displeasure at being locked away for her own safety.

The ones I botched went down the toilet, since I'd determined that entry into the sewage stream would diffuse the poison and render it harmless. In fact, I was a little dismayed to find out just how much terrible stuff was already in our local sewage stream, though too tired to care.

When I was finished, I repackaged everything, boxed it, wrapped it, tucked the card among the packing peanuts, and sealed the white carton. I changed my appearance a bit and took it to a shipping store in a business park facility during a busy spell. I kept my nerves mostly under control, though I did drop my purse and have to gather its contents at one point.

Then I went home to take a nap. There was no reason yet to monitor the Internet, and I was increasingly tired anyway, sometimes sleeping sixteen or eighteen hours a day. I even kept my phone turned off much of the time because there wasn't anybody I wanted to hear from.

I'd paid for next-day delivery and it was Wednesday, so the present would arrive tomorrow. On Thursday mornings, according to the *San Diego Union-Tribune*, Laverne always attended a business breakfast, so she'd be gone before it was delivered. If she paid attention to packages that came to her house, as women tend to, she'd open it tomorrow night and be unable to resist taking a bite out of a succulent chocolate morsel.

Her last succulent chocolate morsel.

I slept well and soundly, setting an alarm to wake me for my eight a.m. meds and returning to bed, then sleeping clear past noon. I spent the afternoon reading newspapers from around the world online, pretending I wasn't aware of every minute that passed.

Then I was tired again, so I took another nap after my four p.m. meds. When I awoke, it was nearly dark.

I went to the computer and found the story third on the headline list of my favorite news service: *Western Health Executive Dies Under Suspicious Circumstances.* It was breaking news with few details, just that Leonard Patterson had called 911 when his wife suddenly collapsed and that homicide detectives were investigating and had no comment.

I'd expected to feel some kind of satisfaction and relief, vindication for those who had suffered at Laverne Patterson's hands and would be saved from her future attempts to mold health care. But I didn't feel much of anything, really.

In a corner, Gwendolyn batted her favorite pink ball and I remembered running across the room to grab the cyanide-treated truffle that was rolling toward the bathroom door. I remembered reaching down and picking it up with the gloved hand that wore the heavy silver poison ring. I wondered if Molly knew what I had done.

Then I checked my e-mail and found a message marked *Urgent* from my doctor's office.

I had been approved for the clinical trial, he told me, after somebody dropped out at the last minute. They'd been unable to reach me by phone but time was an issue, and I needed to get to Philadelphia for pretesting as soon as possible. There were no guarantees of the new orphan drug being tested, but it had proven promising in animal studies. Like most clinical trials, there was no way to know if I'd receive the actual drug or a placebo, but they were certain I would be as pleased by this surprising development as they were.

Somebody had "dropped out" of the study. Had dropped dead, more likely, but that hardly mattered.

I had a chance again. I might be cured. I might live and cheat those charities out of their speedy inheritance. Of course, I might also get the sugar pills, but then I was no worse off than I'd been to start with, except that I'd be in a hospital in Philadelphia.

It was all terribly confusing, and I was getting tired again. I wished Molly were here, or somebody else I could talk to.

If I joined the study and lived, I'd get a double pass, from both death and the criminal justice system.

I'd taken every possible precaution to avoid spending my final days in a literal cell instead of the figurative one of my impending death. I obscured my identity two different ways at the candy store and the shipping service, made cash payments with twenties from East County ATMs, wore gloves at every stage of the maneuver except the actual sale counters, where I touched nothing. I used my own cheap ballpoint to fill out shipping forms, flushed or burned the remains of the chocolate-doctoring session, kept only Molly's cloisonné box and the four rings it contained.

The rings.

I watched Gwendolyn continue to bat the pink ball and remembered the heavy silver ring I'd been wearing when I fixed Laverne's final snack. It was back in the cloisonné box, but I'd slipped Molly's opal onto my finger for good luck when I headed out to ship the candy. The ring was a little loose, but that didn't really matter. It didn't fit the character I was playing at the shipping service, so I'd tucked it into my purse.

I moved in slow motion now toward the little drawstring bag, its contents still jumbled from when I'd stuffed everything back in as I waited in line to send my package, dismayed that I'd called attention to myself. I dumped the contents on the table.

No ring.

I took my time about it, checked and rechecked, ran the film back and forth in my brain. I went out and searched the car. Checked my purse again. There hadn't been pockets in the sweat suit I was wearing at the time, and in any case I'd left it in a Salvation Army drop box on my way home twenty minutes later, after changing in a McDonald's restroom.

So I'd dropped it on the floor at the shipping service, where cops were probably already trying to find out who'd sent the candy. Where somebody would surely find it. And trace it to Molly, who bought it on eBay and told me the seller had assured her only three existed in the world just like it.

I opened the cloisonné box and put the chunky silver poison ring on my finger. I sent a brief reply to the doctor's e-mail, saying that I had decided not to participate in the clinical trial. Then I opened the poison ring and removed the capsule it still held.

Instant karma.

THE ANGEL'S SHARE

BY MORGAN HUNT

Hillcrest

Betty Lou Thomas from Muncie, Indiana, complained as though the pot at the end of the rainbow had a flush valve. Thick-bodied, flat-chested, 5'2", with brown eyes, coarse features, and hair the color of stone-ground mustard, she was the sort of woman you didn't notice. And she carried a twenty-carat diamond chip on her shoulder about that.

She resented being short. ("In Indiana we lived for basketball. What chance did I have on the women's team at five-two?") Being female. ("Why don't men have periods and cramps?") Being a lesbian. ("Still waiting for *my* Emancipation Proclamation.")

She was currently issuing a whine-a-thon into the phone about the lack of cleaning power in modern laundry detergents. Jesus.

I lay on rumpled sheets in my bungalow near Front and Spruce streets. San Diego's "June gloom," otherwise known as the marine layer, had finally burned off and sun now warmed my bedroom. Next to me in all of her considerable glory lay Caterina, a thirty-nine-year-old self-styled mixed-media artist and boutique owner whom I'd known for exactly twelve days.

On Caterina's index finger, a crimson nail sharp enough to serve as Occam's Razor traced its way from my ankle, along my calf, to the tender flesh of my inner thigh. There she dug in and drew blood. I would have screamed, but she covered my mouth with her other hand.

This latest maneuver made the phone conversation more difficult than before, precisely Caterina's intention.

Betty was droning on, something about a neighbor in her condo building who kept taking her assigned parking space in the garage.

I twisted my mouth free of Caterina's hand. "Why don't you report him to the building manager?" I asked, knowing she'd reject any practical suggestions that might lead to a resolution.

"Oh, he's just an asshole," Betty sighed. "What are you having for dinner tonight? I never know what to cook. Last night I tried meat loaf with salsa . . ."

"Betty, I'm in the middle of something right now; I really have to go."

"I need to change the settings on my satellite dish tomorrow and I could use some help . . ."

"What time?"

"I'd like to get it done first thing. Could you come over around seven-thirty a.m.?"

"Betty, I have to work tomorrow. If it can wait a few days, I'll—"

"No, I've got my whole day planned. Your work schedule's flexible; go to work later. I need to get this done early."

The talon enameled with Heavenly Heartache now circled a very sensitive part of me. Never answer the phone when you're lying naked in bed.

"I've got a major work project pending and a staff meeting tomorrow. Find someone else to help this time. I've got to go."

"But we haven't talked in over a week. And I—"

"Sorry, talk to you again soon." The snap of my cell felt harsh, but I'd spared myself a clitorectomy.

"I thought Betty was an ex from ages ago," Caterina probed. "I thought you said she was boring."

"True and truer."

"Then why do you still talk to her?"

Why, indeed. Because she reminded me of an underdog boxer who struggles up from the mat on the count of nine repeatedly until she finally wins the bout. Because when she wasn't complaining, she cracked corny jokes. Because for the sixteen months we were together, she tried her damnedest and it was my fault it didn't work out. Because when I broke my ankle years after we split up, Betty walked my dog and made me dinner every day for six weeks. Because I could feel her heart from across a room.

These were not things I would be able to easily explain to Caterina, who had forgotten her own question and was now gliding around the house nude in search of asparagus stalks and cellophane. I like that in a woman.

I got up early the next day to brainstorm a new marketing campaign for my employer, Sciortino's Winery, in the San Pasqual Valley. To save gas, they allowed me to telecommute most of the time. Caterina had, as usual, slipped out and returned to her home in the dark of night. I sipped Brazilian coffee and concentrated on strategies that would inspire critics to hyperbolize about our new Tempranillo.

The first call came at 7:48 a.m.

"I'm so sorry, Nikki," a friend's voice said.

"About what?"

"About Betty. You haven't heard?"

"Heard what?"

"Turn on channel 39."

For the next few minutes I ignored twelve more calls while I watched reporters second-guess the situation pertaining to the body lying on the sidewalk. They were calling it a suicide. They were calling her a jumper.

Traffic being what it is, I knew it would be faster to walk the mile or so from my house to Betty's. I grabbed my house keys and cell and headed out.

I couldn't swallow. Guilt and shame percolated deeper with every footstep. My pulse pounded. Suicide? Why hadn't I been more patient? Why couldn't I have been more helpful? Hanging up on her when Caterina distracted me was a very human thing to do, but hiding behind the species is a cheap excuse.

I walked fast, a dyke on a mission, hardly noticing the Craftsman bungalows, Spanish-style stuccos, gay bars, and boutiques that filled the neighborhood.

Hillcrest used to be dominated by a huge Sears, Roebuck and Co. When chichi condo complexes, an art-film theater, and distinctive eateries squeezed out Sears, blue collars were replaced by lavender boxers. Promises of erotic satisfaction now hang in the Hillcrest air, like the pots of petunias and pansies swinging from summer lampposts.

While not as well known as the Castro or WeHo, Hillcrest received national media attention in '97 as the home of Andrew Cunanan, the twisted serial killer who murdered Versace. Now Hillcrest was on TV again: a dead body, sirens and news crews, with Betty Lou Thomas headlining.

I turned east on University toward the Uptown Shopping Center near where Betty lived. I just missed the Walk signal at Vermont. Too fidgety to wait, I strode another block to Richmond to burn adrenaline.

At Richmond the front door of the Alibi, Hillcrest's oldest neighborhood saloon, stood open revealing a murky interior behind the jukebox. Nothing much going on at this hour. The corner smelled of cigarettes; the sidewalk was confettied with butts.

I caught the light, crossed the street, closed the distance, and insinuated myself into the crowd. Betty's body had landed atop fallen jacaranda blossoms, their soft periwinkle blue crushed and smeared into a bruise-colored shroud.

I squirmed through the scene, inching my way toward the officer in charge. "Why are you calling this a suicide?"

"Who are you?"

"I'm one of her closest friends. I spoke to her yesterday and she didn't seem in the least bit suicidal. Not at all."

Gently: "Sometimes it happens that way."

"But it could've been an accident, right? She could've slipped and fallen?"

The officer—a slow-moving whelk of fiber, muscle, and taut uniform—studied me more carefully. "There's a safety parapet around the perimeter of the roof. If someone slipped and fell, they'd slide into the wall." Seeing I was not persuaded, he leaned down so he could speak directly in my ear. "We found Prozac in her medicine cabinet."

"If you took a survey here," I gestured toward the crowd of looky-loos, "you'd probably find 70 percent of them are pumping their serotonin. The rest are on Adderall and a pharmacopeia of other fine substances."

Officer Whelk did not respond.

I persisted. "Did you find a suicide note?" If the police had, maybe it would explain what had provoked Betty to take such an extreme measure. And if there was a note, had she cited me as one of the provocations? *I used to be able to talk to Nikki, but now she acts as if our friendship is of no importance.*

"Not yet, but we've barely begun our investigation. Now, unless you're a family member, please step back . . ."

I took a few snapshots with my cell and reluctantly started the trek home. In a strange state, I let feet and mind wander on the return route. I paused in front of a Thai restaurant to check the menu posted in the window. *Choo-Chi Prawn. Chicken Volcano. Lard Prik.* Was there a lesbian in Hillcrest who had ordered Lard Prik? Was there a gay man who had not?

I passed Milo's Erotic Apparel and assessed their new window display. A reclining masked mannequin in a black leather bustier sat with one leg crossed over the bent knee of the other. A papier-mâché cucumber dangled from a chain on the spike heel of her silver boot.

This was the Hillcrest Betty had fallen in love with. She'd spent many years in Indiana being neurotic, closeted, and lonely. Finally she'd found the courage to move two thousand miles away from everything and everyone she'd ever known. In San Diego she was like a child who'd run off to join the circus and Hillcrest was the center ring. Everything had been fresh, colorful, exotic—the palm trees, the sunshine, the Pride Parade, the sense that diversity was a good thing. Here, even vegetable bondage was acceptable.

Despite her habit of complaining, Betty seemed reasonably content most of the time. I just couldn't wrap my mind around the whole suicide concept. Yes, she suffered from mild depression, but it had been well controlled for years. Yes, she was single and sometimes lonely. But thousands of married people sit, equally lonely, in front of the TV every night and they don't jump off the roof.

If I was going to find out what really happened, I couldn't be encumbered by guilt. I began to strip it from my soul like so much old furniture varnish. If Betty had been depressed, she could've asked for support instead of complaining about laundry detergent. If she had given me any indication that our last conversation might be our *last* conversation, I would've paid more attention.

At Third and Robinson, I stopped in at Caterina's scarf shop. The moment our eyes met, I knew she knew. "Now don't blame yourself, darling," she oozed. "Nothing you could've done."

"I don't know about that, but there's something I can do now."

"What do you mean?"

"The police are calling it suicide."

"The woman jumped off her roof. What else would you call it?"

"The whole thing doesn't smell right. Maybe it was an accident. Maybe she was pushed."

Caterina draped a gold scarf decorated with black fleur-de-lis over a display. "Don't you love what Burberry does with this new line?"

I stared out the window where orange birds of paradise, magenta bougainvillea, and blue agapanthus made the street look like Odin's coloring book. "I'm going to be busy for a while; I'll call when things calm down."

"We have tickets for the San Diego Rep on Saturday."

"I know." I kissed her and headed for the door.

"Don't spend too much time on the dead; it's the living that matter."

Her words echoed as I legged the last few blocks home.

I called a friend who works as a crime reporter at the *San Diego Union-Tribune*. "You get access to police reports right away, don't you? I want to look at the preliminary report on the death of Betty Lou Thomas."

"That the suicide over on Cleveland Avenue?"

"The police are calling it a suicide, yes. Can you e-mail me a copy of the prelim? Sooner rather than later?"

My friend hesitated; there'd been many favors over the years. There'd be a price.

"Can you get me four bottles of Sciortino's 2006 Mourvèdre?"

Our '06 Mourvèdre goes for about forty-five dollars a bottle. I did the math. "I'll drop them off this evening."

I drove to Sciortino's that afternoon to attend a staff meeting and pick up the wine. Traffic was light on I-15 for a change and I arrived early. I wandered the grounds looking for my boss. Maybe he'd approve an employee discount.

Joe Sciortino wasn't in his office. The vineyard supervisor said he wasn't out among the trellises. I walked by the crush pad; no Joe. I checked the barrel room. When I opened the door, a sensual bouquet curled into my nostrils: the Angel's Share. That's what those in the business call the portion of wine that evaporates from the barrels during the aging process, while the remaining product soaks up oak vanilla tannins. Over the years, 5 or 10 percent of the wine will diffuse into the air, filling the tightly sealed barrel room with potent ambrosia. The angels know a good thing when they see it, and sip their share when no one's looking.

I located Joe among the barrels and negotiated a deal on the Mourvèdre.

That evening I deposited four bottles at my reporter friend's apartment. He handed me a sheaf of papers. "I e-mailed these too. I'll update you every few days for a week. Fair?"

"Fair. Happy uncorking."

At home that night I studied the report. There had been nothing unusual about the condo; no packed boxes, no suicide note. In fact, the only note was a handwritten to-do list on Betty's kitchen table. The list had seven items on it. The first was: *Take garbage out.* That item was checked off, and the police confirmed that garbage had, indeed, been taken out.

The second item was to change the settings on her satellite dish receiver—the favor she'd asked me to help with. To SDPD's credit, they had called her satellite dish company to see if there'd been a problem. There had. The company had advised her to try a new setting configuration, and if that didn't work, to bring the receiver back to the office and exchange it for a new one. SDPD had removed the satellite dish and tagged it as evidence, although evidence of what I wasn't sure.

Betty never got to items 3 through 7.

The police had called Betty's closest living relatives, a younger brother and an older sister back in Muncie. They told police that Betty was an unhappy, immoral woman, alienated from church and family. That, along with the Prozac prescription, led SDPD to the suicide verdict, but I still wasn't buying it.

I poured myself three fingers of Irish whiskey on the rocks. I work for a winery, but sometimes I need something stronger than sour grapes to take the edge off.

After a few sips I returned to the report. It seemed blatantly obvious to me that the fall had been an accident. Women aren't jumpers, not in my experience. To validate my intuition, I Googled *women and suicide methods* and discovered that only 3.5 percent of female suicides in the U.S. are jumpers.

I needed to see Betty's roof and its safety wall for myself. I was wondering exactly how to accomplish that when my phone rang.

"Some friends of mine own a condo in the building where Betty lived. I know you want to snoop, so I wrangled us a dinner invitation for tomorrow."

Betty may have longed for my attention but Caterina knew how to get it.

She was in fine form for dinner with her friends the following evening. There was an uncharacteristic chill in the air, enough that I wore a black leather vest over my shirt. She selected one of her new pashmina shawls in jade green and a long, loose skirt. The outfit complimented her lithe body and she knew it. She flirted wickedly throughout the meal. Her friends, Glenn and Mike, wondered aloud if she'd met her match.

At the earliest acceptable moment, I excused myself, took the elevator to the fourth floor, and found the roof access door. No crime scene tape barred entry.

Out on the roof I paused to breathe the cool air. The western horizon over San Diego harbor was slashed by bands of neon scarlet, gold, and fuschia. To the east, the sky was the color of blue pen ink. City lights outshone the stars.

Betty, was this the venue of your chosen farewell?

The roof was flat; no angle jeopardized my safety. The material beneath my feet offered good grip, a skid-proof surface. A thirty-inch parapet did, indeed, encircle the roof. I knew from the police report where the satellite dish had been located and it was nowhere near the roof's edge. Even if Betty had slipped and fallen, the officer was right: she might have slid into the parapet, but it was very unlikely she'd have gone over it.

I scanned the roof looking for indications of a scuffle, for any signs that Betty might have slipped or that someone might have given her a shove. No oil or grease on the roof surface. Lots of footprints, but no distinct skid or scuff marks. Nothing much except bird droppings and sewer vents. My inspection was punctuated by the caterwauling of an ambulance coming from the direction of Mercy Hospital.

As the sky deepened to octopus ink, I clicked on my flashlight and turned to go.

Behind me stood a slender man in his thirties, wearing jeans and a short-sleeved camo shirt. He must have entered the roof while the siren was blaring. Anxious and twitchy, he carried a day's worth of beard and was attractive in a rough-hewn way.

"Hello," I said, walking up to him, hand extended. "I'm Nikki. Thought I'd come up and check out the view."

He shook my hand. "Caleb Trout." He looked me over with an expression that was hard to read. Was he a nosy neighbor who wanted to see where Betty had fallen? Was he keeping an eye out because he suspected something about her death? Was he a meth addict waiting on the roof for someone to deal his next fix?

Suddenly Caleb asked, "Find anything interesting while you were here?"

I looked him in the eye. "Now that the sun has set, there's nothing here to see, Caleb. Nothing here to see."

I had one more errand before I returned to the dinner party. Caterina would fuss about how long I'd been gone. Let her.

The parking garage was a vault of shadows and exhaust. I heard soft laughter and the scrape of shoes coming from the next row of vehicles. In Betty's assigned parking space sat a blue Ford pickup. Her silver Jetta was parked in a nearby visitor's space. I wrote down the Ford's license plate number, and made my way back to the dinner party.

In bed that night Caterina wore violet silk, and I wore quite a smile.

The next day I drove to Sciortino's to give a PowerPoint presentation on the marketing event I'd come up with: The Grapes of Ra, a wine-tasting party where we'd decorate the grounds with hieroglyphs, stuffed crocodiles and cobras, and cheap statuary of Horus and Osiris. We'd hire a belly dancer to perform. Guests would be encouraged to dress like ancient Egyptians. And, of course, the guest list would be restricted to people who could afford half a case of Tempranillo!

I must've sold the idea well because everyone bought into it. Sometimes I wonder about people.

That evening I took Caterina out to dinner at the City Deli, a hallmark eatery that was popular even when Sears ruled the hood.

Afterward we went for a walk. Caterina was in an interesting mood. She talked about remembering the smell of violets in her grandmother's basement when she was a child. She confessed to wearing braces until her sophomore year. She told me her favorite flower was the black Baccara rose, a *rose noir*. Perhaps this conversational intimacy was provoked by the incident with Betty. Maybe she did a bit of soul-searching herself.

When we arrived at my house, the evening was too pleasant for us to stay indoors. We decided to walk across the little-known footbridge that connects one part of Spruce Street, across Kate Sessions Canyon seventy-five feet below, to the other part. The footbridge hangs among tall eucalyptus and acacia trees, suspended by cables secured with concrete at both ends. Walking across this bridge is like swinging in a cab at the top of the Ferris wheel. That half-scary, half-giggly sensation of swaying delighted both of us. Fortunately we were both sure-footed and had no fear of heights.

After strolling through the neighborhood on the other half of Spruce, we returned. That night our lovemaking drew its power from new and deeper wells.

Afterward in bed, my thoughts returned to Betty's death. "If I'm right and it wasn't suicide, then it had to be an accident or murder. And I have to agree with the police—an accident, while possible, does seem unlikely. But who would want to murder Betty?"

"I assume that's a rhetorical question."

I nodded. "In Betty's case, you don't have the 'usual suspects.' She lived off a fat work comp settlement she got from Caterpillar in Indiana years ago. She'd made good investments and never held a regular job after that. So there aren't any coworkers who might be jealous of a promotion, or that kind of thing."

"Yes, darling."

Caterina began licking the inside of my elbow, but I refused to be distracted. "Betty was alienated from her family, so no family feuds."

"And she didn't have a partner, so she wasn't murdered because she cheated on someone," Caterina observed.

"No; no partner, no spouse. No adultery. No family feud. No big inheritance. No coworkers. So what's that leave us?"

"Neighbors?"

"Exactly! And guess who owned the truck parked in Betty's parking space?"

She rolled over onto her stomach and squished a pillow beneath her breasts. "Caleb!"

I nodded. "I bought access to an online database of California vehicle licenses. Looked up the plate number and it was his truck. The day before she died, Betty said she'd argued with someone who kept taking her assigned parking space."

"Plus he was keeping an eye on the roof. He wanted to know what you saw."

"I'd say Caleb is my number one suspect." I failed to mention he was my only suspect. "Let's get some rest." I held her in my arms and drifted off. I had hoped she'd stay the night, but around three in the morning, I heard her scurry out of the house, off to her own bed as usual.

On Saturday Caterina sold one of the most expensive scarves in her inventory to an Elton John impersonator. I received an unsolicited pay raise for my marketing work at Sciortino's. And the production at the San Diego Rep carried all the weight of a marshmallow but was great fun.

After the play, I invited my new lover to do some snooping with me. I dropped her off at Glenn and Mike's, where she borrowed their pass to get me through the security gate of their parking garage. Betty's assigned space was unoccupied. I pulled into it. Caleb must be out prowling.

"The second Caleb shows, slide down and stay in the car. I mean it, Cat. Roll down the window to listen if you want, but I don't want him to know you're here. If anything goes wrong, call 911. Got it?"

"I love it when you think you can tell me what to do."

She and I steamed the windows pretty good while we waited to see if he'd make an appearance. A little after one a.m., Caleb pulled his truck up to Betty's parking spot. It was obvious from his facial expression that he was royally pissed to find the space occupied.

If I was ever going to do this, now was the time.

I got out and confronted him. "You like parking in this spot, don't you, Caleb?"

He relaxed when he saw it was me. "I just got back from serving three tours in Iraq. I think I deserve whatever parking space I want, don't you?"

Caleb was taller than me by a few inches, but he was also scrawnier. He didn't appear armed but you never know. I had a damned good switchblade in my jeans pocket.

"Do I think you deserve a good parking space? I think you deserve a life sentence. I think you liked this parking space enough to kill for it."

I saw his body go tense, but he regrouped quickly. "I don't know what the fuck you think you know, but that woman's death was a suicide. It's all over the papers."

"That right?"

"Yeah, that's right."

I stared him right in the eye. I lie more effectively that way. "I'm a programmer for a high-tech company that subcontracts to Google Earth. You've heard of Google, haven't you, Caleb?"

"Of course; I'm not a moron."

"Well, Google Earth gets mapping data from hundreds of satellites that orbit the earth 24-7. And guess what one of those satellites caught you doing the morning of the seventeenth? You shoved Betty Lou Thomas, owner of this parking space, to her death."

For a long moment, Caleb just stood there. I could almost hear his mental gears click. Would he bite the bait? I had no idea whether any commercial satellites, let alone Google's, could pick up that level of detail. But depending on what he did in the military, Caleb probably wouldn't know either.

"You can't prove anything. If you could, you'd have given evidence to the police and I'd be under arrest."

There it was, his admission of guilt. Now I knew this scuzz had pushed Betty off her roof. Frankly, I didn't care if he had PTSD or a bad case of athlete's foot. It's an all-volunteer service and counseling is available. Another vet might've gotten my sympathy but not a jerk with a hypertrophic sense of entitlement.

"Just tell me why, Caleb. Maybe then I can have some peace."

"I ran into her that morning when I took my garbage out. She was at the dumpster too. The minute she saw me, she started in with her whiny nagging. Said she was going to report me to the building manager if I parked in her space again." Caleb shifted in the long shadows. "I didn't serve years in Iraq to come home to that kind of crap."

"So you were bitching at each other when you took the garbage out . . . and then what?"

"Then a few minutes later I saw her go up to the roof by herself." He glanced down at the oil-stained floor. "Perfect opportunity."

I shook my head in disgust, turned away, and walked back to my car. I kept my hand on my switchblade, hoping with each step that he wouldn't attack me from behind.

I got in the car and drove away.

Caterina asked, "What if he follows us?"

"I'm counting on it."

She regarded me with something that might be admiration.

"You think our little boudoir games are edgy?" I asked. "Baby, if you want to know what edgy really is . . ." I looked in the rearview mirror and saw Caleb's truck two blocks behind us. "I want justice for Betty. I can use your help. Are you in?"

The adrenaline rush affected both of us, but Caterina practically glowed in the dark.

We hadn't been at my place more than three minutes when Caleb pulled up. "You understand what to do?" I asked my coconspirator. If there was a wild card in my plan, it wasn't Caleb.

"Of course, darling."

As expected, he messed with my circuit breaker and snuffed the lights. The window creaked as he raised it to crawl in. I heard a *whump!* followed by a nervous giggle. I reached into the blackness and fumbled for a moment before landing a second blow that guaranteed Caleb a permanent journey to Nod.

I felt the limp weight of his limbs as we carried him into the moonless night. Heard the rustle of critters with chatoyant eyes, then the metal chime of the suspension coils. Counted steps across the wooden planks. As we tensed for the final effort, I smelled Caterina's breath. The crash was quieter than expected.

In the soft deep black of night, I felt her fingernails pierce my forearm.

The next morning I awoke alone, still chasing vague snatches of dream. I brewed coffee, watched *Meet the Press,* and set about accomplishing a number of deferred chores. Driving home from a grocery run, I flicked on the radio and heard, "*. . . body was found in Kate Sessions Canyon today beneath the Spruce Street footbridge. The deceased, an apparent suicide, has been identified as Caleb Trout, an Iraq War veteran and resident of Hillcrest.*"

At midnight I walked alone through the memorial rose garden in Balboa Park. It was a new moon; the only illumination came from distant streetlights. The fragrance of roses calmed me. In such darkness, every rose is black.

Betty's not in Hillcrest anymore, of course, but something of her remains. In the queen ordering sprinkles for his Ben and Jerry's cone, in the corny joke told in a Fourth Avenue café, in the ubiquitous rainbow stickers, I sense both her absence and her presence. She's the Angel's Share.

HOMES
BY KEN KUHLKEN
Newport Avenue

Greg Mairs took a Restoril, his third tranquilizer of the afternoon. He washed his face and sat down to organize bills. Sort out which they could afford to pay. Decide which creditors might allow them to coast another month.

Visa, $150 minimum. No grace on that one. Business loan for the truck-mounted dry cleaner that would've doubled his commercial accounts, except he'd only had it two months before he turned into a wimp who could barely work an hour without collapsing. And even though he'd needed to sell it for half of what he owed, no grace.

Doctor Ramos. Doctor Schuetz. Sharp Cabrillo Hospital. X-Ray Medical. These days, more often than he prayed for miraculous healing, he prayed for a windfall that would allow him to at least pay off his medical and funeral bills. So he wouldn't die as the louse who'd left Barb this stack of horrors, so she wouldn't have to sell their home. He couldn't blame his girls if they boycotted his funeral.

Latin American Childcare. He wasn't about to shirk his pledge to orphans in El Salvador. Gas and electric, down now that summer had arrived, thank God, and the phone bill too. Barb hadn't gabbed as long as usual with her sister in Minnesota. Her sister wanted to talk about Greg, his death, and the future. Not Barb's favorite topics.

He slammed the lid on the rolltop desk and went to the kitchen. While he drank carrot juice, he thought maybe tomorrow, if James could abide his company, he'd join his amigo in a big glass of bourbon. "What good does carrot juice do a dead guy?" he muttered.

He sat on the porch staring down Newport Avenue, at the very place where the Silva brothers would've stomped him to death for knocking up Angie, their little sister. Except James saved his life by mashing Junior Silva's head with a Little League bat.

Then James runs from a murder charge, and only returns after twenty years. He risks it all, comes back home in hopes of rescuing Olivia. And Greg does what, after James gave him the chance to live, know love, meet Barb and Jesus, become a father. "Nothing. Zip," Greg mumbled.

He looked up and watched the fog muster out to sea and begin its advance toward the shore, and tried to imagine some grand gesture, something James would remember whenever he thought of Greg Mairs. But grand gestures usually required money.

He returned to the desk, raised the lid, and sat down. He forced himself to list the bills, almost a full page, add the total, and take the ledger out to the dining nook table where he would remember to go over it with Barb. This time they would talk about his death. Always before, she stopped him and insisted they expect a miracle. He supposed that was her excuse for not giving Chez the truth.

Chez only knew her daddy was sick and couldn't go on the long hikes they used to take in the Cuyamaca forests, across the desert dunes, or along the beaches of Silver Strand and into the Tijuana sloughs. She knew he couldn't work anymore, so they'd had to sell the kayaks and Mom's car, and they watched the blurry TV, no more cable, and they couldn't go to a cabin in snowy mountains or to Arizona for Padres spring baseball.

Tonight, he decided, he'd tell her the whole crappy truth. He tried to imagine her face when she learned he was as good as gone. Pale, he thought, with her cheeks caved in, tears big as goldfish. Shivering.

His horror at the image got interrupted when the old Toyota pickup made the turn off Guizot Street and pulled to the curb in front of their house. Chez waved. Such a beauty, he thought, with her raven hair and Kobe Bryant grace.

He waved back and hustled to meet her. He picked her up, kissed her cheek, and would've held her on his hip while he carried the cleaning gear in, but she squirmed and jumped down. Barb, exhausted from cleaning three houses, came around the front of the car, blew him a kiss, and trudged up the steps to the porch holding Chez's hand.

While he delivered the vacuum cleaner, broom, mops, and buckets into the garage, Chez zoomed past. She was already in her play overalls that matched her dad's outfit. Over her shoulder, she shouted, "Mom's mad cause you didn't make the spaghetti like you were s'posed to."

She leaped over the low rock wall between their yard and her friend Maria's.

Inside, Greg found Barb stepping into the shower. He leaned against the sink. "Babe, tonight, we're going to tell Chez about you-know-what."

Over the splashing, she hollered, "Since you didn't make the spaghetti sauce, how about microwave chicken and that summer squash with cheese that you and Chez like. Okay?"

"Yeah, sure." He stayed a minute peering through the beveled glass, admiring her curves that had trimmed and defined over the past few months since she began jogging. He gazed at her breasts, which he still loved to fondle after thirteen years, more than ever since the hepatitis caught hold. For at least a minute he admired the henna-auburn hair she wrapped like a scarf around her neck while she rinsed her backside.

Greg sighed, then winced from a pain like a high-voltage whack to his liver. He groaned, and staggered toward the bedroom, panting and blowing the way he'd learned at Lamaze classes while Barb was carrying Chez. He lay down and kept panting. As the pain dulled to a bearable ache, he sat up and heaved his feet over the side of the bed. He took the pillbox from the breast pocket of his overalls, opened it, and fingered through the pills. No OxyContin, his most trusty painkiller.

He returned to the bathroom, where Barb was out of the shower and wrapping her hair in the Snoopy towel. She said, "You asked what was for dinner, didn't you?"

"Uh-huh." Greg opened the medicine cabinet and reached for the big new bottle of Vicodin. A lifetime supply, he thought, provided he died on schedule. He loosed a grim "Ho-ho."

Barb, so accustomed to his laughs she didn't question them anymore, gave him a patient smile while she slipped into her panties and lounging sweats. He swallowed his third and fourth Vicodin of the day, unless he'd forgotten others.

He followed Barb through the cramped living room to the kitchen, where she looked into the fridge and a cabinet, then turned with an exasperated grimace. "Should I go to the Safeway or do you want to?"

"I'll go. Babe, we need to tell Chez. Tonight."

Barb retreated as though he'd sneezed a mouthful at her. "Greg, she's only seven. She doesn't even know what death means, not really."

"She found her bunny stiff in the strawberries."

"I mean people."

"Grandma Ruth. She knows Grandma Ruth's in heaven."

"So?"

"So how did she get to heaven if she didn't die? Did you tell Chez she flew United?"

Barb plucked the magnetized notepad off the fridge and began jotting a grocery list.

"See, if we tell her now, there's less chance it'll knock her silly. I can smile while I'm talking about it, tell her you guys ought to have a party to celebrate me going to the most bitchin' place."

"Oh sure, that'll make up for her daddy leaving her." With a reproachful frown, she asked, "Have you given up praying for a miracle?"

He shook his head, a half-truth. He hadn't quit praying, but he'd quit believing when he began to sense that God figured his work on earth was done. Though how God could reach that conclusion was a mystery. For all his good intentions, Greg thought, he hadn't done much except mess things up.

She gave him the list and two bills, a ten and a five. "Don't stop and talk with the street people, okay? I'm pretty hungry and Chez said she's starving."

"She'll eat about six bites and say she's stuffed."

"I know." Barb went to the sink and ran hot water to wash the dishes Greg had forgotten about.

Outside the Safeway, he ran into Chad, a homeless amigo who needed five of his dollars. He returned with one bag of groceries. Barb had already called Chez home and was helping her with Sunday school homework about daily life in biblical days.

While passing the couch, Greg kissed the crowns of his girls' heads. He set the groceries on the sink-board, reached to a top cabinet for corn oil, and grabbed the cast-iron frying pan that hung from the wall behind the stove. Rust had formed along the rim. He hadn't used the pan for months. He poured the Mazola oil, turned a burner to medium high, and set the pan on the burner.

He was chopping lettuce when Barb came in. "What's that smell?" She went past him to the counter. "You bought a pre-cooked chicken?"

"Yep, faster."

"Not much faster than the microwave. What're you making?"

"Tacos."

She frowned. "Well, all right, but you can't fry the tortillas."

"I already started."

"Then stop and microwave them. You can't eat greasy tortillas." She leaned closer and whispered, "They'll kill you."

"Yes, dear." He winked at her.

He was turning to the stove when she asked, "Did you get the milk and Cheerios?"

"Nope. Ran out of money. I'll go back later. Say, Chad's hanging around the Safeway. How about I run back and invite him to share the feast I'm preparing?"

"Darn it, Greg," she whined. "We have to watch every penny."

He might've argued, if not for the fire. Flames spurted up from the corn oil, orange and blue, two feet high, to the cabinet. "Oh no!" Barb shouted, and pushed him aside. While she jumped to the fridge and opened the door, he grabbed a potholder from its hook. He meant to grip the handle and carry the flaming pan to the sink, pour off the grease, and let the fire burn itself out. But again, Barb pushed him out of the way.

Standing arm's length from the fire, she poured heaps of baking soda from a box into her hand and slung them at the fire, until it died out.

The stove looked like a winter scene, Greg thought, and stalactites spiked down from the cabinets where the wood-grain plastic veneer had melted. Barb stomped out of the kitchen. Covering his eyes and leaning on the counter, Greg listened to her footsteps drum the wood floor, all the way to the bathroom. He knew she would lock herself in, sit on the edge of the tub, and weep.

As he lifted his hand from his eyes, he saw Chez beside the table, shooting a laser glare at him. Then she turned and marched out, stiff legged as a Nazi on parade.

He fought a chill. Bright flashes blinded him for a minute. Then he returned to preparing dinner. He was going to the fridge for lettuce and tomatoes when he noticed, on the door, a flyer from the Roxy Theater. A blurb for the movie that inspired James to dream up the murder game.

Night before last, when they were goofy, James on liquor and Greg on his prescribed sinsemilla, they rehearsed bumping off Maurice, the creep whose lawyers would steal James's little sister's nice home.

As Greg threw open the fridge, he recalled the rush of excitement and purpose he had felt beneath the stairs to Maurice's apartment.

He finished chopping the lettuce and tomatoes, put out the mild salsa fresca Chez liked, for which he always remembered to make special trips to the People's Co-op. He zapped tortillas in the microwave, wrapped them in one of the red, orange, and yellow napkins they had bought in Tijuana. He set them on the table alongside the chicken meat he had peeled off, shredded and piled neatly on a serving platter. Before he called them, he poured Barb's red wine, Chez's lemonade, and his own juice.

Barb must've prayed for patience and coached Chez, reminding her that Daddy was sick and needed their love. Four times, Barb told him what a special dinner this was. Every time he glanced at Chez, she beamed a phony smile. But their acts played out. By the end of the meal, Barb was staring dreamily out the window or sneaking furtive glances. Checking to see if he had died yet, Greg imagined.

He wondered if Chez had, on her own, guessed he was dying. While she dipped her last hunk of chicken in salsa and gobbled her peanut butter cookie, he caught her staring at him as though at a strange and scary creature. Maybe she already saw him as a ghost.

His girls watched *Veggie Tales*. He washed and dried the dishes, put them away, cleaned the stove and polished it shiny white. Then he fetched his pillbox and picked out two tranquilizers. A Restoril and a Soma. He tried to decide which he should use then laughed and swallowed both without washing them down. Feeling a new pain like steel teeth biting his liver, he opened the box again and debated between one and two Vicodin. Might as well use them up. "Waste not, want not," he muttered, and made himself chuckle.

In the living room, he flopped on Chez's beanbag beside the sofa where his girls were snuggling. He pretended to watch the adventures of a cucumber and a tomato. Actually, he peered out the corner of his eye at his pretty family and grieved doubly, feeling sure that his life meant nothing to them anymore except trouble.

Chez complained of a headache. Barb said, "That's funny, I have one too."

Yeah. Me, Greg thought.

They gave Greg his goodnight kisses, brushed their teeth, and retired to Chez's bedroom. He listened to his daughter read a couple pages of *Charlotte's Web* before Barb took over for a minute then stopped in midsentence. When he summoned the energy to heave himself out of the beanbag, he went to Chez's room and found both his girls asleep, tucked under the covers of the skinny bed, where Barb spent half the nights these past few weeks. To escape Greg's snoring, she claimed, as if he snored worse now than ever before, which he didn't believe.

The only cure for self-pity Greg knew was to shift from brooding over his problems to thinking of somebody else's. The effort delivered him to memories of James's sister.

Since Greg's ninth grade year, when Olivia was in seventh, he would've quit surfing or anything else to please her, if she'd asked. But she never even hinted. After high school, she moved to Vegas, pranced onstage in a feathered costume, and met Maurice, an older guy whose smooth talk and fists full of cash she fell for, Greg supposed.

Every summer, he saw her at the beach with her kids. The last time was two or three Saturdays ago. He sat with her awhile, thinking he might not see her again. But he didn't tell her about his disease. She didn't need any problems of his.

A few times, Greg had invited Olivia to the One Way Inn to watch his favorite Christian musicians. She would pat his hand or arm and say, "Not this time." He knew what she meant was *I'll go when Jesus shows up at my door and drags me kicking and screaming.*

And now, with her and Maurice separated and him awaiting trial for conspiring with his Vegas connections to take over the action of an Indian casino, some Beverly Hills sharks were going to snatch her home in exchange for their fees. Banish Olivia and her kids to a roach-infested welfare apartment next door to the one where his death would send Barb and Chez.

On a sudden impulse, he stood too fast, got woozy, but managed to stagger to the hall cabinet next to Chez's bedroom door. One of his girls made breathy whistles in her sleep. He tiptoed and pulled the door closed, taking pains to latch it quietly even though he saw double knobs.

He went to the dining nook for a chair and returned to the hallway. Twice he started to mount the chair but wobbled. The third attempt succeeded because he grasped the cabinet handles in time.

When he opened the cabinet, he bonked his forehead with the door's sharp corner, drawing a little blood but not enough to dribble into his eye. The object of this expedition, his high school annuals, were in the back of the cabinet. He had to move things, a pewter vase and picture frames, and the shoe box sealed with duct tape in which he had stashed his .25-caliber six-shot revolver. The maker, he suspected, was German, something like Plfstk he couldn't pronounce. He'd bought it at a pawnshop and used to carry it on risky assignments, back when he was a security guard.

He climbed off the chair, balancing with one hand, all of his high school annuals tucked beneath the other arm, though only his senior year would have photos of Olivia. He must've left the shoe box teetering on the edge of the cabinet. As he stepped down, it fell, grazed his shoulder, made a *bong* sound as it hit the chair, and landed on the floor with a sharp thud. Ouch, Greg thought, and waited for Barb to shout, *Hey, be quiet!*

But if the crash had woken her, she ignored the disruption. He picked up the shoe box, set it on the chair, and went to the dining nook table. He opened his senior yearbook, turned one page, and found the first picture of Olivia, above the caption *Most Popular*. She wore a pleated skirt, an inch or so above the knees, and a purple short-sleeved sweater Greg remembered he'd always wanted to rub his nose in. She was made up heavy like the Portuguese babes from tuna fishing families. Like Angie Silva.

Olivia's dark lipstick looked especially exotic haloed by her wavy golden hair. But gorgeous as she was, what set her above the other beauties was her goodness. She wasn't shy or proud, but natural and gracious. Loyal to her friends, pleasant to everyone. She earned good grades without showing off. Greg remembered a girl saying, *Olivia can afford to be sweet, cause she's got nothing to prove.*

"Phooey," Greg mumbled, and turned the page. "Everybody's got stuff to prove." He found six more pictures of Olivia. The booster club, the French club. "French, huh?" Something else he'd forgotten. Maybe French classes had helped prime her to choose a guy with that name.

"Maurice," he snarled.

Then he found Olivia in candid shots at a football playoff game and at dances. He caught nostalgia dragging his thoughts back toward his incipient death, which he chose to call it ever since Doctor Ramos used that bookish word that made it feel less real. He craved a smoke. He kept his stash of sinsemilla and papers in a top kitchen cabinet beside Mazola oil, Raid, and other items Barb considered dangerous.

He sat at the table and rolled a fat number. Before he lit up, he realized that after smoking he was likely to forget or blow off returning the annuals and his stash to where they belonged. He set the joint on the table, tossed the baggy into its cabinet, stacked the annuals, and carried them through the living room. As he lifted his right foot onto the chair, he noticed the shoe box beside his left foot and felt a mild electric warmth. A power surge.

He managed to replace the annuals without dropping anything, and when he closed the cabinet doors, they didn't bang.

He fetched a Diet Slice and carried the shoe box out front. In the fog, thick and greenish, Greg sat on the folding beach chair with plastic slats. He smoked a few hits and discovered that tonight the weed's first effect was to revive the sucking pain in his liver. He popped the tab on the Slice to lube his dry mouth and to wash down another Vicodin.

Green lights the size of fireflies began flitting around him. With each hit, more tiny green lights appeared in the fog. By his last puff they were a legion. Harbingers of death, he imagined. To soften his rising terror, he muttered, "I'll shoot the bastards," and reached down to pick up the shoe box, on the porch floor at his feet. But when he leaned, he toppled forward, and only braced his fall by grabbing a post, just short of a nosedive off the porch into Barb's tulips.

The folding chair had collapsed behind him. He knelt, turned and unfolded the chair, set it upright, and sat in it with the shoe box on his thigh. He ripped off the duct tape, tore off the lid, and tipped the gun onto his lap. It was wrapped in a dish towel, which he unwrapped before he remembered that when he packed away the gun, he'd put a round of six cartridges with it.

Without thinking why, he loaded the gun. But the instant he gripped it with his finger on the trigger, even before he catalogued the reasons or checked the time, he knew why.

Suddenly, as though he'd gotten bewitched, turned from a frog into a prince, he saw everything with different eyes. His chest swelled with tangy air, though he couldn't remember breathing. His brain dismissed all the dread, gloom, and sorrow for a lifetime of wasted opportunities and lame decisions. He believed the act he was created to perform had presented itself. For once, he felt like a champion.

But the next instant he thought, *Murder?*

He wasn't going to kill anybody. The idea was just another of his fantasies, like when he used to imagine playing lead guitar for Bob Dylan even though he only knew six chords and lost the rhythm a few times every song he tried to play.

The guy he ought to shoot was himself, he thought.

He tried to remember the last time he'd gotten this mired in despair. If he could remember, maybe he'd also remember a way to climb out of it.

"David," he muttered. King David made a habit of sinking in despair and climbing out. David was usually in danger. Because he was always killing people. "Saul killed his thousands but David his tens of thousands," he quoted. David killed people because God told him to.

Greg lay the gun in his lap, sat motionless though the heat surging through him made him ache to move, and counted the signs he'd been given, maybe by God.

First, the movie flier that reminded him of the murder game. Barb had posted that flier. She never posted fliers. Next, Barb and Chez fell asleep at eight-thirty, when every single other night Chez would throw a fit if they tried to put her down before the SeaWorld fireworks.

And a few minutes later the gun appeared, after so long he'd forgotten he owned the damned thing.

"Man," he mumbled, "how many signs do you need?"

He jumped up and stuffed the loaded gun into his baggy front pocket.

God wasn't urging Greg to bomb abortion clinics or risk hurting innocent people. Nobody could call Maurice innocent.

Only a few years ago, he was Pete Pinella's "bodyguard" until the gangster went to Pelican Bay on a murder charge.

Greg rushed inside. He strode to the kitchen and looked at the clock. Ten minutes before ten. Another sign. The SeaWorld fireworks would blast off at ten, just when Maurice was supposed to leave his bartender shift at Rick's Lounge, and just enough time for Greg to get there. If he hustled.

Greg tiptoed through the living room to Chez's bedroom door and turned the handle slowly until it stopped. He pushed the door open wide but only leaned his head and shoulders into the room.

Gaping at the beauty of his girls, the soft cheeks, glossy hair, the moons of their eyelids, he wondered how such a loser as himself had won the mother and helped create the daughter.

He crept out of the house, staggered down the porch steps, then steadied himself. He tried jogging, but the slap of his feet on the pavement spooked him.

Down the hill in thickening fog, he remembered Abraham. God commanded the patriarch to sacrifice his son not to get the deed done, only to test the man's faith.

Giddy with relief, he thought God wasn't going to make him kill Maurice, only make sure he was willing.

Between gasps to catch his breath, he told himself, *Just go there, get ready.* Then God would show up and stay his hand, like he did Abraham's.

The red light at Sunset Cliffs Boulevard was a dull splotch in the fog. He listened for a moment. Though he knew that in fog he might not hear an approaching car, he jogged across, hoping nobody was crazy enough to drive lights-out tonight.

He tripped over the curb and fell to his knees, heaved himself up using the streetlight pole for balance. He staggered down Newport, allowing a thought he'd suppressed up till now. The signs—the movie, his gun that appeared as though out of nowhere at the right time, the soupiest fog this year, and the others—they didn't have to be from God. Some demon could've rigged them.

His pace slowed for a few steps, and the fog seemed to whirl around him. The world had turned weirder than back before Barb and Jesus, when he now and then shot dope with his biker amigos, earning himself the death sentence. Maybe he was dying right now. He walked faster, then faster, almost a jog.

Halfway down the block, he weaved through a crowd of Friday-night smokers outside The Jail, a pickup bar. He stumbled and bumped into a girl with buzzed hair, a sparkly halter, and tight jeans. She caromed into a large Filipino who was lighting her cigarette. The guy burnt his finger on account of Greg.

"Dude," the Filipino said, and took a step toward him, but stopped when a muffled boom sounded. He returned to the girl and lit her cigarette while Greg reeled and thought the sound had to be from God. From SeaWorld, sure. But also from God. Satan wasn't crafty enough to arrange all these signs.

He double-timed the rest of the way, across Cable Street and past the Newport Café to the walkway east of Rick's. He didn't look into it. Not yet. First he glanced both ways through the fog and saw nobody watching him from the porch of the hostel or the crowd a block west outside the Cave dance club or out the window of El Nopal Taqueria.

The walkway led along the west wall of Rick's to the alley and the staircase to the second-floor apartment where Maurice had gone to live after Olivia kicked him out.

If anyone noticed him disappear into the dark walkway, Greg told himself, they'd think he was some drunk looking for a hole to piss in.

Two booms sounded. Greg stumbled backward, out of the streetlamp glow and into darkness where he slipped on an oil slick or something and clattered against a roll of chicken wire or something before he groped his way to the staircase and grabbed hold. He peered underneath it and saw the trash cans were still where he had set them during the murder game, leaving a roomy space between them and the stairs. He steadied himself by leaning against the wall to Rick's. He gasped a few breaths and noticed a smell like beef broiling, maybe seeping out a vent from Rick's, and another like fresh crap, so close he thought it might be what he'd stepped on.

Pulse slammed his groin and his skull. The fireworks kept booming, and Greg waited. After a minute, he checked the gun, found the safety on, released it, and leaned the barrel on the seventh step, unless he'd miscounted. To make sure, leaving the gun on the step, he squatted, reached out, and touched each step. He counted to seven. He tried to remember the equation he and James had settled upon. If he shot from between the seventh and eighth steps when Maurice's foot touched down on the fourth, the bullet ought to slam his midsection. Or maybe he'd got that backward. "Fuck," he said aloud for the first time since his last doctor's visit.

Five rockets boomed in rapid succession. A man rounded the corner. Greg peered between steps. The man's hair was silver-tipped black and high on top, short on the sides. Like Maurice's. He was smoking, but he kept the cigarette cupped so the fire didn't illuminate his face. He wore a shiny jacket that looked like polished leather, a checked shirt, dark slacks. At the foot of the stairs, he fished in his pocket and lifted out something that jangled. A key ring. Greg nodded. A visitor wouldn't be using keys. He slipped his finger inside the trigger guard.

The man hacked a cough, bent forward, and coughed again and again until he was honking like an asthmatic. He appeared to rock back and forward to the rhythm of Greg's raging pulse.

As the man climbed to the first step, he grabbed the rail. A flurry of booms, then a dozen of Greg's heartbeats, passed before he made the second step, but the next pair of steps came fast, as if something had warned him to make a dash.

Greg pulled. Time lost its authority. The world spun faster.

Two shots cracked, a hundred times louder than the skyrockets. They echoed off both walls of the walkway. The pistol's second kick launched Greg backward. He fell butt first on the rim of the metal trash can. The can toppled and spilled him into the alley.

The man on the steps groaned from deep in his gut. Then he hacked out something like, "Who the hell?"

As Greg heaved and pushed to stand, the groaning fell silent.

A pain more wicked than any struck. Not in the liver. Higher. Around his heart. Greg tipped forward, grabbed the stairs, and thought, *Maybe I only hit him in the arm. Maybe he's only passed out.* He needed to know, before the pain took him under. Using the rail for balance, he managed one step toward the foot of the stairs.

The next boom came, and a cannonball slammed then sucked into Greg's middle, just below the ribs. His head tipped backward. He saw Maurice, with gritted teeth and red eyes. In one hand, a pistol shook.

Despite everything, a new kind of love washed over Greg. He wanted to reach out and touch the fellow. He tried to say, *Hey, amigo.* But he began spinning. When his knees buckled, he was facing down the alley, toward the ocean where a mammoth wave rose, emerald green and luminescent.

As Greg sensed commotion around him, he watched the emerald wave sweep high, above the two-story shops, and flood over the sea wall, across the road, and into the alley.

Peace, Greg thought. *It's only peace.* He turned, meaning to tell people not to worry, but all he saw was one fellow. Either Jesus or Chad, with a small but earnest smile that meant, *I get it, brother. I've been there.*

It was Chad, not Jesus, Greg thought, as he whispered a last "Ho-ho." Because Jesus wouldn't be nodding goodbye.

PART III

LIFE'S A BEACH

AFTER THIRTY

BY DON WINSLOW

Pacific Beach

Charlie Decker is a hard case.

Ask anybody—his shipmates, his captain, his family back in Davenport if they'll talk to you about him. They'll all tell you the same thing.

Charlie's no good.

He's trouble and always has been. Drunkenness, absent-without-official-leave, brawling, gambling, insubordination— three stretches in the navy and Charlie's been in and out of the brig and up and down the ranks. The navy probably would have thrown him out if there wasn't a war on and they didn't need a man who knew how to make an engine run. Give Charlie Decker thirty minutes and a wrench and he can fix anything, but you also know that he can wreck anything too, and just as easily.

People tried to tell Millie this, but she wouldn't listen. Her roommates saw it clear as day. One good look in Charlie's eyes, that cocky smirk of his, and you knew. They told her but it went through one ear and out the other. Now she opens her eyes, looks at the clock on her bed table, and slaps him on the butt. "Charlie, get up."

"What?" he mumbles, happy in his sweet, warm sleep. They sat up and drank when she came home from her night shift at Consolidated, and then they did it and then drank some more, so he don't want to get up.

She shakes his shoulders. "It's thirty *days*."

Millie knows the navy—up to thirty days it's AWOL, after thirty it's desertion. He's been shacked up with her for almost a month now. Almost a month in the little bungalow that was already crowded with four other girls, and he said he was going back before the thirty days were up.

But now he mumbles, "To hell with that." And closes his eyes.

"You're going to get in big trouble," Millie says. AWOL, he would get a captain's mast, but probably no time in the brig because he's set to ship out soon anyway. But for desertion he's going to get a court-martial, maybe *years* in the brig, and then a DD.

"Charlie, get *up*."

He rolls over, kisses her, and then shows her what trouble is. That's the thing—she knows he's bad news but he's just so damn handsome and so good in the sack. She knew from the moment they met at Eddie's Bar that she couldn't keep her legs shut with Charlie.

Charlie makes her see fireworks.

Charlie rolls off her, reaches for the green pack of Lucky Strikes by the bed, finds his Zippo, and lights one up.

"Go fix us some breakfast," he says.

"What do you want?"

"Eggs?"

"*Try* buying eggs, Charlie."

"We got any coffee left?"

"A little."

Like everything else, it's rationed. Coffee, sugar, meat, cigarettes, chocolate, gasoline of course. The girls swap ration coupons but there's only so much and she doesn't like it when Charlie deals in the black market. She tells him it's unpatriotic.

Charlie doesn't give a damn. He figures he's done his patriotic duty all over the Pacific, most recently on a tin can in the cordon line off Okinawa, and he deserves a little coffee and sugar.

The first cigarette of the day is always the best.

Charlie sucks the smoke into his lungs and holds it before letting it out his nose. It makes him feel good, relaxed, at ease with the decision he has to make.

"Then after breakfast you'll go back," Millie is saying.

"I thought you loved me," Charlie says, flashing his smile. He's proud of the smile—his teeth are white and even.

"I do." She does love him, despite everything. That's why she doesn't want to see him get into a really bad jam. He's always going to get in a little trouble, Millie knows, that's part of what she loves about him.

"Then why do you want me to go?" Charlie teases. "You know we're shipping out."

"I know."

"Will you wait for me?" he asks.

"Of course I will."

He knows she won't. Millie needs it, like most women. The story is that men need it and women just put up with it, but Charlie knows better. Maybe not virgins, maybe they don't, but once a woman's had it, she wants it again. And Millie wants it. Takes a couple of drinks to loosen her up enough to admit it, but after that, hell, look out.

If he ships out she'll be with another guy by the time he gets back. He knows this for a fact because she was cheating on some poor jerk when she went to bed with *him*. Anyway, Charlie knows she won't wait and tells himself that's why he's not going back. She'll find another guy to sleep with, another guy's back to scratch with her nails, another guy to tell that he makes her helpless to stop him.

That's what he tells himself most of the time, and when that story doesn't sell—usually in those cold gray hours of the early morning when he's so drunk he's almost sober—he tells himself a different story—that he doesn't want to go back to the brig.

Charlie has felt an SP's baton in the kidneys, along with the metallic taste of his own blood when they decided it was more fun to bust up his face, and he don't want any more of it. They do whatever they want to do to you in the brig, and then hose it down like that washes it all away. Thirty days AWOL, the captain might send him to the brig and it's not a chance he wants to take.

That's what Charlie tells himself, anyway.

Now he watches Millie walk into the kitchen and likes the way she looks in the little white silk robe he bought her.

Millie's a looker, all right.

That Saturday night he had liberty and headed down to Eddie's because he heard that's where the factory girls go. The ship had just limped back for repairs so they had a lot of free time, and after what they'd been through they were all ready to for it too. The scuttlebutt was that Eddie's was the place to go, so he skipped the usual dives in the Gaslamp and headed to Pacific Beach. The joint was crowded with sailors and Marines all after the same thing, but he saw her and gave her that smile and she smiled back.

Charlie went up to her and talked and then she let him buy her a drink and then another and they talked and he asked her a lot of questions about herself and found out she came out from a little town in North Dakota because she'd always wanted to see the ocean and she wanted an adventure.

"I heard there were jobs for women in San Diego," she said. "So I got on a train and here I am."

"Here you are," Charlie smiled.

"In Pacific Beach, California," she said.

"Do you like it?"

She nodded. "I like the money and it's fun living with the other girls most of the time."

They talked some more and then he asked if they could get out of there and she said okay but where did he want to go?

"Can't we just go to your place?" he asked. "You said you have a place."

"I do," she said, "but I don't want to go right away. A girl likes a little romance, you know."

Oh, hell, he knew. He was just hoping this one girl didn't. But if she didn't, she'd be the first ever. At least of the ones you didn't pay. The whores, they didn't want romance, they just wanted you to get your business over with as soon as possible so they could get on with theirs. It was like eating on a ship—hurry up and finish because there's a sailor waiting for your chair.

But Millie, she looked at him with those dark blue eyes and he decided that a walk along the beach would be just the thing. You expected blue eyes with a blond girl, but Millie's hair was jet black, and cut short, and she had these cute lips that made you think of Betty Boop. When he walked close to her she smelled like vanilla, because, she told him, perfume was hard to get.

But the vanilla smelled good behind her ear, in her hair. She was small, what did she call it—petite—and fit nice under his arm as they walked on the sand under the pier. A radio was playing somewhere and they stood and danced under the pier and he held her tight.

"You feel nice," he said, because it was all he could think of to say and because it was true too.

"So do you," she responded.

Now he remembers how nice she smelled and how good she felt under his arm and how life was the way he always hoped it would be. There were no flames that night, no acrid smoke that burned his nose, no screams that seared his brain, and the waves touched the beach like kisses, and if he told the truth he would have stayed there forever with her on Pacific Beach and not even taken her back to her place and her bed.

But he did and they made love and he slept through his liberty. He meant to go back that day, he really did, while it was still no big deal, but it was just too good with her in the little bungalow.

Millie shared the bedroom with another girl from the factory, a girl named Audrey from Ohio, and they'd run a rope across the room and draped a blanket over it for a little privacy. Sometimes Millie didn't want to make love if Audrey was home because she felt shy with the other girl just across from the blanket. But Audrey worked the day shift and was gone a lot of nights with an airman, and sometimes Millie did it anyway with Audrey there and Charlie suspected she liked it because it made her feel dirty.

The bungalow was crowded, but so was all of Pacific Beach since they built the factories and all the people came for work. There was hardly any place to lie down—some people lived in tents in backyards—so Millie felt lucky to stay there even though it was hard to get into the bathroom sometimes and there were two girls sleeping in the living room.

Charlie liked it there too, that was the problem, even though it often felt as crowded as a ship. But it was quiet in the morning with the girls gone on their shifts, and he and Millie got up late and had the kitchen to themselves and they'd take their coffee and cigarettes out into the tiny yard and enjoy the sun.

Audrey had a car and sometimes they'd drive down to Oscar's for hamburgers, or go to Belmont Park and ride the roller coaster, and Millie would scream and hold on tight to his arm and he liked that. One time when Millie got paid they went to the Hollywood Theater downtown to see the burlesque and she dug her elbow into his ribs when he gawked at Zena Ray, and they both laughed at Bozo Lord even though his jokes were corny. And afterward he got her to admit she thought the girls were pretty, and she was a pistol in bed that night.

On the nights she worked, he'd stay home or hit the bars on Garnet or Mission Boulevard, keeping a sharp eye out for the SPs even though there were a lot of guys walking around in civvies—the 4Fs, sure, but mostly men who had served their bit, or been wounded, or were on leave. So the SPs didn't look at him too hard and anyway they were busy keeping an eye on the sailors and marines who flooded the sidewalks and had fistfights that spilled into the street.

Charlie would make sure he arrived back to the bungalow before she got home, tired from work but too jazzed up to go to sleep, and he thought it was funny that this tiny girl was building PBYs and B-24s.

"You've probably killed more Japs than I have," he said to her one morning.

"I don't like to think about that," she said.

The nights were fun but the days were the best. Most days they'd sleep in late, then have breakfast and walk down to Pacific Beach and swim, or just sit or lie down on the sand and take naps, or walk along the boardwalk and maybe stop someplace to have a beer, and the days just went by and now July has become August, and he has a tough decision to make.

Charlie comes into the kitchen in his skivvies and a T-shirt and sits down at the table.

"Aren't you going to put some clothes on?" she asks.

"The other girls are all at work, aren't they?" he asks.

She pours him a cup of coffee and sets it down in front of him. Then she puts a little margarine in a pan, waits for it to bubble, and throws in two slices of bread and fries them.

He can feel her impatience and aggravation. He hasn't done a damn thing but hang around for a month, and even though she says it's all right with her, he knows it isn't. Women can't stand a man not working. Just a fact of life—it was that way with his mother and his old man and it's the same way with Millie and him now. She knows he can't get a job, knows he can't ever get a job with a DD on his record, so she's wondering how long he plans on living off her and he knows that's what's on her mind.

Has been for the past couple of weeks, if you want to know the truth. Since that night he woke up with Millie shaking his shoulder, telling him he was having a bad dream.

"It's okay, baby," she was saying. "It's okay. You're having a nightmare."

He didn't want to tell her it wasn't a nightmare but real life, and she asked him, "Where were you?"

"None of your damn business," was all he said, and he felt that his cheeks were wet with tears and then he remembered that he'd been crying and moaning, over and over again, "I don't want to go back, I don't want to go back . . ."

She asked him, "Where? Where don't you want to go back to, Charlie?"

"I told you it was none of your damn business," he said, and slapped her across her pretty little Betty Boop mouth. When she came back in from the kitchen she had ice in a towel pressed against her lower lip and there was a little streak of blood on her chin and she said, "You ever hit me again, I'll call the SPs and turn you in."

But she didn't throw him out.

She knew he had no place to go, no money, and would probably get picked up by Shore Patrol. So she pressed the ice to her lips and let him stay, but nothing was ever as good between them after that and he knows that he broke something between them that he can't fix.

Now she sets the plate down just a little hard.

"What?" he asks, even though he knows.

"What are you going to do?" she asks.

"Eat my breakfast," he answers.

"And then what?"

He almost says, *Slap that look off your puss if it's still there.* Instead he shoves a piece of fried bread into his mouth and chews it deliberately. A woman should let a man have his coffee and breakfast before she starts in on him. The day is going to be hot—the summer sun is already pounding the concrete outside—and she should just let things slide so they can go down to the beach and enjoy the breeze and the water, maybe walk down to the end of the pier.

But she won't let it go. She sits down, folds her forearms on the table, and says, "You have to go, Charlie."

He gets up from the table, goes back into the bedroom, and finds last night's bottle. Then he returns to the kitchen, pours some of the cheap whiskey into his coffee, sits down, and starts to drink.

"Oh, that will help," she says. "You showing up drunk."

Charlie doesn't want to listen to her yapping. He wants to get drunk even though he knows that no amount of booze can wash away the truth that no man can stand to know about himself.

That he's *afraid* to go back.

Since that moment the Jap planes came crashing onto the deck, spewing fuel and flame, and he saw his buddies become running torches and smelled them burning and he can't never get that smell out of his nose. Can't get it out of his head, either, because it comes in his sleep and he wakes up shaking and crying and moaning that he doesn't want to go back, please don't make him go back.

Charlie knows what they say about him, that he's no good, that he's a hard case, but he knows he ain't hard. Maybe he used to be, though now he knows he's as broken as the spine of the ship.

But the ship is repaired now and will be steaming out across the Pacific, this time to the Japanese home islands, and if they think Okinawa was bad, that was nothing compared to what it's going to be.

It ain't the thought of the brig and it ain't even the thought of losing her, because the truth is he's already lost her. He can take the brig and he can take losing her, but he can't take going back.

Something in him is broken and he can't fix it.

Now what he wants to do is get drunk, stay drunk, and lay on the beach, but she won't shut up.

"You have to go back, Charlie," she says.

He stares into his cup and takes another drink.

"If you go back today it will be all right."

He shakes his head.

Then she says it. "It's okay to be afraid."

Charlie throws the cup at her. He doesn't really know if he meant to hit her or not, but he does. The cup cuts her eye and splashes coffee all over her face and she screams and stands up. She wipes the coffee out of her eyes and feels the blood and then stares at him for a second and says, "You son of a bitch."

Charlie doesn't answer.

"Get out," Millie says. "Get out."

He doesn't move except to grab the bottle, take a drink directly from it, and lean back into the chair.

Millie watches this and says, "Fine. I'll get you out."

She heads for the door.

That gets him out of the chair because now he remembers what she said she'd do if he hit her again, and he did hit her again, and Millie is the kind of girl who does what she says she'll do, and he can't let her go and call Shore Patrol.

Charlie grabs her by the neck, pulls her into his chest, and then wraps his arms around and lifts her up, and she wriggles and kicks as he carries her toward the bedroom because he thinks maybe it can end that way. But when drops her on the bed she spits in his face and claws at his eyes and says, "You're real brave with a woman, huh, Charlie? Aren't ya?"

He hauls off and pops her in the jaw just to shut her up, but she won't shut up and he hits her again and again until she finally lays still.

"Now will you behave?" he asks her, but there's blood all over the pillow and even on the wall and her neck is bent like the broken spine of a ship and he knows he can't fix her.

She's so small, what do they call it—petite.

Charlie staggers into the bathroom, pushes past the stockings that hang from cords, and washes his bloody hands under the tap. Then he goes back into the bedroom, where Millie is lying with her eyes open, staring at the ceiling. He puts on the loud Hawaiian shirt he bought at Pearl, the one Millie liked, and a pair of khaki pants, and then sits down next to her to put on his shoes.

He thinks he should say something to her but he doesn't know what to say, so he just gets up, goes back into the kitchen, finds the bottle, and drains it in one long swallow. His hands shake as he lights a cigarette, but he does get it lit, takes a long drag, and heads out the door.

The sun is blinding, the concrete hot on his feet.

Charlie doesn't really know where to go, so he just keeps walking until he finds himself at the beach. He walks along the boardwalk, which is crowded with people, mostly sailors and their girls out for a stroll. He pushes his way through and then goes down the steps to the sand and under the pier where him and her held each other and danced to the radio.

Maybe it's the same radio playing now as he stands there listening to the music and looks out at the ocean and tries to figure out what to do next. They'll be looking for him soon, they'll know it was him, and if they catch him he'll spend the rest of his life in the brig, if they don't hang him.

Now he wishes he had just gone back like she told him to.

But it's too late.

He stares at the water, tells himself he should run, but there's nowhere to run to, anyway, and the music is nice and he thinks about that night and knows he should never have left the beach.

Then the music stops and a voice comes on and the voice is talking like he's real excited, like the radio did that day the Japs bombed Pearl Harbor.

Charlie turns around to look up at the boardwalk and all the people are just standing there, standing stock-still like they're photographs or statues. Then suddenly they all start to move, and whoop and yell, and hug each other and kiss and dance and laugh.

Charlie walks to the edge of the boardwalk.

"What's going on?" he asks this sailor who has his arm around a girl. "What's going on?"

"Didn't you hear?" the sailor answered, swinging the girl on his hip. "We dropped some kind of big bomb on Japan. They say it's the end of the war. They say the war is over!" Then he forgets about Charlie and bends the girl back and kisses her again.

And all along Pacific Beach people are hugging and kissing, laughing and crying, because the war is over.

Charlie Decker, the hard case, goes and sits in the sand.

He peers across the ocean toward a city that has burst into flame and people burn like torches and he knows he will never get the smell out of his nose or the pictures out of his brain. Knows that he will wake up crying that he can never go back.

Ask anybody—his shipmates, his captain, his family back in Davenport if they'll talk to you about him. They'll all tell you the same thing.

Charlie's no good.

Now, broken, he sinks back onto Pacific Beach.

DON'T FEED THE BUMS

BY LISA BRACKMANN

Ocean Beach

Welcome to Ocean Beach.
Please Don't Feed Our Bums.

The stickers were all over the place. On the bumpers of cars. On store windows. Kari had even seen one on a surfboard stuck into the sand by the pier.

They sold them at The Black, a souvenir and head shop that was ten years older than she was, that had been around for forty years. The stickers were round, yellow and olive green, with a silhouette of a tall, hunched man carrying a knapsack. It made Kari think of the Boy Scouts.

It wasn't that she liked the bums. The homeless crowd that had moved into Ocean Beach recently wasn't like the old hippies who lived in their beat-up vans and had been around forever. These bums, they were younger, mostly, single guys, and some of them were a little scary. A lot of them were meth-heads, or so the local gossip went, and she believed that was true; with their greasy hair, the blemishes on their skin, the way their faces had hollowed out and their eyes seemed to have come loose from the sockets, rattling around like marbles in a shot glass.

But she didn't like the stickers.

"I don't know, I think it's mean," she said.

Sam rolled his eyes. "You're just way too nice."

They sat in the small gray patio of South Beach Bar and Grille. It was Taco Tuesday, and the tacos were all $2.50. Sam loved the mahi tacos, claimed they were the best fish tacos he'd ever had.

"I don't think so," she said. "It makes it sound like they're animals or something."

"If they were animals, you'd be feeding them," he pointed out.

She blushed a little. "I like feeding the cats. They don't hurt anything."

"It's cool that you feed them," Sam said, taking a bite of his taco.

She did like feeding the cats. The routine gave her focus, and a kind of satisfaction.

It was funny, because Before, she didn't even want to have pets.

There was a Before and an After, and she knew that she was two different people. Except that the After just felt like Now. Everything always happened all at once; she had a hard time putting one moment before another, one moment after the next.

She knew as well that she wasn't able to think the way she used to. Knew this mostly because people who knew her Before would let that slip sometimes. But every now and then, she'd know it herself. She'd start to think of something, something quicksilver and elusive, and she could almost catch it, but it would flash between her fingers, gone, leaving just its emptiness behind.

Maybe I'll be able to someday, she'd think, but she didn't like to think too much about that. Sometimes, if she tried too hard to grab onto such thoughts, she'd get so frustrated, the anger bubbling up in her like a teapot boiling on the stove. She'd break things, sometimes, when she felt like that.

But that didn't happen much. It hadn't happened in a while.

She always set a timer when she boiled water too. So she wouldn't forget.

That was the key to managing her After life. They'd taught

her all these things in rehab. Make lists. Check off your to-do's.
Stick to a routine.

"So you want to go, you know?" Sam asked. He stretched out his
arm and settled his hand on hers, his thumb gently rubbing the
muscle between her thumb and forefinger. Kari liked it when he
did that. Her right hand cramped sometimes, at odd moments,
since the accident.

She got out her notebook. Looked at her list for the day. "I
can't," she said. "David's home tonight."

Sam tilted back his head and sighed. "Okay."

Sam didn't like David. Which made sense, she guessed. They
were about as different as two people could be. Sam was relaxed.
Shaggy. That was the word that she used for him. He smoked
a lot of pot and liked to surf. He made money doing carpentry
and odd jobs, and he wrote things, stories and poems. She didn't
know if what he wrote was any good or not. That was one of the
problems she had After. Reading, keeping the words in order, was
hard for her; they were like unruly kids who wouldn't stay in line.

But she didn't really care if Sam was a good writer. She liked
him. He was nice, she thought, and she liked the way he smelled,
and she liked how he fucked her.

Made love, she corrected herself. That was how you were
supposed to think of it.

She liked how David made love too, but he was really different. He was bright. Sharp. Those were her words for him.
She liked to look at him, just to take in his glow. He probably
wouldn't like Sam, if he ever met him. David didn't have a lot of
patience. He lost patience with her sometimes, though he tried
hard not to.

But David was from Before. She'd had to tell Sam about David, but she couldn't see any reason to tell David about Sam.

David was from Before, so he came first. She could keep that
much in order.

She knew that sleeping with two different men at the same time wasn't something she was supposed to be doing. Helen, her therapist, talked to her a lot about that. "You have some problems with impulse control," Helen said. Kari remembered this because Helen had said it many times, and she'd written it down.

"When you want to sleep with somebody, you really need to stop and ask yourself why. And if this is something you'll be happy about the next day."

Kari had actually thought this was pretty stupid advice, but she'd kept that to herself. "Why" was because it could be fun and it might feel good. How she'd feel about it the next day was impossible to predict—it hadn't happened yet.

Still, she remembered that she had to be careful about things, about getting pregnant, about getting diseases. They'd wanted to give her some kind of shot or some other thing, some device, for birth control, so she wouldn't have to remember to do anything, but she convinced them that she could remember to take the pill, and she could remember to use condoms, and she did.

Write it down. Stick to a routine.

And she didn't think that she was being that impulsive. She wasn't picking up strangers in Newport Avenue bars.

Two men didn't seem like too many.

It was just better if David didn't know about Sam.

The check came. They'd each had two fish tacos and a beer. As usual, they split the bill. Sam liked coming here on Tuesdays because it was so inexpensive, and he didn't have a lot of money.

It didn't bother her that Sam couldn't pay for things. She guessed it would have bothered her Before, but not now. She had plenty of money now, and she didn't care if men could take her out or not, even though she was supposed to. Actually, she wished she could just buy Sam lunch all the time. But that might raise too many questions.

Sam didn't know that she had money, and she wasn't sure it would be a good idea to tell him.

That was another thing she and Helen talked about. How she needed to be careful, or people could take advantage of her.

After lunch, she stuck to her Tuesday routine.

First, she went down to the beach, then south, past the faded stucco apartment with the tattered peace flag hung in one window and the yard of sand that had once been a saltwater pool, onto the tide-pool flats where generations had carved things into the soft rock; their names, mostly. Why did people do that? Kari wondered. They wanted to be remembered, maybe, but she read their names now, and she had no idea who they were. She watched crabs scuttle in and out of the crevices, listened to a man sitting on a rock play his guitar, his feet dangling over the ocean, catching spray.

After that, she walked onto the pier off Newport and bought a cup of coffee at the café there. Walked past the guys fishing, the Mexicans and the tattooed Anglo with the Volcom cap, the rusting blood on peeling paint, the faint shimmer of scales on the railing.

At the very end of the pier, she paused and stared out over the ocean, today the color of midnight with sapphire peaks where the wavelets arced and crested.

One Leg was there today. She got out the Tupperware container in her tote bag and retrieved a sardine from it, put it on the splintered rail.

One Leg was a big gull, all white with a yellow beak, one leg amputated above the joint so that it waved around like a conductor's baton when the bird hopped over to grab the sardine.

"Hi, One Leg," she said. "There's another one for you."

He didn't seem to be doing badly, even with one leg, but she still liked feeding him.

Then it was time to go north, to Dog Beach. She liked to

watch the dogs running free in the sand, splashing in the surf, their owners tossing Frisbees and tennis balls. The other reason she liked to go there was that a bunch of stray cats lived over among the rocks on the jetty, and she liked to feed them.

There were only a few out now: the little gray cat with green eyes, the big white one with black patches, and a half-grown calico kitten she hadn't seen before.

"Hi, Cow Kitty," she said. Cow Kitty let her get really close most of the time. Once she'd even extended her hand for Cow Kitty to sniff, and he'd rubbed against her fingers.

She had a baggie full of kibble, and she scooped out a couple of handfuls and left them on the flat rocks.

And after that, it was time to go home.

Her little cottage wasn't far from Dog Beach, just off Voltaire. It was old, wood, with peeling paint and boards gnawed by termites, and the wrought-iron gate had rusted in places. Inside, the house was similarly rundown. The couch sagged in the middle; the area rug was frayed; there were cobwebs hanging from the high splintered rafters, but she didn't care.

It was comfortable. It was hers.

The gray bank of clouds that waited offshore had started to roll in, as it often did late afternoons or early evenings in June. Settling in for the night. She liked that thought. As if the clouds and fog were tucking her into bed.

She would watch TV, maybe. Have something small to eat. Lift some dumbbells, since it was not a gym day, and it was important, her physical therapist told her, to maintain her strength, to reinforce those frayed connections between her brain and nerves and muscle.

Oh, and David was home tonight.

"Spare some change?"

The bum stood just outside her fence, leaning against the telephone pole. She caught a sharp scent of sour sweat, and tar.

"I . . ." Did she have change?

"So I can get something to eat," he said. "A dollar."

He was young, skinny, his body taut to the point where it almost seemed to vibrate. His green eyes were big in his face, too big, his hair greasy and ready to mat, his jeans crusted with grime.

She reached into the pocket of her shorts. She had a couple of dollars there. "Here," she said, extending her hand.

He reached out and took it. His nails, she noticed, were chewed and rimmed with black.

"God bless you," he said. "We're bathed in the light of the Heavenly Host."

"Kari?"

"Oh. Hi, David."

She'd fallen asleep on the couch. The television blared on regardless. She'd done her weights like she was supposed to, had a banana, and then settled down to watch television, but it hadn't been very interesting, she guessed. What was even on now? It looked like a show about pandas.

David stood in the center of the living room, dressed in a suit and tie. The energy rolled off him, she thought; he was almost as tense as the bum she'd given money to.

She sat up. Waited a moment for the dizziness to pass. "Did you have a good trip?"

He nodded. His eyes flicked around the living room. "Jesus, Kari. This place is a disaster."

"It is?"

She hadn't noticed. She tried to see the room the way he saw it. Her sneakers, jacket, and tote bag on the floor, dumbbells scattered around, an empty glass and a crumpled can on the coffee table.

"I'll pick up," she said. She'd meant to do it. She'd just forgotten.

David shook his head and grabbed the glass and plate, took

them into the kitchen. She stood up and followed him. He started putting dishes in the dishwasher, picking them off the chipped tiled counter.

"I can have the cleaning lady come more," she said.

His back was to her. "It's not that. It's this house. All of it."

David didn't like the house. He never had.

Kari's dad had left her this house. She remembered staying overnight when she was a kid, sleeping on the couch, her brother curled up on the floor in a sleeping bag, the two of them going to the beach with their dad.

Before, she and David had lived in a rented condo in Escondido, and it was funny, because when she was a kid she'd loved coming here, but as an adult, Before, she'd felt more like David felt now: that it was run-down, not clean, not nice.

Finally David turned to her. "I'm sick of being panhandled every block. Did you see that kid who's parked himself in front of the house? Two days running now! That's the kind of neighborhood we're living in, with fucking bums puking on the sidewalks. We can afford something better than this."

"You mean, *I* can afford it," she said.

Something dark crossed his face. He slammed the glass down on the counter and stalked out.

She hadn't meant to make him mad. She was just stating a fact.

When she went out into the living room, he was sitting on the couch, flipping through channels with the remote.

"I'm sorry," she said. "I wasn't trying to, to . . ." She thought about what she wanted to say. Sometimes it took her awhile to turn the feelings in her head into words. "Insult you."

"I know." He put down the control and leaned back against the couch, his body still rigid as a plank. "Things are turning around," he said. "The market's coming back up. Probably better to wait and sell this place then."

"But I don't want to sell it." She sat down on the couch next to him. "I like it here."

"Great. With the hippies and drunks and stoners."

"Why don't you like it?"

"Jesus. Because it's a dump. Because nothing ever changes. Other parts of town, they build nice houses. Have new businesses. Improve things. Not here."

She thought about it. She liked that Ocean Beach didn't change. "Why do you like me?" she asked.

"What?"

"I mean . . . you liked me before, but I'm different now. You liked someone else. Who isn't here anymore. So why do you like *me?*"

"I don't like you," he said. His voice was dark, like his face had been. "I love you."

"Why?"

"How can you even ask that?" He let out a sigh. "It's not your fault. I know it's not your fault."

"That doesn't matter," she said. "If it's my fault or not. I don't . . . I don't expect you to . . ." She stopped there, puzzled. What was it that she didn't expect?

"I promised to always take care of you. Remember?"

"You don't have to," she said. "I know I make mistakes, but . . . I'm doing all right. I can take care of myself."

"I want to," he replied, his jaw tight, then sighed again. "Take care of yourself? You probably don't even remember what day it is tomorrow."

She thought about it. "It's Wednesday."

He closed his eyes. "It's our anniversary."

Oh.

It was not on her list for the day, but it was on the San Diego Zoological Society calendar in the kitchen, noted there beneath the photo of the cheetah cubs in David's blocky print: *Our Third Anniversary.*

David had changed into sweats and a T-shirt. He sat on the

couch, watching some financial news show. She couldn't really follow those now, or maybe it was just that she wasn't really interested in them anymore. The market this. The market that. Who cared?

"I'm sorry," she said. "I'm sorry I forgot."

"That's okay." He tried to smile. That is, he *did* smile, but she didn't think he meant it.

She wasn't good at remembering where she put things, or what she was supposed to do, or a lot of facts and figures. But she was good, she realized, at judging emotions, whether people's words and expressions matched their feelings.

"How do you want to celebrate?" he asked. "Or do you even want to?"

She thought about it. *Our Third Anniversary.* Underneath the photo of the cheetah cubs.

"Let's go to the zoo."

On Wednesday mornings she had her appointment with Helen, her therapist. It was nice, because Helen's office was just off Newport Avenue, and she could walk to it. She hadn't driven since the accident. She didn't have seizures or anything like that; she probably *could* drive. She just didn't think she wanted to.

"I don't know why he likes me," she told Helen.

The therapist leaned back in her chair. She was fluffy. Cloudy, in Kari's way of picturing her, but with sharp beams of light that refracted through the clouds: a mass of graying brown hair, horn-rimmed glasses, chunky jewelry and layers of gauzy clothing, and a penetrating gaze, a way of pinning down feelings with sharp words, like the feelings were dead butterflies.

"You're a very likable person, Kari."

"Maybe. But I'm not the same person. I'm not . . ." She struggled to find the words. "We used to want the same things. I was quick, like he was. I was . . . ambitious. We were going to, to make a lot of money. Live well. Have nice things." She shrugged.

"I don't care about that stuff now. But he still does. And he says that he loves me, but I don't know why."

"Because you're lovable."

"What does that mean?"

"You're kind. You're caring. You're pretty . . ."

"So is it about how I look?"

Helen sighed. "It's about a lot of things. Have you asked him?"

"I tried. But he won't tell me."

Helen tapped her pen on edge of the desk, like she was summoning up her words. "Kari, you keep talking about how he feels about you. How do you feel about him? Do you want to be with him?"

She considered this. "I don't know."

"You really need to think about that, Kari. And you need to think about what you want to do, long-term. You've made a remarkable recovery. It's time for you to start thinking about the future."

She tried to smile. "It feels so far away."

"I know. But it comes before you know it. Look." Helen hesitated; she wasn't sure of something, Kari thought. Maybe not about what she wanted to say, but the words she needed to use, so that Kari would hear them. Finally Helen continued: "Your life is very different than it was, and you can't do some of the things you used to do. You're not going to be a lawyer."

"That's okay. I don't want to be one."

"Good. So why don't you think about what you *do* want to do? And we'll start focusing on that." Helen opened up her day planner. "Next week?"

When she walked home, the bum was there, leaning against the telephone pole.

"Spare a dollar? So I can get something to eat?"

I gave you a dollar yesterday, she started to say, but then she thought, *That was yesterday, and today he needs to eat again.* She had a dollar and some change in her pocket. She gave it to him.

"Jesus loves you," he said. "But the Shining Ones, the deceivers, they take a pleasing form."

There were a lot of gaps in her memory. The stuff she'd learned in school, especially law school. Some of it was there, but she couldn't connect it all together. And other kinds of things: incidents. People she knew. Places she'd visited. She'd remember, sometimes, if someone reminded her, that, oh yes, she'd been there. She'd seen that.

Other people and places were gone, no matter how well they were described to her.

The zoo was something she did remember. She'd been coming here since she was a little kid, for all her life, really.

Walking through the front entrance, seeing the flamingos across from it, smelling that strange chlorinated bird-shit smell, she thought of coming here with her parents, back when her parents were together, and her little brother.

Before everyone died.

"Let's get some tacos," she said to David.

Her father had died first. A heart attack. Had left the house to her and her brother. They'd talked about selling it, but Jake wanted to live there while he went to college. It was something the two had argued about, because she'd wanted the money to pay off her law school loan, but they'd decided to table the discussion for at least a year. There was insurance money from her dad, at least, to compensate her for the lost income, the money that Jake couldn't afford to pay.

She'd graduated. Passed the bar. Her stepfather and mother wanted to celebrate. They'd all ridden together in her stepfather's car: Kari, Frank, Mom, and Jake.

* * *

There was life insurance money from Frank and her mom. Money from the sale of the very nice house they'd owned in Del Mar. Money from their IRA. She'd had her own insurance, though it hadn't begun to cover the total cost of her hospitalization and rehab.

The real money came from the lawsuit over the accident, which had just been settled.

"You're going to need advice and guidance," Helen had told her. "But you're competent to make some basic decisions about your future."

David wanted to be her advisor. He was her husband, it only made sense. But the things he wanted to do with the money—investments, expansions, new houses—didn't interest her.

She hadn't said no yet. But she hadn't said yes, either.

"How much longer do you want to stay?"

He was already bored. They'd been there nearly two hours, including the time it took to eat, and they'd only gone to the Children's Zoo and the Insect House and the Reptile House, then through the Monkey Trail and down to see the pandas.

"I don't know," she said. "We haven't been to the tigers or the elephants yet."

She thought that he sighed. "Okay. Let's go see the elephants."

The elephant exhibit was new. When you entered it, there were signs welcoming you to see the animals that were here in Southern California thousands of years ago. There were statues of mastodons and saber-toothed tigers, equipment for kids to climb on, all sitting in beds of ground-up tires; metal monoliths two, three times her height, with cutouts of gas pumps and faucets and bulldozers, slogans like *Reuse and Recycle* and *Sustainability*. There was a tar pit with animal skeletons—fakes, she figured.

And then there were the real animals. Rattlesnakes. Condors with wingspans as big as Chinese kites. Lions, with signs warning you that their spray range was seven to ten feet.

The elephant enclosure wound around the mesa like a broad, lazy river of packed brown dirt and sand. They followed it, watched an elephant use its trunk to retrieve items stashed up in the branches of a metal tree. "Look at that," she said, pointing. "Look at the end of his trunk! It's like . . ." She stopped, puzzled. "I don't know. Like a finger, but with no bones. Like what an octopus has."

"A tentacle."

She laughed. "Yes! Like that."

They reached the Elephant Care Center. From the front, it looked ordinary, a small building that could have been a vet's, or a dental office, or anything. Then around in back, it opened up, like someone had unfolded a pop-up book, into a huge sort of barn, as big as a jet hangar. Banners of elephants' legs hung above massive steel bars—cages. It looked like a science fiction movie, she thought. Like there should be monsters inside. But it was empty. Dark.

"Is that where the elephants sleep?" she asked. "Or just where they go when they're sick?"

"I don't know," David muttered. He wiped his forehead with the back of his hand. The sun had finally come out, late in the afternoon.

The greatest danger to elephants is the encroachment on their habitat by man, she read on one of the plaques. It took her a few times but she understood it. She got it right.

"We need to leave soon," David said, "so we can go home and get changed for dinner."

"Dinner?"

"We have a reservation at Tapenade. I told you that."

She nodded. She didn't think that he had, but it wasn't worth arguing about. Sometimes she thought that he pretended to tell her things and didn't, but she wasn't sure why.

Maybe so she would think that she needed him more than she did.

They took one last walk through the rainforest, into cool mist and vegetal darkness. There was one place she particularly liked: a giant walk-through aviary, taller than jungle trees. Birds flew overhead, emitting alien cries and chatter. She and Jake used to play here when they were little, race up and down the greening cement paths until their parents lost patience. She remembered that, suddenly, smelling the mossy water, hearing the birds call.

"Let's walk a little longer," she said. There was still so much she hadn't seen.

Below the aviary was a series of paths and grottoes. There were sun bears. Tapirs. Monkeys with names she'd never seen before. Golden-bellied Mangabey, with the *Do Not Feed* warning next to it. A sleeping snow leopard. A North American lynx. She read the placards on each, mumbled the names of the animals to herself.

Status—Endangered. Status—Threatened. Loss of habitat. Extinction.

"Are you crying?" David asked. "What's wrong?"

"Just . . . it's sad."

Do Not Feed.

"Let's go home," David said. "You're tired. You get stressed out when you're tired."

"I'm not. I'm not . . . tired. Or stressed." She pulled her arm away from him and continued down the path.

Here were some smaller enclosures, containing little monkeys and birds.

Did you know . . . the sign said on one.

"*Did you know,*" she repeated aloud. "*Like people, not all animals are . . . are physically perfect. It is the, the policy of the San Diego Zoo to allow . . . to allow these . . . individuals to, to live normal lives . . .*"

"Let's go home, Kari," David said. "We're going to be late."

"I know what I want to do now, with the money," she said over dinner.

David had just taken a sip of his wine. He held onto the glass, frozen in place. "Oh?"

"I want to, to do something . . . for animals."

David put the glass down. "What?"

"I've been thinking a lot about it," she said slowly. "Like when I'm out feeding the cats. And then today, at the zoo."

"Kari, what are you saying?" His voice rose. "You want to give your money to *cats*?"

"No," she answered, her voice sharp. "I still understand a few things. I'll have . . . a foundation . . . or a nonprofit. I'll pay myself a salary from it. I'm not stupid."

"Look, honey . . ." He took a gulp of wine and lowered his voice. "You're doing a lot better. You've really come a long way . . . but you're not ready to take something like that on."

"I know," she said, and she felt calmer again. "I'll hire someone to help me decide what kinds of projects. I was thinking, maybe, helping animals that get hurt. Or buying land where they live so they'll be safe."

"Kari . . ."

"It's my money," she said. "I get to decide."

Maybe that hadn't been very nice.

It had been a few days, and David was still mad at her, she could tell, no matter how many times he said he wasn't. "We just need to think about this a little more," he kept saying. "Talk it over."

That wasn't all he wanted to do.

He'd called a lawyer. He thought that she wouldn't find out. But that was one thing she remembered about David, that she was beginning to remember better: he thought he was smarter than he was.

It had been easy to find out. He liked to take long showers, so when he went into the bathroom, she checked his cell phone. There were two numbers that weren't identified, and she wrote them both down. After David left for work, she called them.

The first was a restaurant. The second, a law firm specializing in divorce, family law, and mental health issues.

Competency.

She Googled the name of the firm, and that's how she learned what they did.

She wasn't what she used to be, but she wasn't stupid.

That was yesterday.

She hadn't said anything to David about what she discovered, not yet. She was still trying to work out what it all meant.

Today was Saturday, a day that she went to Dog Beach and then to feed the cats on the jetty. She walked down a little street that fronted the beach, lined with a row of houses, all low-built with sharp angles—left over from the '60s, maybe. In the middle of these was a house under construction. Three stories high, strange swooping curves. It looked so wrong next to the little Jetsons houses. Like a mistake. A big sign was posted on the chain-link fence surrounding it, with the headline, *What's Happening Here.*

Single Family Home. Approved by Planning Commission. Approved by Coastal Commission.

Maybe he wanted a divorce. That would be okay with her, she realized. She didn't think she liked him very much anymore, and she was starting to wonder, how much had she liked him Before? There was something, something she could almost remember, that happened before the accident, that she hadn't liked. Something about the way he did business.

Frank, her stepdad, what had he told her?

"He plays fast and loose, sweetie. That's my read. Gets in over his head and looks for an easy out."

"You can do better," her mom had said.

What's happening here?

She thought about all this as she dressed for the gym on Monday, fumbling at the laces of her sneakers, which were still hard for her to tie.

An easy out.

If they divorced, he wouldn't get the settlement money. Would he? That money was for her, for her pain and suffering and loss. Loss of ability. Loss of income. Loss of family.

There were other assets: some money left from the various insurance policies, the Del Mar house.

If he wanted half of all that, he could have it.

But how much was left? She didn't know. There was a financial advisor, who David met with more than she did. He handled their personal bank accounts. Paid the bills. There had been a lot of bills, even with her health insurance.

Competency. That was the other part.

"Spare a dollar, so I can get something to eat?"

There he was, squatting against the telephone pole by her house. He looked worse than ever. Skinnier. Hair tangled into dreadlocks. A crusted sore on his cheek. He smelled worse too.

She had some quarters, a couple dimes. "Here," she said.

"That all you got? Come on, lady."

"Sorry, I don't have any change."

He stared at the coins, muttering under his breath. "Lucifer was the most beautiful of God's angels, radiating light and glory. I'm not deceived by his honeyed words. Jesus watches over me, just like he watches over you."

She fumbled with her little teardrop bag, the one she took to the gym. There was money in there, she was pretty sure. Some bills.

"Here." She didn't look at what she gave him. She had more important things to think about.

* * *

After her session with the trainer, she stood outside the gym and called her own lawyer.

"I want a divorce," she told him.

Yes, she was sure. Yes, she knew the financials would be complicated.

"Give him whatever he wants, except for my house and the, the settlement. He can't have those."

Yes, they could have access to her bank accounts, her financial records. She'd sign anything they needed her to sign. Was there an accountant? There was, she remembered signing papers, but the accountant would be David's, not hers.

"If you can rec . . . recommend one, just hire him," she said.

She had a sense, a feeling that she needed to act quickly. Before he did.

"The other thing is . . ." What was the other thing? "Competency," she managed, only stumbling a little on the word. "He's going to, to chal . . . challenge my competency."

"Great," her lawyer said with a sigh. "That could make things complicated. You know, I told you that guy was an asshole."

"You did?"

He laughed. "Yeah. Back when you wanted to divorce him the first time."

She hadn't wanted him to come along, that day they all went to celebrate.

How could she have forgotten that?

She took an extra long time after the gym, feeding the cats. She walked out onto the pier to look for One Leg, but he wasn't there. Stopped at the Chinese restaurant on Newport for takeout. By the time she rounded the block to her house, it was dark.

David would be home by now.

She decided that the best thing to do was to pretend that she didn't know what he'd been up to, and to not tell him about her own plans. Wait until her lawyer told her he had "all the ducks in a row," whatever the ducks might be.

The light was on in the living room, and she thought she saw movement behind the curtain.

"Spare some change?"

Kari flinched, her heart pounding. "You scared me."

The bum wasn't leaning against the telephone pole. Instead, he stood next to it, close to the fence that surrounded her house.

"I need some money," he said. "So I can get something to eat."

"I gave you some earlier today."

"Bitch!" he whispered. "Deceiver . . . full of fucking lies . . ."

What was that in his hand? A knife?

"I cast you out," he said. "I reject you."

He clutched the knife, the tip a short lunge from her belly. She stared at it.

"Okay," she said. "But here's some food." She slowly lifted her hand, the one holding the bag of Chinese takeout. "If you're hungry. It's good. You can have it." She held it out to him.

For a moment, they both stood there, frozen, him with the knife, her with the bag.

She heard the front door of her house creak open, a sliver of light spill out. Was that David?

Suddenly, the bum started to sob. "I'm sorry," she made out. "I'm sorry. I listened to the Shining One. He said you were a fallen Host. He said he'd give me gold. But he lied again. He always lies. I asked for food, and you fed me."

The sliver of light vanished. The door had closed. David must have seen her, seen her and the bum. But he stayed inside.

What's happening here?

An easy out.

She wasn't sure she was thinking it through, exactly. It was more like the thought just came to her.

"I know how that is," she whispered back. "Cause the Shining One, he lives with me. Right inside that house."

The bum nodded, his head bouncing up and down, like he wasn't in control of it. "Yes. Yes, he does. He speaks to me. He told me lies about you."

"I want to get him out of there," she said. "But it's hard to make him leave."

He nodded again, and even in the dark she could see the change that had come over his face. He'd been like one of the cats she fed. Now he was more like a dog on the beach, and she'd just thrown him a bone.

"If you cast him out, he can't lie to you anymore," she said.

One way or another, she was through feeding that bum.

MOVING BLACK OBJECTS
BY CAMERON PIERCE HUGHES
Mission Beach

May 2007

FIRST PROTOCOL: FIND OUT WHERE THEY ARE

Moses Johnson takes his job way too personally. He knows it, his colleagues know it. It's why his wife of twelve years divorced him four years ago, though it was mostly a peaceful divorce and they're better friends than they were a couple and he's a good dad. See, people who go into Moses's line of work go through steps. First they do it because they need the work. Then they start taking it seriously as if it's their patriotic duty, and before you know it, it becomes, "Asshole, you owe *me* the money." Moses skipped the second step and embraced the third step—by his sixth month. He cultivates looking imposing. Black suits (*always* black), blood-red tie, and shoes so shined that they could probably blind someone. He doesn't wear sunglasses, even when the temperature is at its highest and the sun at its brightest. He was hit in the face with shrapnel on a classified op somewhere overseas which makes his left eye droop. It makes him scarier when he's after a deadbeat. A deadbeat know he's screwed if he sees Moses coming toward him with the attaché case he always, *always* has with him and that look in his eye like when Michael Jordan has his sights set on the basket and there ain't nothing in this world that's going to stop him. When looking for someone, you become your mark, you eat where he eats, you talk to who he would, you order his drink and eat the same food. It's the reason Moses is so good at this, he can think like a deadbeat. He's close friends with his ex and he spoils his daughter, who was born with spina bifida and is in a wheelchair, rotten and visits with her every chance he gets. You can see him racing her in her chair all over the boardwalk most afternoons. It's his military special ops background. Be All You Can Be extended to all parts of his life.

He's been working for The Guys downtown for twenty-one years. He's forty-four.

The current deadbeat he's looking for owes tens of thousands of dollars. He's an Internet pornographer named Theodore "Teddy" Bear.

"Teddy's a piece of work," George Leedom, his boss, had told him three weeks ago.

Leedom is a legend, been around for decades, completely hairless with less of a tan than Casper the Ghost. When out of earshot, and making sure he's not even in the same neighborhood, his underlings call him the Greasy Old Bastard because he always gets his money no matter what and his skin has a peculiar sheen to it. His voice sounds like Darth Vader, if the Sith Lord smoked three packs a day. He sees Moses as his successor and always sends him on the tough jobs, except east of the 5, because Moses's skin is a few shades too dark in places like Santee (Klantee) and Lakeside (Whiteside).

Teddy was your average kid at USD in the late '90s pursuing a career in computers and getting his hands on all the porn he could, really kinky and filthy shit. It wasn't long before he put his passions together and he was a multimillionaire by twenty-four. File-sharing by the early twenty-first century was a godsend for him. He created a powerful search engine to find streaming videos of filth and it wasn't long before advertisers were lining up and he became the King of Filth on the Internet. Then he sold the software for millions and went back to his passion of making and distributing porn to stream on the Internet. Now it's come to light that he has been cheating the guys who run the city for quite some time. It's not like he couldn't afford to pay what he owes and still be richer than God, he's just greedy.

"We don't know who's protecting him, and every time we think we have him, he slips away. I need you to get him," Leedom rasped.

So Moses has been following him around San Diego and every time he thinks he has him, the guy suddenly gets in a car or lost in a crowd. It's gotten perversely funny for Moses, every other time he gets close, a sleek black car stops to let Teddy in. These cars are so featureless that Moses has started calling them Moving Black Objects, slang from his days in the military. The dude even changes where he lives frequently. Moses figures he has something serious going on in San Diego, because most cheats would be out of the country by now if they knew they were in trouble. He tracks him to Mission Beach, where he's been seeing him for the past few days, always slightly out of reach. A buddy of his once said that the only mission to be found there was getting laid, pounding beers, catching a wave, and *maybe* riding the roller coaster.

It's Moses's first break. He's lived in San Diego all his life, and was born and grew up in Mission Beach. He still lives there now in a two-bedroom condo by the bay that would cost a fortune, your soul, and your first-born child today, but was a steal back in the late '60s. His eight-year-old daughter Summer lives with him there every June and every other weekend. He knows the best place to get a burger, the best place for Mexican, the best coffee of all blends. Hell, he even knows a great little Greek café called Kojak's that plays Creedence Clearwater Revival on the juke box. He knows that the best place to get fish-and-chips is at this little joint by the harbor where he keeps the small tuna fishing boat he inherited from his dad who was in that line of work for over thirty years. He knows every single lifeguard by name and has dated most of the daughters of the aging owners of the small convenience stores and restaurants that have been around forever. He knows the ecosystem of the neighborhood, that the best dirt comes from the storekeepers, the bartenders, the guys in the restaurant kitchens, the security at the Sound Wave, a popular club that has live bands at night. He knows that the carnies at the fair games at Belmont Park see and hear everything. They all make the wheels turn in Mission Beach, not the landlords and rich people who rarely even come down here. This is where he eats. Where he sleeps. His comfort. His solace. His *home*. It's easy as pie to use that ecosystem to find Teddy's latest featureless white condo and safehouse, and that's where he is now, looking for clues.

He's been doing this a long time and knows how to search. He's not inside the condo because breaking in could get him arrested, but it's fair play if Teddy's trash is on the sidewalk ready to get picked up. Of course, Teddy has slipped the noose again and isn't there, but after some disgusting digging that only makes Moses angrier at Teddy, he finds a scrap of paper that says, *Go see Legacy.*

SECOND PROTOCOL: TRACK WHAT THEY DO

Brandon "Legacy" Penter is that kid every big city has who you just hate. Tall and athletic with spiky brown hair with blond tips and an I-just-got-away-with-something grin. He's the son of a former San Diego lawyer turned judge, his mother a real estate mogul, his brother a councilman, and his uncle is CIA. Legacy is a junior at USD where his entire family went and is part of a snooty frat. Legacy is so dumb that he wouldn't be able to find a seashell on the beach he lives twenty feet from. Daddy has to pay off the right people so he can pull off Gentleman's Cs. If San Diego has royalty, the Penters are it, living in their mansion at the top of the very exclusive Soledad Mountain in La Jolla.

Moses goes to Mission Boulevard, the heart of Mission Beach.

In Mission Beach, every foot of space counts and is bitterly fought for and protected. Five surf shops, four bars, a handful of restaurants, a resort hotel, a Turkish-style coffee house, and a small amusement park named Belmont Park with the last wooden roller coaster in California are packed in tight here, wedged in and amongst the beachside homes. At North Jetty Road, the southwestern cap of Mission Beach, there is a well-known locals-only spot where Moses surfs with a group of middle-aged professionals called the Gentleman's Hour; at the north end is the Catamaran Hotel, a ritzy vacation spot with suites costing up to eight hundred bucks a night and worth every penny. Compared to its sisters Pacific Beach and Ocean Beach, Mission Beach is a baby in age and much smaller than both.

Pacific Beach is losing to gentrification and crime spurred by alcohol, and Ocean Beach tries way too hard to be funky and pretend it's still 1975. Hanging on to a true beach-town feel amid the commercialism of the age is no easy task for those who live there, but Mission Beach keeps it real. Fourteen streets and forty-six walkways cross Mission Boulevard, emptying out onto the brown mud banks of the bay on the east and the sand of the Pacific Ocean on the west. Delicious views of blue sky peek out from between the rows of homes; clouds pass slowly overhead. Here, boxy stucco houses with neatly manicured lawns sit next to fading wooden shacks whose gardens sprawl on their small front yards like they don't have a care in the world. Towels sway lazily on clotheslines; wet suits hang over balcony rails to dry; surfboards lie piled on porches and on top of cars and in garages, still wet and slippery from morning sessions. Paint has peeled, façades dulled, and cars rusted, but this only adds to the funk of the place. Neighbors gather on the sidewalk to talk about the weather. For a city where the sun shines three hundred days a year, its citizens are obsessed with the weather and act betrayed and more than a little scared when it's cloudy or, God forbid, raining. Moses doesn't judge, he's had his share of weather conversations.

Several people can be seen walking their dogs. People nod

and wave at each other from the windows of cars. Surfers wax and hose their boards, talking story about the mythical perfect wave, and the height and ferocity of the wave gets bigger the more they drink. Shop owners linger outside storefronts, smoking and chatting and watching the street traffic. Restaurants don't dare have dress codes (*No shirts, no shoes? You can come in!*) and more often than not have outdoor seating. Beach-front condos have every variety of life. You can see what looks like an MTV beach party on one patio, next to a group of retirees drinking red wine while enjoying their golden years, and a happy middle-aged gay couple holding hands as they absorb the sunset.

Houses face the streets and walkways, few blocked from view by trees or hedges, which gives the area a casual and friendly look. A puppy eager to please. Street performers like jugglers or reggae bands do their thing on the boardwalk. The *whoosh!* of the Giant Dipper roller coaster can be heard every few minutes and Moses remembers the huge block party thrown when it was reopened in 1990. If you didn't know the locals, very few appeared to have a care in the world; for Moses, it's everything a beach town should be and the fact that scum like Teddy and Legacy infect it makes him sick.

Legacy lives with some other trust-fund California kids in a nice stucco house and when Moses gets there, he finds the guy washing down his obnoxious yellow humvee with Creed blasting on the stereo. The awful, crime-against-humanity music only worsens Moses's month.

"Hey, Legacy. You and I need to have a Come to Jesus meeting. You free?" Moses turns off the stereo; Legacy is lucky he doesn't hurl it into the ocean.

Before Legacy can run into the house and lock the door, Moses has him by the neck. Moses is a big guy, 6'2" and 220 pounds, who was an all-state quarterback at Mission Bay High, and worst of all, he's black, which, like, *terrifies* entitled assholes like Legacy. He has him backed up to his car with nowhere to run.

"C'mon, man! I didn't do anything? Why you aggro?" Legacy whines. Moses doesn't know what aggro means, but he's guessing something like upset. Moses is fairly upset.

"Theodore Bear. You know him."

"I don't know anyone by that name!" Legacy tries to get by, but Moses pushes him back against the car.

"Legacy? I can smell bullshit from the next county."

"I'm gonna call my dad!" Legacy screeches. It's a good threat. Moses's career is stalled because he pissed off Legacy's dad by hassling him back when he was a powerful downtown lawyer and partner at the prestigious Burke, Spitz, and Culver law firm.

Moses doesn't really care now though. He slams Legacy against the car again.

"Oww! Dude! Fine! I see the guy every now and then, sell him some X or weed."

"That all?"

"We surf a little. He can get me in the good clubs and the best tail. Man likes his comfort and fun. Dude! I wouldn't lie to you!"

"You know more." Moses kicks the car.

"He's got something going down on Memorial Day on Monday. Don't know where, don't know what. C'mon, man! You're hurtin' me!"

Moses releases him and and starts to leave, but then changes his mind and takes the CD out of the stereo and breaks it in half, figuring it's his good deed of the day, maybe the week.

It's the next afternoon when he strikes gold.

THIRD PROTOCOL: LEARN WHAT THEY HAVE

It's Memorial Day weekend and Mission Beach is hopping. There's an estimated crowd of 800,000 people filling the beach, both local and tourist. Moses loves tourists. They always dress wrong for the beach and think just because it's San Diego it doesn't get cold. This May weekend is a somewhat cold one as San Diego's sun takes its rare coffee-and-cigarette break before coming back with a vengeance in the later summer months. Moses likes the kayakers and wannabe surfers best who return to land like they just got back from storming 1944 Normandy; they have this great shell-shocked look on their faces and their eyes are wide and terrified. It's like *Apocalypse Now*, "The horror . . ." Those who don't bother with a wet suit are the best.

So Moses hears the mugging before he sees it, and only because he catches the name *Teddy*. He's leaving his humble little condo for another day of chasing pavement, and after looking around for the source of the voice he sees this big guy cornering a pretty girl in an alley out of sight from the crowds. Moses recognizes him as a local thug and your garden-variety bully, so he hurries over.

"Leave the lady alone, Vinnie."

Vinnie McBride smirks and steps away from the girl and gets close to Moses. They're about the same build, but Vinnie has size on Moses from steroids and being a gym rat.

"You gonna make me, nigger?"

Vinnie always did have a talent for making situations worse for himself.

"Guess I gotta, Vinnie." And Moses kicks him in the nuts. It's a good ball-shot that should have sent the guy clear across the 5 into El Cajon, but he's a 'roid freak and gets back up and rushes Moses, who dodges just in time and kicks him in the shin. Catching Vinnie as he stumbles, Moses shoves him into the wall and tosses him into a dumpster, slamming the lid shut. Vinnie will be napping for a while.

The racial slur just makes the fight a happier experience for Moses and he likes the location. Alleys are narrow, lots of hard edges, and usually a dumpster to dispose your trash, and the day he can't take on a street thug like Vinnie is the day he walks off Crystal Pier and drowns himself.

Moses walks over to the girl. She's about 5'8" with long, messy black hair that looks unwashed and eyes the color of melting butterscotch. She has a heart-shaped mouth and her nose is slightly bent like it's been broken once or twice in her life. She's wearing a wrinkled, red summer dress and scuffed sneakers. Moses guesses she's in her late twenties.

"My name is Moses Johnson. You okay?"

"Yeah, I think so. Not like I haven't been roughed up before." He doesn't like her laugh, it's too harsh, and he hears it on too many young girls these days. "Thank you though. My name is Hope. I don't have any money . . ."

"Money's not necessary, just doing what was right. Can I buy you an ice cream? I know a place on the boardwalk that makes a mean cheesecake on a stick."

"I'd like that. Guys usually want to buy me a drink, get me drunk." She smiles ruefully and smoothes out her dress.

"Doc told me if I kept drinking my liver would mutate into something out of a Godzilla movie that would stomp on the city."

Hope laughs and it's a better one with more life to it, and as she calms down he thinks he can hear Texas in her voice. It's a short walk on the boardwalk from the south end where he lives by the bay, where most people own their condos. It's more sedate than the north end where all the rentals and college kids live, but close enough that you can always hear the buzz of activity from the beach, Moses's favorite thing in the whole world is taking Summer to Belmont Park and doing all the games and riding the Giant Dipper.

Moses and Hope arrive at Sweet Treats and he orders them two chocolate-covered cheesecakes on a stick and they sit on a bench along the boardwalk. She licks her cheesecake and her face lights up in pleasure. He wonders when the last time was that she had a hot meal.

"What was that all about?" Moses asks.

"Why should I tell you? How do I know you didn't just beat

up Vinnie so you can bring me back to Teddy yourself to get paid?"

"You don't know that, it's true. What I can tell you is that by the look of your dress and hair, you've been living in a car for at least a week and haven't eaten well for a while. That won't be the last Vinnie you encounter. Whatever you're running away from, it's bad. Pretty soon thugs won't be paid to bring you back, they'll just shoot you." Leedom always said that sometimes the hard truth is better with a potential witness or informant.

He can tell she hadn't considered that. She looks like she's suffering from exhaustion and stress and can't think straight. She starts to shake and he steadies her. "What's so special about Teddy?" she whispers.

"I've been looking for Teddy. He owes me and my bosses some money."

"Teddy owes a lot of people money. He likes to bet. Who do you work for?"

Moses tells her and she blinks in surprise.

"Well, I didn't know he owed *them* money. Porn is a license to print money, I should know. He's a greedy little bastard."

Moses shows her his ID card and, not by accident, a picture of his daughter. Most people trust a parent. Leedom always said to use every tool. "I can help you; I've caught a lot of bad guys in my time."

She studies him for a moment and smiles at the photo. "I don't really know where to start."

"Why not the basics first? What is it you do, Hope?"

"I was a star, honey. Lotta films in L.A. My name is Hope Love—you never heard of me?"

"I don't watch much porn, honestly. It gets kinda boring."

She smiles almost shyly and leans back. "Mama was a hippie, hence the name Hope. I was your average girl from East Texas. Homecoming queen. Class president. Cheerleader. *Goooo Panthers!* I was at a concert in Austin when this dude approached me. I was a little high, he was a smooth talker. Said I deserved better than hicksville Texas and have I ever considered Los Angeles and making movies? Daddy was a preacher man and thought he could beat the sin out of me. I was just smart enough to know my life was already over and I'd probably marry right out of high school and be fat and drinking myself to death by thirty. It's not like I was a virgin either. I was on a plane the next day. L.A. was a trip, man. I had never seen so many people. Anyway. It's always the same story, agents won't see you, so you get desperate. I agreed to some nude pictures, and it's not a long slide to doing some freak on camera for four hundred bucks. You figure that'll set you up for a nice start, until you realize that L.A. is a little bit more expensive than East Texas."

"You did a lot of movies?" Moses asks, watching some kids run with a kite on the beach. It's a nice windy day for it.

"Tons. Turns out I had a knack for it. I liked the money and the attention. And the kinkier stuff is where the green is. I made some good bank in a couple years. A ton of features for creepy men. That's about how long most girls last if you don't have a major production company behind you. Turns out the smooth guy I met wasn't a player. I wasn't fresh anymore. Couldn't get a deal with the big guys. I looked tired. Everyone had done me. So I started doing gonzo and reality."

"I'm already lost. Gonzo? Reality?"

"Reality is, like, five minutes of plot. Home video stuff. Straight into the sex. It's for the freaks. They can watch me sleep with a regular guy as a cheerleader or even a teacher. I was good at it, but gonzo is where the real money is. It's the crazy stuff."

Hope pauses to take a bite of her cheesecake and smiles at a little girl running with a puppy on the beach.

"This is *wonderful*. Anyway, you rationalize it. I can make the rent for the next two months if a couple guys do me at once. Slammed against a wall and punched? Bruises fade and the green makes up for it. Sodomy and rape simulation, you start telling yourself, isn't *that* bad. I even did gay-for-pay for a while when people started getting tired of watching me get humiliated. You really never heard of me? That's kinda sweet."

They throw their trash away and start walking. The gray is melting away and the sun is peeking through. Hope raises her face to it and smiles.

"L.A. is a rough place. It shows you how ugly it can be, like it's proud. Here is better." She stares out into the ocean. "At least San Diego tries to cover up the ugly."

"How'd you get here?"

"Last year I was preparing to get it on with a midget lady. Hell of a way to turn twenty-eight, huh? That was when I decided to get out. For a laugh I tried to go legit as a sitcom actress, since a couple guys told me I was a good actress and I was dumb enough to believe them. I got beat out by this blond tart, which was literally what the part was, and now it's the biggest sitcom on TV. I met Teddy at a party and he gave me the same line I got at seventeen, that I could have a better life. And like when I was seventeen, I believed it. We moved to San Diego and it was cool for a while; he did his Internet porn thing and the shoots were actually kinda classy and professional. I was his executive assistant, because I knew the business, and his live-in girlfriend. I loved the city. It's not like L.A. where you can forget that there's a beach, it's everywhere here. It's the culture. You can actually *see* the sun. It's what Texans think of when they imagine California. Like I said, though, San Diego is good at hiding its ugly. Teddy started moving us around a lot, had a bunch of secret phone calls and meetings with creepy men in suits. I heard some things, read his e-mail. I had to get out of there. Teddy's a respected member of society, gives to charities, has a couple boats, several houses. Lots of powerful friends. Who was I going to turn to for help? I'm just a washed-up fuck star. "

Hope watches a father chase his squealing child across the sand. Volleyball players run around yelling for others to get the ball. Teenage girls giggle and gossip as they sneak glances at the bronzed surfers heading out into the water.

"I like you, Moses. If I thought you weren't a good guy, I'd ask if you wanted to be with me tonight."

He blushes. "Hope, what did you find out about Teddy?"

She turns to him, and she's all serious now, tears in those amazing butterscotch eyes. "You gotta help me. This is bad. Really, *really* bad."

So she tells him everything.

She tells him about Memorial Day.

She tells him about the empty houses with the filthy mattresses.

She tells him about the smuggling.

She tells him about the filmed rapes.

She tells him about the Moving Black Objects.

FOURTH PROTOCOL: EXECUTE WHAT THEY FEAR

It's Memorial Day at nine a.m. and the sun is shining down and the streets are packed full. Restaurants are at maximum capacity and lifeguards are on edge since so many people are in the water. You pretty much have to sacrifice a virgin to find parking. The perfect weather is why everyone pays such a high price: paradise ain't cheap. Getting drunk and laid is everyone's goal, not honoring those who fell in combat. Hardly anyone notices the van pull into a lonely alley and unload a group of Muslim women in burkas and hurry them inside the small red house.

Moses and Hope had spent the weekend going over the details of Teddy's scheme, and he has to admit it's sort of slick. "Teddy thinks this is patriotic what he's doing. He thinks he's saving American lives," Hope had told him the night before. Teddy, like most of America, had totally freaked when the Twin Towers went down and became a 9/12 conservative. Normal on 9/10, scared to death on 9/11, and ready to kick some ass in revenge on 9/12. At first he had donated large amounts of his fortune to the war effort in Iraq and any politician hungry for

Muslim blood, but that wasn't enough. Like everyone, he saw the torture scandals on the news, but instead of being sickened, he saw opportunity. He hooked up with his old roommate, Councilman Douglas Penter; Douglas introduced him to his uncle, Agent Jack Penter of the CIA. Teddy told them his idea and they too saw opportunity.

Muslim women were smuggled in; Councilman Penter had the right people look the other way, and Judge Clark Penter took care of the rest. The women were taken to houses secured by Mrs. Helena Penter and raped. The brutality was filmed and sent to secret CIA prisons and shown to whomever the hell they suspected of terrorism or had alleged ties to terrorism, as a way to get them talking. Teddy sold copies on the pervert black market.

It's a beautiful world.

So Moses, Hope, and a swarm of FBI agents are closing in on the little red house on this gorgeous San Diego morning where you just *know* there's a God, and Moses feels pumped. It's been a long time since he's seen action like this and taken down a real bad guy. He remembers what Hope had told him the night before, that Teddy's terrified of losing his status in high society, but more importantly, all his *stuff*. Moses can't wait to get his hands on the man.

"You ready?" asks his buddy, Special Agent Brooks Fairley, who looks more like a surfer than a G-man.

"*Born*. Let's kill this bitch." Moses grins and their small army kicks in the door.

Instant chaos. It's an abandoned house with a slim brown-skinned woman on a dirty mattress and five others in black burkas handcuffed to a pipe. Moving Black Objects. Not real women to Teddy and his partners. It's old military slang to dehumanize them in order to make it easier if you have to kill one of them.

Legacy is on top of the terrified girl on the filthy mattress and it's being filmed by a fat guy with one hand simultaneously on his crotch. Multitasking. Teddy is in the corner laughing and chatting it up with some shady-looking guys in suits. Teddy's an attractive man with curly black hair and classic Roman features. He's almost prettier than handsome. Moses bets the guys in suits are spooks. The men scatter when the door is slammed open and Fairley's men with their guns drawn come streaming in like a murder of crows. Through the confusion, Moses can hear Legacy yelp as Fairley throws him against a wall a little too roughly, and it warms his heart and he makes a mental note to buy Fairley a beer when this is over. Summer tends to the women.

Moses sees Teddy slip out the back and races after him.

Moses is fast for his age and size, but Teddy's a younger guy by about a decade and he slips easily onto the crowded boardwalk. They push through fat and pale tourists. Teddy shoves a little girl to the ground and she starts crying. The reggae street band orchestrates the chase. "Ramble Tamble" is blasting out of Kojak's. Moses can't let him make it to the parking lot or Teddy will be out of his reach for good, so he steps it up, and in a last ditch effort, like throwing a TD pass from his football days, he hurls his attaché case at Teddy, who stumbles at the sudden impact. Moses grins in triumph and soon has Teddy in a headlock, moving back to the authorities.

"That bitch rat me out? You stop this operation of ours, American soldiers and American citizens will continue to get killed by the rag-heads!" Teddy gasps.

"Teddy, her name is Hope and she's a smart girl who I'm going to help get a good job downtown. No, what screwed you is cheating on your taxes. Holding back on your 941s was cute since it's the welfare of your employees, and not you, but the geeks in auditing caught it. You owe me thousands of dollars, asshole. You should have known that the IRS always gets their man. As a bonus, I get to see the Penters burn. The sun is shining, the birds are singing, it's a great day to go to jail."

PART IV

BOUNDARIES & BORDERS

THE ROADS

BY GABRIEL R. BARILLAS

Del Mar

Roads. That's what everyone thinks about when you mention Southern California. The locals are obsessed by their roads and their epic traffic. Everyone has a shortcut and a hundred horror stories of hours spent crossing town on a rainy day. But during the summer, nobody minds if the beach roads are stopped. The cars and streets are filled with young beautiful people wearing not much at all.

San Diego is the most southern part of Southern California, but there aren't that many roads. There's Interstate 5, the long ribbon that runs the entire length of California's farmland and great cities. The 5 effectively bottoms out in San Diego, where it hits Mexico. You get the picture. Not too many places to go when you get here. San Diego is a repository for detritus that falls off Interstate 5. Nobody is truly from San Diego. Everyone came from somewhere else.

The hundred-mile drive from L.A. to San Diego is beautiful. Halfway down from L.A. you hit Camp Pendleton and the Pacific Ocean appears as you pass the sprawl of San Clemente. I drove past ritzy towns like La Jolla, Rancho Santa Fe, and Del Mar, but after only a few days of living here, I noted one thing. Behind its slick and sunny veneer, San Diego can't escape the fact that it's a border town. I quickly learned that late night in downtown San Diego can be quite a grab bag of adventures. Drug cartel members take busman's holidays here. Human traffickers set up bases and patiently wait for the time to be right so they can move

224 // SAN DIEGO NOIR

their cargo north. Drunken sailors and marines litter the streets, on leave for the weekend, and in their wake follow the whores, both male and female, a tribute to the diversity of our military. The Gaslamp Quarter, the developed section of downtown and the pride of San Diego, rolls right into what some locals consider the seedy side of town. This was the San Diego that I came to call home.

I spent hours driving around the city looking to familiarize myself with my new hometown. The city is inviting, nestled on the Pacific in a place where the sun shines nearly three hundred days a year. I drove past the airport, which sits mere yards from the bay. There's even an outdoor escalator that thrusts you right into the warm San Diego sun. You get sucked into this city mostly because you have nowhere left to go, but I'd learned that that's what the California dream can come to. That's how I felt now, holed up in a desperate little room. This was not my California dream.

I didn't have any money coming in since I walked out, or rather ran out, of my job after the first three hours. I was going to have to sell some of that shit I brought down. Maybe apply at one of those Indian casinos all over the hills to the north that I kept hearing about. All the concerts seemed to be held in one of the dozen or so out there. It might be nice to head into the mountains for a bit.

I ended up in San Diego because a cousin of mine suggested it might be the place to lay low for a while. I came by way of the big town, L.A., but that's not where my journey began. Sitting there in the dark, I had a lot of time to think about how I'd gotten to that point. I worked my way down the 5 from Fresno where I'd grown up. My parents were migrant workers from Central America. They moved north when I was three years old and never left. I grew up in a series of plywood shacks in various fields during the picking season and we'd rent a one-bedroom apartment in Fresno the rest of the year. I never saw my parents go to bed on anything but sleeper sofas or futons, whichever was available or cheapest at the local thrift shops. My parents could outfit a home for around $250 but it seemed like they could only afford $200 of it. They were always trying to make ends meet.

I remember the tourist kids coming through town in the summer asking what we did in Fresno for fun. I could never think of anything to tell them. All I ever wanted was to get the fuck out and never look back. There isn't shit to do in Fresno once you turn eighteen. Jobs are scarce. I sold some weed to make money in high school. Nothing big, I'd buy an ounce and split it, the occasional quarter-pound if I could get it cheap, but never more than that. I basically sold weed so I could smoke weed. I had to stay off the police radar since my parents were never able to apply for green cards, but mostly I kept out of trouble.

I had to make a living so I did about the only thing you could do in Fresno: wait tables. I started at the Denny's working late-night shifts and worked my way up to the local Applebee's. After a few years of busting my hump in the restaurant business, I decided to make my move to L.A. I had a universal skill and enough of a resume to be able to get a waiting job almost anywhere. And let's face it. It wasn't like I was going to try to get a job in the movie business. I'm not a handsome man. If you were to ask people who I looked like, they wouldn't name anyone famous. In my community they might call me *pura cara de indio*, or "full-on Indian face." It's not a compliment.

So before I left town, I stopped by my weed man, picked up a quarter-pound, just in case I had trouble finding a hook-up in L.A. or needed to sell some for quick cash until I got work. I went by my Tío José's place to say goodbye. My uncle didn't think it was such a great idea to drive 230 miles with four ounces of marijuana, but I told him, "It's only weed, Tío. You get like a hundred-dollar ticket for selling an ounce or less, and you know me. I don't break the law." I waved goodbye and jumped in my beat-up, skunky-smelling Ford Taurus and headed south.

My uncle knew what I meant. I always drove the speed limit and my lights always worked. My car was always registered. I couldn't afford to get pulled over since I couldn't get a driver's license. I couldn't afford to get busted and sent back across the border. That would kill my chances of getting my immigration papers in order. You get caught without papers and your name goes on a list and you can never apply for legal residency, and that was what drove me. I had to get legal. My father was on such a list. He got caught in an immigration round-up in the '70s, leaving us alone until he was able to sneak back into the country. He eventually died here but was never allowed the opportunity to immigrate legally.

My first job was a diner on Third Street near the La Brea Tar Pits. A stepping stone until things started to look up. It didn't happen right away. I toiled there for a couple of years before I saw any daylight. Not until the mid-'90s when casinos started going up in L.A. One of my fellow waiters told me about a job at the latest casino opening next door to the racetrack in Inglewood. I was lucky and I got in on the ground floor, working in their fine dining room.

I loved the hectic pace of the casino. I took some classes and learned how to deal cards and soon moved from the dining room to the casino floor. I worked the Pai Gow and black-jack tables dealing cards to old Asian women with too many diamonds on their hands and gray-skinned locals. I discovered I liked the gambling environment so I got a second job at the racetrack. I found myself dealing cards at night and during the day punching tickets for the most miserable bunch of optimists you ever saw. There were guys I'd see every day the track was open and there were people I'd see both at the casino and at the track. Where did they get the money to gamble full-time?

I ask because after too many years of dealing cards and keeping up with the ponies and not doing shit about my illegal status, I was mired in a financial shitstorm. This casino, unlike most gaming establishments, allowed its employees to play the tables as long as we weren't in uniform. Some days I'd blow $200 at the track and another $200 at the card tables at night. Oh, I'd win a few, but the odds are always in the house's favor. Soon, due to fiscal pressures brought upon by my creditors and unsound investments, I found I owed over forty large to various parties, none of whom I could afford to pay or continue to owe. I owed Eddie P. the biggest part of the nut, $25,000. I borrowed from him to pay Lazy Louis some of the $20,000 I owed him and another guy who I owed over $10,000. I'd been juggling for a while but it finally caught up with me. Living off credit is one thing, but owing these guys was another. Banks garnished your wages. Guys like Eddie P. and Louis took body parts for payments and killed you if you didn't fulfill your obligation.

That's when I finally listened to my cousin's pitch about San Diego. I'd never paid him much mind before. The last thing someone without a green card wants to do is drive south, but I had few options in L.A. I left my two jobs suddenly and without much notice. The world I inhabited there was small and my creditors were everywhere. I had to get out fast. So when my cousin said, "Hey, we have a racetrack here. I bet you could get a job," I told him see you in three or four hours. I picked up my two paychecks, snuck out the back door, visited my weed man, and didn't stop until I got to San Diego—not the "real" San Diego but the barrio my cousin lived in.

Getting a job at the track was easy. The racing season in Del Mar is a big affair. People come in from out of town and businesses thrive. The hotels are packed and the restaurants and bars are full of revelers. Ask any local waiter or waitress about working opening day and you'll hear horror stories. To me they were hilarious, tales of inebriated men and women coming in for dinner after a day of partying at the track. Some arrive already too wasted to place their next drink order. It's not unusual to see a breast fall out over dinner, and there always seems to be some girl in a miniskirt splayed ass-over-tea kettle on the walkway. The thong has made this particular vigil worth waiting for. Occasionally there is no panty to speak of.

Del Mar, like all other tracks across the country, is open all year. The regulars don't have a racing season. They come in year round betting on races as far away as Belmont in New York or Pompano Beach, Florida. There's always a track racing. Regardless of this, opening day is opening day. And the people turn up. Women in hats and parasols showing off new clothes purchased strictly for this day, wearing sunglasses too big for their faces. Companies host parties in private booths where men in sunglasses drink too much and wear vulgarly logoed designer wear. The train pulls into the station half a mile away and unloads cars full of already-drunk partygoers. In Los Angeles it's burnouts, and only on major race days does anyone dress up or host a party in private booths. Not in San Diego. They hang celebratory bunting. You'd think it was the World Series for six weeks.

I took my place behind the ticket machine on opening day, excited about the possibilities. I was in my element and it was a glorious day in North San Diego County. My slate was clean and the first thing I was going to do when I saved a bit was see about my immigration papers.

I was feeling optimistic. The weight of worry that had followed me from L.A. was beginning to disappear. I sat at my station and began to make plans to contact an immigration lawyer, but the crush of people soon had me working too hard to follow that tract. I had no idea the number of people who came in from L.A. every single day, but I learned quickly enough. I'd been at my window for three hours when I took my first break between the third and fourth races. I ran to the bathroom. They are large at the Del Mar track and this one was mobbed. I stood in line waiting for a urinal to open up, all the time staring at my watch. It's a sin to be back late from a break. We were all on tight schedules and you don't play around on opening day. The stall next to me opened up and I ran to the door. The guy coming out tripped on my foot. I looked up at him and mumbled an apology and shut the door quickly. I was in a hurry but something in my brain made me turn and look. The guy was washing his hands and he glanced back as I was staring at him, trying to catch a glimpse of his face in the mirror.

I now know what people mean when they talk about their blood freezing. I started to piss on my shoes I was so shaken. I hoped to God he wasn't still looking and I whipped around so he wouldn't see my face.

Of all people.

Eddie P.

The guy I owed twenty-five grand and to whom I had sworn upon my mother's grave that I was good for it.

I wasn't sure he saw me clearly but he seemed to have some sense of recognition. I tried to stay cool and keep my eye on him. As soon as he left, I exited through the opposite door. I ran into the employee room, opened my locker, and grabbed my keys. I ran to my car, jumped on the 5, and headed south to safety.

I'd never been a tough guy. I'd never needed to be. Life had been pretty easy so far. How had I allowed myself to get into this spot? My heart raced all the way home and a couple of hours beyond. I was shaking uncontrollably. I couldn't think of what to do. I now had no job, which was better than the alternative. I'd become too accustomed to my skin to want to lose that. I figured I only had enough money to last a month. I went out for dinner after I calmed down a bit but still couldn't relax. I was hoping to get lost among the mass of people but unfortunately San Diego's population isn't that dense. I walked down Ash and all I could see was my shadow bouncing around as the streetlights illuminated me and only me. I headed south to a more crowded section of town but thought better of it. I was sure some of the track people would end up down in the Gaslamp to continue their party. I grabbed a couple of tacos off a roach coach and hurried back to my room.

I could barely eat the small tacos. My stomach was convulsing. My walk had made me feel exposed and I'd begun to shake again. I didn't deserve this. I wasn't a bad sort. Hell, I was an altar boy. Got a perfect-attendance award when I was twelve, a heavily lacquered portrait of Jesus with the index finger of his right hand pointing up. My mother said I succumbed to my baser instincts, the first time, when she discovered a *Playboy* under my mattress. It became a litany whenever she flushed a bag of weed she'd found in my pockets when doing laundry. I always thought she looked through my pockets hoping to find something incriminating, and she was almost effusive when she did, but I knew it broke her heart every time. It didn't help when I said, "Shit, Ma, it's only weed." No Latino mother wants her kid to be a marijuano. I was glad she wasn't around to see me like this. I'd never felt more like a punk.

After a week holed up in my room, I was going batty. I had to man up, and besides, I needed supplies. I put on some shades and a Padres baseball cap and went for a walk. I ended up on E Street walking past the library, glad to be breathing the air and out of my room. I was worried about my weed stash. It was stinking my room up so bad you could smell it as you walked by the door. I had to get rid of it and get some money.

E Street is full of small businesses—barbershops, cheap women's boutiques, and hair supply places—and they were all just opening up for the day. I glanced into the window of one. There's something soothing about the old-fashioned barber shop. It's a place where guys go to shoot the shit. You never see women in there. I looked past my reflection to the barber chair. Sitting there, getting himself a nice trim and staring back at me, was Pablito. Some called him Diablito.

Eddie P.'s left hand.

The hand that did all the dirty work.

Fuck!

I turned as calmly as I could, then I ran back to the library. By the time I got into the back stacks I'd half convinced myself I was hallucinating. Paranoia was starting to take over.

I walked slowly through the stacks, trying to relax. I didn't really know how to behave in a library. I didn't have a library card and had never been much of a reader. After a few minutes of aimless wandering, my heart had started to slow down again. I figured it was safe to leave, but as I got to the door I saw him, cell phone in hand. This time I knew I wasn't imagining it.

I ran out a side door, through the parking lot of my motel, and up the stairs to my room, pulling out my keys so I would be exposed as little as possible. I was deciding whether to head to Vegas or Arizona. I grabbed my bag from the closet and filled it with my clothes. Luckily, I hadn't had any time to shop so everything fit. I went back to the closet for my weed tin which still had three ounces and the rest of my money. I've never had a bank account. No papers, no driver's license, no social, no bank account, so I always carried my fortune with me. I put the weed in the trunk and my money in my pocket.

I drove up the 8 into the mountains, where I figured I could hide off some side road for a while, at least while I split up my weed and formulated a plan. I saw a sign for a casino a few miles ahead and the light went on in my brain. Where there's gambling there's alcohol, drugs, and whores. The casino supplied the gambling and the booze but the whores and drug salesmen were independent contractors. I'd see if I could perform a service and unload some of this shit in the casino.

It felt good to have the beginnings of a plan. It gave me hope that I could get out of this mess I'd made. Maybe I could parlay the weed money into something in the casino and begin to pay Eddie part of the twenty-five large I owed him. That would take a load off my mind. I wasn't made for living like this. Maybe I could talk to Eddie and Louie and enslave myself to them until my debts got paid. Man, I'd do anything to get those monkeys off my back. There was no way I could live another day looking around every corner. I turned the radio up and punched it. I was suddenly feeling as good as I'd felt in a few years. I was going to pay Louie and Eddie P. I was going to get that lawyer and fix my papers so I could get a driver's license, a checking account, and real credit cards. I was going to make my mother proud.

As I got further east, traffic started to slow. Damn, there was always construction on these highways. You can't get anywhere in a hurry anymore. Pretty soon the traffic stopped and I could see that a lane closed ahead. Holy crap, you never know how many cars are on the road until you see a jam like this. Maybe there was an accident. I leaned out of my window and stared back at an endless stream of traffic heading up the hill behind me, then I turned forward and saw border patrol trucks.

Fuck.

Nowhere to go.

I took three deep breaths and crept along, reassuring myself about everything. They won't ask to look at my papers. I can pass for a citizen, I'm just going to the casino. It's all good. As I got closer, however, I saw the sign. *Working Dogs.* Shit, this was bad. I'd double-wrapped the weed. Maybe the dogs wouldn't smell it. I moved closer to the front of the line. I could feel myself shaking. I had to calm down before I gave myself away. As I got to the front, the damn dog started jumping up and down right next to my car. It was going crazy. The fed handling the animal brought it around the car and it kept leaping.

The guy leaned in and asked, "Sir, are you a U.S. citizen?"

I said, "Yes." Called his bluff.

"Sir, could you move your car to the side of the road, over there next to that ramp, please." It wasn't a question.

I glanced around. There was nowhere to go. I wasn't meant for running.

"Please step out of the car, sir."

I got out. What else could I do?

"I'm going to pat you down now."

They were going to find it. They were going to find everything. I'd blown it. The dog was all over the car and I saw the fed pull the package out of the trunk.

"Sir, I'm going to read you your rights. Anything you say can . . ."

His words simply faded away. I couldn't hear anything. Fear fell through me like a lead weight. It was over. At some point in the future I might be able to sneak back into the U.S., but I'd never have that golden ticket, that green card I'd wanted my entire life, and I was probably going to jail before being deported.

"Do you understand these rights as they have been read to you?"

I just nodded and looked back down the road.

There was nothing to see.

LIKE SOMETHING OUT OF A COMIC BOOK

BY Gar Anthony Haywood

Convention Center

E veryone who's ever seen the pages knows there's something special about them. They can see it right away. Not because the pencil work itself is exceptional, because it isn't, nor is there anything worth shouting about in the writing or the story or the substandard superheroes depicted in the panels.

It's the inks.

You look at the four pages and the ink work jumps out at you, black lines flowing over mediocre pencils with an almost magical, mesmerizing gloss. Get too close and the broad, powerful strokes draw you in like a fish, make you forget where you are and what you're doing until your nose is right up against the paper and you snap out of it, the spell broken.

It's only at that moment that people understand where I get the nerve, asking them to pay me $1,000 for four pages of a comic book that never made it into print, pages that were written, drawn, and inked by a writer/artist whose name is only vaguely familiar to them, if it's familiar to them at all. Before then, when their first impression of the clumsy, anatomically incorrect artwork and third-grade dialogue almost has them walking away without hearing my pitch, they think I'm crazy—*$250 a page for this drivel?* There's original artwork of a higher, more professional caliber to be found at every third booth at the Con, and at far more reasonable prices.

But then the ink work sinks its teeth into them, without their even knowing it, and they start asking questions. They want to know more about the pages—the who, the what, and the why—not so much because they're interested in buying, but because they know there must be a story behind them. A story that will help them understand how comic book artwork, so ordinary otherwise, could have such a paralyzing effect upon them.

So I tell them the story, the way it was told to me.

It was Ken Fenderson's first Comic-Con and he was hoping to God it would be his last. He wasn't a comic book person. Far from it. He considered himself above such foolishness, costumed superheroes and flimsy, shorthand fantasy stories told with pictures. Fenderson was a writer, not a clown or a child, and he took his work as seriously as a bomb squad tech took his. But comic books were where it was at, the very eye of the latest Hollywood storm where every multimedia and merchandising deal worth a paragraph in the trades was forged, and hell if Ken Fenderson wasn't going to make a spot for himself at the feeding trough. Fenderson was nothing if not an avid follower of the The Money, wherever it chose to lead.

So here he was in San Diego on this weekend in July, bouncing off and among the freaks and geeks filling every square inch of the San Diego Convention Center like plaque clogging an artery. Spandex in a rainbow of colors was everywhere, taut as a second skin here, as loose as a rumpled bedsheet there, and almost invariably in the service of a body that nobody on a full stomach would have wanted to set eyes upon. Fat Batmen and hairy Wonder Women, bald Wolverines and impish Captain Americas, and hundreds of other, pathetically rendered costumed superheroes and sci-fi movie characters of unrecognizable origin. It was like a madhouse for retired circus performers, a hot and sweaty rodeo corral teeming with nutjobs whose minds had never advanced beyond the age of eleven.

Fenderson was appalled. It was all he could do to keep his

breakfast down. This fiasco happened once a year in this place? This gigantic, eight-block long, landlocked cruise ship on Harbor Drive they called a convention center? How was such a thing possible? And what the fuck had happened to San Diego?

Fenderson had no use for the city, he'd been living in Los Angeles ever since his father moved the family there from St. Louis over thirty years ago, but he'd been here once or twice back in the early '80s when you could still get a thirty-nine cent beer down in Tijuana. Back then, L.A.'s "sister city" was a pit as far as Fenderson was concerned, a navy boomtown way past the boom, as old and slow and lifeless as a Mormon bingo party.

But now? Jesus H. Christ, downtown San Diego looked like Vegas crammed into a mason jar. The nautical-themed convention center anchoring the old navy yard was just the tip of a re-development iceberg that had apparently run amok, surrounded as it was by new restaurants and hotels, shops and cafés, and—most incredible of all—a goddamn baseball stadium, PETCO Park, sitting smack dab in the middle of the Gaslamp Quarter like something a tornado had uprooted from the suburbs and dropped from the sky.

Fenderson couldn't have felt more disoriented were he hanging upside down on a float at the Doo Dah Parade.

But business was business, and business today was here at Comic-Con in San Diego. Distractions aside, Fenderson had to focus and look for what he'd paid a ticket scalper the preposterous fee of $100 to find among all these funny book-obsessed weirdos: a great illustrator willing to work on the cheap.

For all his talent and ingenuity, after fifteen years of trying, Fenderson had yet to make it big as a writer, either of crime novels or screenplays, and he was at his wits end, attempting to figure out why. It surely had nothing to do with the work itself; compared to the crap some name authors were getting paid six figures or more a book to churn out, Fenderson knew his stuff was as good or better than anyone's. His premises were startlingly original, his characters were unforgettable, and his dialogue crackled with realism.

He knew all this because some of his best drinking buddies in the business—who had no reason to lie to him, right?—had often told him so, and the host of the public television show *Bebe's Bookshelf* gave his last book, *Murderer*, a rave review. So his problem, as near as Fenderson could tell, could only be chalked up to one thing: timing. He was simply in the habit of missing the crest of the wave.

It was an error he was determined to correct immediately. This time, he was going to be ahead of the curve, and the curve at present led directly to the graphic novel. Glorified, oversized comic books with hardback covers—that was what everyone was buying, especially the suits in Hollywood. You wrote the right graphic novel, big-dollar option deals were almost certain to follow. The fan boys in the movie business couldn't get enough, and there seemed to be no end in sight to all the money they were willing to throw around in search of the next *Hellboy* franchise or *Watchmen* blockbuster.

Fenderson didn't know Hellboy from Superboy, but he knew a gravy train when he saw one, and he'd driven down to San Diego for the express purpose of hitching a ride on this one. He had the "novel" part of his graphic novel already in hand—typical of his ability to produce amazing work in a short period of time, he'd written the 400-page manuscript in less than a month—and now all he needed was an artist to illustrate the ten-page proposal he'd put together. He'd done enough research to know that no editor would glance at five pages of his book without illustrations, so an artist was a must. Preferably, someone extremely talented, desperate for a break, and dumb enough to do the job for free, based on Fenderson's bullshit promises of a big payday on the back end. *Gullible*, that was the word. He needed a brilliant artist who was also gullible.

He couldn't imagine he'd have much trouble finding such

a geek in this room; pimple-faced kids dragging portfolio cases bursting with artwork from one booth to the next were everywhere. Some were in costume, more just wore geeky T-shirts, but they all looked ripe for the picking. All Fenderson had to do was find one who could actually do professional-grade work, then give him the big pitch: a once-in-a-lifetime opportunity to collaborate with one of the most critically acclaimed authors in crime fiction on a graphic novel project that editors and movie producers were already lining up to see. Who the hell could say no to that?

Fenderson roamed the halls for two hours, peeking over shoulders, eavesdropping on conversations, taking his sweet time. He wanted to get this right, and it would be all too easy to make a mistake in light of his inexperience in such matters. Having as little interest in comic books as he did, all the artwork on display at the Con pretty much looked the same to him. The godawful stuff was fairly obvious, but everything else struck him as equally juvenile and absurd. His contempt for the entire medium made it difficult for him to view the work of the artists in attendance with anything approaching a critical eye.

But then he saw the fattest Luke Skywalker he'd ever laid eyes on showing a stack of large black-and-white pages to a mildly attentive fanzine publisher, and he thought he had his man. Chubby wore a five o'clock shadow and was dressed as if for a blind date on Tatooine, but the artwork he was flashing with obvious pride had a noirish power to it that even Fenderson couldn't miss. Fenderson waited for his conversation with the publisher to peter out, being jostled on all sides as he did so by cardboard-clad Stormtroopers and video game characters swathed in felt and Velcro, then moved in on him as he started to walk away, a shark chasing fresh blood in the water.

"Ken Fenderson?"

Fenderson spun around at the sound of his name, startled. Fat Luke slipped off the hook and disappeared, swallowed up by the crowd.

The young woman who had called out to him did not look familiar. He made a point of forgetting homely girls as soon as he met them, and this one, at first glance, was as homely as they got: lifeless, shoulder-length black hair, zero makeup, and the posture of a plow horse, all wrapped up in the standard uniform of a violin teacher.

"Yes?" Fenderson said warily.

She showed him a small smile he could not quite read. "You don't remember me, do you?"

Had she been a looker, a lie would have been called for. But for this sad sister, the truth was good enough. "No, frankly, I don't."

She offered the odd smile again. "Jennifer Alcott. I was a student of yours once. 'Writing the Can't-Miss Screenplay,' class of winter '96."

Oh shit, Fenderson thought. *One of those.*

For two years, back in the mid-'90s, he had taught a be-ginner's screenwriting class at the Learning Bridge, a low-rent extension-course outfit in the San Fernando Valley that no lon-ger existed. The pay had been shit and the students had been worse, retirees and wannabes from all walks of life who laugh-ingly thought they had the chops to become the next big A-list Hollywood scribe. None of them could write their way out of a paper bag, and it was all Fenderson could do to read their stuff week after week without retching all over the page.

"Oh. Hey," Fenderson said. The name Jennifer Alcott rang a very dim bell, but the face meant nothing to him.

"It's such a surprise to see you. What are you doing here?" Alcott asked, not appearing to be *pleasantly* surprised at all.

"Actually, I'm looking for an artist. For a graphic novel I'm doing for Dark Horse." He'd read somewhere that Dark Horse was one of the top publishers in the graphic novel arena, and implying he already had a deal in place there was a lie he was prepared to tell at the Con all weekend long.

"An artist? Really." Fenderson thought she would flash that

bizarre smile of hers again, but this time all she did was nod. "Well, what a coincidence."

"Coincidence?"

"That's what I am now. A comics illustrator." She gestured with the portfolio under her right arm, bringing his attention to it for the first time.

"No kidding," Fenderson said, searching for the nearest exit. There wasn't a doubt in his mind that Alcott had to be as lousy an illustrator as she had been a screenwriter, even if he couldn't remember, exactly, just how lousy a screenwriter she was.

"Maybe you'd like to see my work."

"Uh . . ."

"Just for old times' sake? You never know. I might be exactly what you're looking for."

Fenderson figured there was zero chance of that, yet he couldn't bring himself to blow Alcott off. It bothered him that she was such a blank page to him; her name was familiar, so why wasn't her face?

"Well, okay," he said. "Let's see what you've got."

"Here?" Alcott looked around, scrunching up her nose at all the bodies flying by them. "I'd rather we found a place to sit down. Maybe have some tea or something."

Tea. Right, Fenderson thought. "Okay. But finding a seat in this zoo—"

"Not here at the Con. Somewhere else. I'll drive, if you want. I know just the place."

Fenderson couldn't imagine why he should go anywhere with this cow. He tried to retreat. "Gee, I don't know, Jen. I've got a couple of meetings to take later, I wouldn't want to be late."

"I understand. You don't want to waste your time on somebody who can't deliver the goods. And all you've got so far is my word that my stuff's decent, right?"

That was exactly what Fenderson was thinking. "No, no. It's just . . ."

"Here. I'll give you a small peek." She unzipped a corner of her portfolio and peeled it open for him.

Fenderson leaned in, squinting. What he could see of the artwork inside was pretty damn impressive: crisp, bold, even slightly cinematic. It wasn't as dynamic as the stuff the big man in the Luke Skywalker outfit had been hawking earlier, but it was close. Maybe even close enough.

"Not bad, huh?" Alcott said. "Some people tell me that my work reminds them of Jack Kirby."

Fenderson had no clue who Jack Kirby was, but if he could draw like Jennifer Alcott apparently could, he'd probably go far in the comics business.

"So," Alcott said, zipping the portfolio back up before Fenderson could ask to see more of what it contained, "shall we go?"

Fenderson wanted to say no. He'd been hoping to partner up with somebody who was more than just another face at the Con, maybe one of the superstars sitting in on a panel or signing books for a line of people winding through the hall like an endless snake. But that hope was a long shot and Alcott was a bird in the hand. If the lady was as good as the sample she'd let him see, and she could be bought for next to nothing, he could avoid all the hassles of negotiating with a stranger by cutting a deal with her instead. Rather than a pain-in-the-ass distraction he could have done without, maybe running into Alcott like this had been a genuine stroke of luck. The kind of luck, he knew, that only came to people destined for greatness.

"Sure. Lead the way," Fenderson said.

She drove an old shitbox Honda that would have had him laughing out loud had it not been a big step up from the ancient Toyota he'd driven down to San Diego at a crawl. The A/C was on the fritz so they had to ride around with all the windows down, Alcott's hair blowing in her face like a damn sheep dog.

She took him to a café that sat on a corner at the feet of the old El Cortez Hotel, up in the hills above downtown where the one-way streets could make you crazy if you didn't know the territory. The café was mundane and the place wasn't even a hotel anymore—all the building played host to these days were business seminars and wedding receptions—so Fenderson couldn't figure what they were doing there until they were seated at a table and Alcott explained the irony in her choice of setting. Apparently, during its infancy, Comic-Con used to be held at the El Cortez, down in a basement that was far too large for the meager turnout it was able to generate at the time. Alcott knew this because she'd been coming to the Con forever, even back then when she was just a pimply faced kid, having dreamed of drawing comic books years before the thought of being a screenwriter ever entered her mind.

Fenderson nodded and pretended to give a shit. He still couldn't recall anything about Alcott as she'd appeared in his Learning Bridge extension class, but her mention of screenwriting gave him an idea as to how he might discretely refresh his memory. "So how's the script going?" he asked.

"The script?"

"The one you were writing in class."

"Oh. That," Alcott said, clearly embarrassed the subject had come up. "I gave up on it. Everybody I showed it to said it was awful." She flashed that eerie smile again. "Just like you did."

"Me? Did I say that?"

"In so many words. You told the whole class. But I didn't take it personally, because you liked to say similar things about everyone's writing."

Fenderson briefly considered denying it, then decided to save his breath. Of course he'd said some terrible things to the morons in that class; they'd paid their tuition to have a working professional assess their writing in an honest and straightforward manner, and he wouldn't have been doing them any favors by killing them with kindness. The sooner they realized they'd just be muddying the waters real writers like Fenderson had to swim in, glutting the market with unsolicited screenplays that were all but unreadable, the better. Cruel? Fenderson liked to think he was simply giving them their money's worth.

"Remind me what it was about. I'm drawing a blank," Fenderson said.

"It's not important. I've moved on. And it's not my writing we came here to discuss anyway. It's my abilities as a comics illustrator."

"Yeah, I know, but—"

"Why don't you tell me a little about your novel. So I'll know whether or not it'd even be worth your while to see more of my work."

Rather than argue, Fenderson gave her the bare bones of it, as careful as ever not to say more than was absolutely necessary. People were always on the lookout for what Fenderson had to offer, a fresh, new idea with endless commercial possibilities, and even a nobody like Alcott could get him ripped off if he took her too far into his confidence.

She listened to his pitch without comment, sipping her tea and picking at her salad, her face as devoid of expression as a porcelain doll's. If he hadn't known better, Fenderson would have thought she was bored by it all, until he wrapped things up and she nodded her head and said, "Wow. That's really something."

"It is, right? It'll make a hell of a movie, but I thought selling it as a graphic novel first would be the best way to get a film deal done."

"Sure."

"Which brings us back to you and your work. I'd love to have you onboard as the illustrator, but I haven't seen enough of what you can do to know whether or not you'd be right for the project. Have I?"

Without further encouragement, Alcott opened the portfolio propped against the chair beside her and eased a page out of it, handling it with the care of an obstetrician delivering a newborn. It was the pencil-and-ink page she'd allowed Fenderson to have a look at earlier; the text seemed to suggest some kind of weird superhero/sci-fi hybrid. The words meant nothing to Fenderson but the artwork was striking, proving that his initial impression, based on just the first panel, had been accurate. Alcott was damn good. Certainly good enough to illustrate his proposal. And beyond that, who gave a rat's ass? Once he had his novel sold, the publisher could sign Alcott up or replace her with whomever they liked.

"Yeah. I think you're my illustrator," Fenderson said.

Alcott took her artwork back and returned it to her portfolio. "Wonderful."

He thought she'd be excited, but she almost looked more sad than happy.

"Now, about what I can pay you . . ." he started to say.

But Alcott cut him off: "I know. It won't be much. I'm just a beginner and you're a real pro. I'm sure whatever you offer me will be more than fair."

Fenderson couldn't believe it. This had to be fate, the Big Break he'd been waiting all his life to get. There was no other explanation for how easily it was all falling into place. He would have felt better if the fog lifted and he could remember something, *anything*, about this frumpy broad from her time as a student in his classroom, just so he'd have a frame of reference as he continued to play her for the fool he was counting on her to be. But what he knew about her now was enough, at least for the moment: she was talented, hungry, and willing to work with him at any cost.

"Cheers," Fenderson said, lifting his beer mug.

"Cheers," Alcott replied, tapping it with her water glass. And now the smile that stretched across her face seemed to hold no hidden meaning at all; it was just the smile of a lady on the brink of having her greatest dream come true.

"Ken Fenderson. Wow," she said. "Do you know how long I've been hoping to run into you again?"

Fenderson couldn't remember much of anything after that. He ordered another beer, went to the bathroom, they finished their meals and asked for the check.

Then, boom, the next thing he knew, he was in Alcott's apartment, or what he assumed was her apartment. Between the dim lighting and the excruciating pain he was in, it was hard to be sure where he was.

As near as he could tell, he was sprawled facedown across her bed, naked, hands and feet hog-tied to the frame like somebody about to be drawn and quartered. His mouth had a sock or something stuffed into it and his head was pounding so hard every blink of his eyes came at a price. He tried to scream, yanking at his bonds with the fury of a rodeo steer trapped in the gate, but the gag swallowed up his voice like a sponge. All his muffled cries managed to do was draw Alcott over from another room.

"Ah. Finally awake," she said, peering down at him.

She was wearing nothing but a bra and panties, both simple and white, without a hint of decorative lace. The sight should have disgusted Fenderson, even in the relative dark, but to his utter amazement, he found himself aroused by it. Rather than the shapeless blob her dowdy clothes had promised, Alcott's body was full and curvaceous, a balanced blend of generous bosom and wide hips.

"I know what you're thinking," she said. "This isn't the body you were expecting. I don't dress to impress the way I once did, do I? Or do you still not really remember me, even without my clothes?"

She was crazy. Fenderson had no idea what she was talking about. Why the hell should he remember what Alcott looked like without—

Oh, Jesus.

Jennifer Alcott. *That* Jennifer Alcott. One of several female students he'd had the hots for during his teaching days, and one of the few he'd taken to his bed. Some willingly, some not so willingly. Every woman was different. Alcott had been one of those who needed a little chemical push.

As the memory of that night finally came into focus, the mystery of how Alcott had managed to get him here today, in this place and in this unenviable position, without any conscious cooperation on his part that he could recall, was all too easily solved. No wonder he had a splitting headache. She must have slipped the drug into his beer while he'd been in the bathroom.

Now Fenderson was afraid. Really afraid.

He tried screaming again.

"Screaming's good," Alcott said. "I screamed a lot after you did what you did to me. I know. I hated myself almost as much as I did you, so I let my appearance go to shit and screamed when I needed to scream. Screaming makes you feel better." She leaned in close to whisper in his ear: "But it doesn't really change anything."

Blinking back tears, Fenderson became vaguely aware that the room around them was awash in black-and-white comic book art, taped to a huge drawing board and pinned in overlapping layers to the surface of every wall. With flickering candlelight his only guide, straining his neck as he was to see anything beyond the mattress to which he was tied, it was hard for Fenderson to be sure, but none of the drawings in the room looked anything like the one Alcott had shown him earlier. This artwork was crude and listless, devoid of all the power the page he'd seen at the café exhibited.

Alcott followed his gaze. "Angry, isn't it? That's what everyone always says about my stuff. Aside from that it's not very good. I'm a better inker than an illustrator. They say I've got a real talent for inking." She pulled some rubber gloves onto her hands and rolled a tea cart over to the bed near Fenderson's head where he could get a good look at the macabre collection of sex toys—oversized, heavily studded dildos, mostly—that was arranged upon it.

"The page I showed you at the El Cortez, by the way? That really was Jack Kirby," Alcott said. "I bought it at the Con just before I ran into you."

And with that, she picked up one of the phalluses—a giant chrome number lined all around with sharp little barbs—and proceeded to show Ken Fenderson a whole new perspective on the crime most commonly referred to as "date rape."

Fenderson was never heard from again. Nobody cared enough about him to really notice he was gone. Alcott took her own life shortly thereafter.

I bought the four pages of art you see here from her sister, who inherited her meager possessions and told me the story I've just shared with you to explain my otherwise inexplicable fascination with them. She said her sister mixed something into the ink she used that gives the artwork that strange, ethereal glow. She didn't say what that something was, but her inference was pretty clear. I don't know if I believe any part of her story or not.

Someday, either I myself or a future buyer—you, maybe?—will have a DNA test run to find out for sure what these pages are really worth.

THE NATIONAL CITY REPARATION SOCIETY

BY LUIS ALBERTO URREA

National City

It wasn't like Junior Garcia only hung with white people now. But he didn't see much Raza, he'd be the first to admit. Not socially. That's why you leave home, right? Shake off the dark.

As soon as he picked up the clamoring cell phone, he had that old traditional homecoming feeling: why'd I answer this? He didn't recognize the number—some old So Cal digits. He stared at the screen as if it would offer him further clues.

When he answered, an accented voice said: "Hey, bitch."

"Excuse me?"

"Said: Hey. Bitch. You deaf, homes?"

"You must have the wrong number," Junior said, about to click off. *Homes*, he said to himself. *What is this, 1986?*

"Junior!" the guy shouted. He used the old, hectoring fake-beaner accent the vatos had affected when mocking him in school: Yoo-nyurr! "I bet you got some emo shit for a ringtone. Right? Like 'The Black Parade,' some shit like that." The guy laughed.

"I've been talking to you for, like, almost a whole minute, and you already insulted me. I don't even know who you are." His ringtone was Nine Inch Nails, thank you very much. Emo? Shit. "I'm out, *homes*."

He clicked off and pulled on his Pumas. Got his jog on along the beach. It was one of those rare sunny days, and everybody was out, looking in their Lycra and spandex like a vast, roving fruit salad. He tucked the celly in his shorts pocket. Who's the bitch now? he wanted to know.

His nemesis caught him again as he was cooling off, jogging in place beside a picnic table, breathing through his nose, pouring good clean sweat down his back—he could feel it tickling the backs of his legs. *"You let me penetrate you,"* his phone announced. *"You let me penetrate you."*

"You again?" Junior said.

"It's me. Damn!"

"Me, who?"

"Chango!"

Junior wiped his face with the little white towel he had wrapped around his neck. "I should have known."

"That's what I'm sayin'."

"Fucking Chango."

"Right?"

Junior could hear him smoking—he still must like those cheap-ass Domino ciggies from TJ. They crackled like burning brush when the guy inhaled. "Why you calling me, Chango?"

"What—a homeboy can't check on his li'l peewee once in a while? I like to make sure my boyz is okay."

"I haven't talked to you in ten years," Junior said. He sat on the table and lay back and watched the undersides of gulls as they hung up there like kites.

"So?" said Chango. "You think you're better than us now, college boy?"

Apparently, the 1,000-mile buffer zone was not enough barrier between himself and the old homestead.

"Nice talking to you, Chango. Be sure to have someone send me an invitation to your funeral. So long. Have a nice day."

"Hey, asshole," Chango said. "I'm gonna live forever. Gonna be rich too. I'm workin' on a plan—cannot fail. You gon' want some of this here."

"A plan?" Junior said.

And when he said it, he felt the trap snap shut over him and he couldn't quite figure out how or why he was caught.

It was a short flight. Lindbergh was clotted with GIs in desert camo and weepy gals waving little plastic American flags. Junior caught the rental car shuttle and grabbed a Kia at Alamo. No, he wasn't planning to take it across the border. Put it on the Visa, thanks. Oh, well—the homies were going to give him shit about the car. It would be badass if they rented '67 Impalas with hydraulic lifters so he could enter the barrio with his right front tire raised in the air like some kind of saluting robot. He didn't smile—he was already thinking like Chango! He poked at the radio till he found 91X and the Mighty Oz was cranking some Depeche Mode. At least there was that.

On his way south, he hopped off on Sports Arena, but Tower Records was gone. What? He pulled a U and tried again, as if he'd somehow missed the store. Gone? How could it be gone? Screw that—he sped to Washington and went up to Hillcrest and looked for Off the Record. He was in the mood for some import CDs. Keep his veneer of sanity. It was gone too. Junior sat there in the parking lot where the Hillcrest Bowl used to be. He could not believe it—all culture had vanished from San Diego. His phone said, *"You let me penetrate you."* Chango. Junior didn't answer.

He'd only come to check it out. It was a crazy adventure, he told himself. Good for a laugh. Chango had picked up a magazine in a dentist's office. New dentures: our tax dollars at work. He thought it was a *Nat Geo*, but he wasn't sure. Some gabacho had written an article about abandoned homes along the I-15 corridor. Repos. Something like six out of ten, maybe seven out of fifteen or something like that. Point was, they were just sitting there, like haunted houses, like the whole highway was a long ghost town, and the writer had broken in to look around and found all kinds of stuff just laying around. Sure, sad shit like kids' homework on the kitchen table. But it's on a kitchen table, you catch my drift, Chango demanded. There's whole houses full of furniture and mink coats and plasma TVs and freakin' Bose stereos. La-Z-Boys! Hells yeah! Some have cars in the garages. And it's all foreclosed and owned by some bank. But the kicker—the kicker, Yuniorr—is that the banks can't afford to resell this stuff, so they send trucks to the houses to haul it to the dump. Friggin' illegals driving trucks just drag it all out and go toss it. A million bucks worth of primo swag.

"You tell me, how many freakin' apartments gots big-screen TVs that them boys just hauled home? You been to the swap meet?" And Chango had noted, in his profound research (he stole the magazine from the dentist's) that the meltdown had banks backed up. Some of these houses wouldn't be purged for a year or more.

"Ain't even stealin', peewee. Nobody wants it anyway. Worst case is breaking-and-entering. So I got this plan and I'm gonna make us a million dollars in a couple of months. But I need you to help."

"Why me?"

"You know how to talk white. Shit! Why'd you think?"

Junior motored down I-5 and dropped out at National City. He was loving the tired face of America's Finest City—San Diego was a'ight, but National was still the bomb. The Bay Theater, where he used to see Elvis revivals and Mexican triple-features. He'd kissed a few locas up there in the back rows. He smiled. He checked the old Mile of Cars—they used to call it the Mile of Scars, because sometimes Shelltown or Del Sol dudes would catch them out there at night and fists would fly between the car lots. That was before everybody got all gatted up and brought the 9s along. Junior shook his head; he would have never imagined that fistfights and fear would come to seem nostalgic.

He drove into the old hood, heading for West 20th and

Chango's odd crib over the hump and hiding behind the barrio on the little slope to the old slaughterhouse estuaries. He wanted to see his old church, maybe light a candle. He didn't mean to go bad in his life. He didn't mean to go so far away and not come back, either. Or maybe he did. St. Anthony's. America's prettiest little Catholic church. He smiled. They'd sneak out of catechism and go down behind the elementary school and play baseball on the edge of the swamp. There was a flat cat carcass they used for home plate.

He turned the corner and beheld an empty lot surrounded by a low chain-link fence. He slammed on the brakes. It was gone, like Tower Records. Things seemed to be vanishing as if all of San Diego County were being abducted by aliens.

He jumped out of his car and beheld a man watering his lawn, surrounded by a platoon of pug dogs.

"Where's the church?" he called.

"Church? Burned down! Where you been?"

"What! When?"

"Long time, long time. Say, ain't you that Garcia boy?"

"Not me," said Junior, getting back in the car.

He drove past his old house. Man, it sure was tiny. Looked like all his old man's gardens were dead. He didn't want to look at it. It had a faded *For Sale* sign stuck in the black iron fence.

The barrio had a Burger King in it, and a Tijuana Trolley stop. Damn. All kinds of Mexican nationals sat around on the cement benches savoring their Quata Poundas among squiggles of graffiti. Junior shook his head.

He dropped into the ancient little underpass and popped out on the west side of I-5 and hung a left and went to the end of the earth and hung another left and dropped down the small slope toward the black water and there it was. Chango's house. His dad's old, forgotten Esso station. Out of business since 1964. Chango lived in the triangular office. He'd pasted butcher paper over the glass and had put an Obama poster on the front, with some Sharpie redesigns so that it now said: CHANGO YOU CAN BELIEVE IN.

He'd given the prez a droopy pachuco mustache and some tiny, irritating homeboy sunglasses—Junior knew that Chango, ever the classicisist, would still call the glasses *gafas*. He knocked on the glass until Chango woke up from his nap.

"Car's for shit," Chango noted as Junior drove.

"Where we going?" Junior said.

"You remember the Elbow Room? That's where we're goin'. Down behind there. Hey, the radio sucks, ese. What's this? You should be listening to oldies."

Junior punched the OFF button.

"Damn," Chango muttered. "Shit." He looked like a greasy old crow. All wizened and craggy, all gray and lonesome. His big new teeth were white and looked like they were made out of slivers of oven-safe bake wear. His fingers were yellow from decades of Mexican cigarettes. "For reals," he was saying. It was apparently a long-standing conversation he had with himself. His various jail tattoos were purple and blurry and could have been dice rolling snake eyes and maybe a skeleton with a sombrero and on the other forearm an out-of-focus obscenity. He had that trustworthy little vato loco cross tattooed in the meat between his thumb and forefinger. "Tha's right, you know it," he added.

He'd shown Junior the article. It was by Charles Bowden, and did, indeed, confess to uninvited recon sorties into the creepy abandoned homes. One found these places by looking for overgrown yellow lawns and a sepulchral silence.

"This guy's a great writer," Junior said. "I can't believe you read him."

"Who?" Chango replied.

"This guy—the writer."

"I was mostly lookin' at the pictures, homie. That's what caught my eye."

They pulled around the old block where everybody used to go to drink at the Elbow Room, except for Junior who was too young to get in. They rattled around into a dirt alley and Chango directed him to stop at the double-door of a garage. They could hear Thee Midnighters blasting out.

"That's some real music, boy," Chango said, and creaked out of his seat, though he managed to sway pretty good once he got erect, swaggering like an arthritic pimp.

Inside, a Mongol associate of Chango's had dolled up a stolen U-Haul panel truck. He wore his vest and scared Junior to death, though lots of vatos liked the Mongols because they were the only Chicano bikers around.

"Sup?" the Mongol said.

"Sup?" nodded Junior.

"Sup?" said Chango.

"Hangin'," said the Mongol.

There was a time when Junior would have written a poem about this interaction and turned it in for an easy A in his writing workshop. *Oh, Junior, you're so street, as it were.*

The van was sweet, he had to admit. It was painted white. It had a passable American eagle on each side, clutching a sheaf of arrows and a bundle of dollars in its claws. Above it: *BOWDEN FEDERAL* and some meaningless numbers in smaller script. Below it: *Reclamation and Reparation/Morgage Default Division.*

"You misspelled *mortgage*," Junior said.

They gawked.

"So what?" Chango said. "Cops can't spell."

"The plates are from Detroit," the Mongol pointed out. "An associate UPS'd 'em to me yesterday." He turned to Chango. "Your sedan is out back."

Chango bumped fists with him.

"Remember, I want a fifty-inch flat screen."

"Gotcha."

"And any fancy jewelry and coats for my old lady."

"Gotcha, gotcha."

"And any stash you find."

"You get the chiba, I got it. But I'm drinkin' all the tequila I find."

Chango, in his element.

Junior had to admit, it was so stupid it was brilliant. It was just like acting. He had learned this in his drama workshop. You sold it by having complete belief. You inhabited the role and the viewers were destined to believe it, because who would be crazy enough to make up such elaborate lies?

He followed the truck up I-15. It was a sweet Buick with stolen Orange County plates. Black, of course. He wore a Sears suit and a striped tie. His name tag read: *Mr. Petrucci*.

"Here's the play. We move shit—we're beaners," Chango explained. "Ain't nobody gonna even look at us. You're the boss. You're Italian. As long as you got a suit and talk white, ain't nobody lookin' at you, neither."

To compound the play—to sell the illusion, his college self whispered—he had a clipboard with bogus paperwork, state tax forms they had picked up at the post office.

Three guys in white jumpsuits bobbed along in the cab of the truck—Chango, a homeboy named Hugo, and the driver— Juan Llaves. Hugo was a furniture deliveryman, so he knew how to get heavy things into a truck. They banged north, dropping out of San Diego's brown cloud of exhaust and into some nasty desert burnscape. They took an exit more or less at random and pulled down several mid-Tuesday-morning suburban streets—all sparsely planted with a palm here, and oleander there. Plastic jungle gyms in yellow yards, hysterical dogs appalled by the truck, abandoned bikes beside flat cement front porches. Juan Llaves pulled into the driveway of a fat faux-Georgian, half obscured by weeds and dry grass and looking as dead as a buffalo skull.

Junior took his clipboard in hand and joined Chango on the lawn.

"This is it, Mr. Petrucci!" Chango emoted. Junior checked his papers and nodded wisely. Nobody even looked out of the neighboring houses. It was silent. "I can't believe we're doing this shit," Chango muttered with a vast porcelain grin.

They tried the front door. Locked. Chango strolled around back. Some clanging and banging, and in a minute the front door clicked and swung open.

"Electric's off. Hot as hell in here. Fridge stinks."

The associates went inside.

The bank notices were there on the kitchen table. Somebody had abandoned a pile of DVDs on the carpet. "Oh yeah!" Chango hooted. *The Godfather!*"

Llaves and Hugo hauled the table and chairs out to the truck. Plasma TV in the living room; flat screen in the bedroom. Black panties on the floor looking overwhelmingly sad to Junior. Chango put them in his pocket. "Chango's in love," he told Junior.

In the closet, most of the clothes were gone, but a single marine uniform hung at the back. They took the TVs, a rent-to-own stereo system with about fifty-seven CDs, mostly funk and hip hop. Chango found a box of *Hustlers* and a Glock .40 that had fallen behind the box. For the hell of it, they took the dresser and the bunk beds from the kids' room.

In the garage, there was a Toro lawn mower and, oddly, a snowblower. They took it all. As they were leaving, Chango trotted back into the house and came out with a blender under his arm.

In and out in less than three hours. They were home for a late supper. The stuff went into the garage.

Wednesday: three TVs, a tall iPod dock, a long couch painting, a washer and dryer, a new king-size bed still in plastic wrappers, whiskey and rum, a minibike, and a set of skis.

Thursday: a Navy peacoat, a mink stole (fake), six rings, another TV, another bed, a recliner chair and matching couch in white leather, a shotgun and an ammo loading dock, a video porn collection, a framed swirl of blue tropical butterflies, golf clubs, a happening set of red cowboy boots.

Friday: aside from the usual swag—how sick were they of TV sets by now—they found an abandoned Mustang GT in the garage. Covered in dust, but sleek black. Chango wiped that baby down and Llaves hotwired it for him and he drove back to San Diego in style.

It was a massive crime wave, and the only witnesses so far had been two kids and an ice-cream man, and the ice-cream man had called, "Times are tough!" and Chango, into some Robin Hood hallucination, took him a thirty-two-inch flat screen and traded it for Sidewalk Sundaes for his gang.

After a month of this, after dealing the goods out to fences and setting up a tent at the flea market, Chango and Junior were rolling in it. They paid their associates a fair salary, but their folding money was in fat rolls held together by rubber bands. Chango had the old repair bay in his house converted to a gym. Nordic Trak, an elliptical, a Total Gym As Seen on TV, three sets of weights, and a shake-weight that nobody wanted to touch because it looked like they were wanking when they were ripping their biceps.

"You don't make this kind of money selling dope to college girls," Chango said.

"No," Junior confessed. "Not lately."

He hadn't planned on selling pot to anyone. He had hoped to teach a good Acting 101 class. Maybe write a script or some poems. And there was a gal . . . well, enough of that happy horseshit. He wasn't going there. Then he chided himself for thinking a cliché like "going there." No wonder he drank—it was the only way to shut his brain down. Fortunately, Chango had collected seven kinds of rum. Junior doctored his Coke Zero and lounged.

He had a cot in the corner of Chango's gas station. It was a little too close to Chango for comfort, and he had to put in his iPod buds to cancel out the old crow's snoring. But it was free, and the snacks and booze were good.

The Mustang sat out on the street. Junior kept telling Chango it would get him busted, that it was too visible. But Chango was invincible. Chango told him: "Live, peewee. Ya gotta live!" There was a tin shower rigged up in the restrooms. Junior's stolen iPod port was blasting "Can't You Hear Me Knocking."

"Stones suck," said Chango, swallowing tequila. "Except for Keith. Keith's ba-a-ad."

Junior was thinking about the old times, how when they'd gather at the bowling alley to play pinball, Chango would smoke those pestilential Dominos and force Junior to lose by putting the burning cherry on his knuckle every time he had to hit the bumpers.

"Fucker," he said.

"You got that right, homes."

"So, Chango—what's next?"

"We, um, steal a lot more shit."

"Shouldn't we cool it for a while? Let the heat die down?"

"Heat!" Chango shrieked. "Did you actually say 'heat'? Haw! 'Heat,' he says. GodDAMN." And then: "What heat?" He laughed out loud. "You seen one cop? We is invisible, homie. We just the trashman."

"I'm just being cautious," Junior said.

"I got it covered, peewee. Chango's got it all covered."

"Covered how?"

"Next stop," Chango announced, "Arizona! Don't nobody know us over there in 'Zoney!"

* * *

They should have never crossed the border. That's what Junior thought as he escaped. They didn't know anything about Arizona. Someone had seen them, he was pretty sure. It was probably at the motel outside of Phoenix. They'd probably been made there.

Whatever. It went bad right away. They drove around looking for abandoned houses, but in Arizona, how could you tell? All the yards were dirt, and the nice yards looked to them exactly like the bad yards. What was a weed and what was a xeriscape?

In Casa Grande, they felt like they were getting to it. A whole cul-de-sac had collected trash and a few tumbleweeds. Junior couldn't believe there were actual tumbleweeds out there. John Wayne–type stuff. They pulled in and actually rang the doorbells and got nothing. So Chango did his thing and went in the back and they were disappointed to find the first house completely vacant except for an abandoned Power Ranger action figure in a bedroom and a melted bar of Dial in a bathroom.

The second house was full of fleas and sad, broken-ass welfare crap. Chango found a bag of lime and chili tortilla chips, and he munched these as he made his way to the third, and last, house. He went in. Score!

"I love the recession!" he shouted.

They drained the waterbed with a hose through the bathroom window. Hey—a TV. These debt monsters really liked their giant screens. Massaging recliners. Mahogany tables and a big fiberglass saguaro cactus. "Arty," Chango said. Mirrors, clothes, a desktop computer and printer, a new microwave, two nice Dyson floor fans, a sectional couch in cowhide with brown and white color splotches. They even found a sewing machine.

It had taken too long, what with the long search and the three penetrations. After they loaded, pouring sweat except for "Mr. Petrucci," who sat in his AC so he'd look good in case any rubber neckers came along, it was four in the afternoon, and they were hitting rush hour on I-10.

The truck was a mile ahead. Junior liked to hang back and

make believe he was driving on holiday. No crime. He was head-ing cross-country, doing a Kerouac. He was going back down to National City to find La Minnie, his sweet li'l ruca from the Bay Theater days. He should have never let her go. He hadn't gone to a single high school reunion, but his homeboy El Rubio told him La Minnie had asked about him. Divorced, of course. Who in America was not divorced? But still slim and cute and fine as hell. Junior knew his life would have been different if he'd done the right thing and stayed on West 20th and courted that gal like she deserved, but he was hungry. Trapped like a wildcat in somebody's garage, and when the door cracked the slightest bit, he was gone.

These things were on his mind when the police lights and sirens went off behind him.

He had to give it to Chango—the guy played his string out right to the end.

The cops blasted past Junior's Buick and dogged the white U-Haul. Two cars. Llaves knew better than to try to run—the truck had a governor on the engine that kept it to a maximum speed of fifty-five. He puttered along, Junior back there shouting, "Shit! Shit! Shit!" Then he hit his blinker and slowly pulled over to the shoulder, the police cars insanely flashing and yowling. The associates were climbing out when Junior went by. He could see Chango's mouth already working.

He didn't know what to do. Should he keep going? Book and not look back?

He hit the next exit and crossed over the freeway and sped back and crossed over again and rolled up behind the cop cars. He set his tie and pulled on his jacket with its name tag and even picked up his clipboard.

There were two cops—one Anglo and one Hispanic.

The associates stood in a loose group against the side of the truck. The cops turned and stared at Junior.

"Officers," he called. "I am Mr. Petrucci, from Bowden Federal in Detroit. Is there a problem?"

"Petrucci," said the Hispanic. "Is that Italian?"

"It is," said Junior.

"This dude," Chango announced, "is some kinda Tío Taco!"

"Shut it," the cop snapped.

A Border Patrol truck pulled up behind the Buick.

"Sir?" said the cop. "I need to ask you to leave. You need to call your bank and have another team sent out to deliver these goods."

"Fuck!" shouted Chango.

"Is there a problem with . . . the load?" Junior asked.

"No sir. This is strictly a 1070 stop."

"1070?"

"SB 1070. Immigration. We have reason to believe these gennermen are illegals." The BP agent was eyeballing Chango.

Junior almost laughed. "Why, I never!" he said.

Chango called, "He don't know shit. Fuckin' Petrucci. He's just a bean counter. Never did a good day's work in his life! That asshole don't even know us." He was playing to the crowd. "I worked every day! I paid my taxes! I, I, I served in Iraq!" he lied.

The cop held up two licenses in his fingers, as if he were making a tight peace sign or about to smoke a cigarette. Llaves and Chango—Hugo didn't have a license.

"Do you have citizenship papers?" the BP man asked.

"I don't need no stinkin' papers! This is America!"

"Have they been searched?" BP asked.

"What are you, the Gestapo?" Chango smiled a little. He felt he had scored a major point. "I'm down and brown!" he hooted. "Racial profiling!"

"Not yet."

"I ain't being searched by nobody," Chango announced.

The BP man wagged his finger in Chango's face.

"I'll break that shit off and jam it up your ass," Chango hissed. "You think some wetback would say that?"

"We ran your license," the cop said. "Your address seems to be an abandoned gas station in San Diego."

The cops and the BP agent smirked at each other.

"Goddamned right I live in a gas station!" Chango bellowed. "My dad owned it!"

"Uh-huh." The cop turned to Junior. "I have to insist, Mr. Petrucci—you need to leave the scene. Now."

Junior stared at Chango and got into his Buick as the cops tossed the guys against the side of the panel truck and he saw, or thought he saw, just as he pulled into traffic, the Glock fall out of Chango's pocket and the cops draw and squat, shouting, and he hit the gas and was shaking with adrenaline or fear or both and didn't know what happened but he never slowed until he was in front of the old station. He was stiff and sore and scared out of his mind. He ran into Chango's bedroom and tore open his Dopp kit and took his roll of cash. He thought for a minute and went out, locked the door, and slipped into the GT. The wires sparked when he touched them and the big engine gave a deep growl and shout, the glasspacks sounding sweet, like coffee cans full of rocks. He was going to go. Going to go. Just get out. Break the ties once and for all. Never look back. He was in the wind. Junior rubbed his face three or four times. He revved the big engine and put his foot on the pedal and stared. Night. Streetlights shining through the palm trees made octopus shadows in the street. Junior rolled down the window. He could smell Burger King. Two old women walked arm in arm, speaking Spanish. He could hear a sitcom through the open window of a bungalow above Chango's station. Junior knew if he headed down toward the old Ducommun warehouse, he could find La Minnie's mom's house. It was funky twenty years ago. With its geraniums. Minnie could be there. Or her family could tell him where she was. She used to like a nice ride like this. Maybe she'd like to feel the wind in her hair. They could drive anywhere. He thought he could talk her into it, if he could find her. The way things had changed around town, the old house might not be there at all. Probably not. Probably gone with all the things he remembered and loved. But . . . he asked himself . . . what if it wasn't?

He shifted and moved steadily into the deeper dark.

A SCENT OF DEATH

BY MARIA LIMA

Gaslamp Quarter

It was an alley, just like all the other back-of-hotel alleys downtown. Nothing to distinguish it, especially after the Clean City initiative had turned most San Diego alleys into something that more resembled Vancouver. Not that this part of the city had been all too bad. The almighty tourist and convention dollar tended to keep things cleaner than, say, Chicago or Manhattan. Bonus for us, really.

After all, this was the back of the Leaf, one of the Ivy Tree chain, originally just one hotel, but now several boutique hostelries run for the sole purpose of pampering the wealthy. Everything at the scene reflected the Leaf's exclusivity, the green of the kitchen door matched by the swirling green leaves painted on the sides of the two dumpsters. The beige awning over the door was the same fine fabric and design as those facing the street view. No one came back here but delivery trucks, the city trash haulers and other similar workers. No matter, though, the Leaf kept up its branding behind the scenes too. This was a true sign of either class or just pure stinking rich.

Admittedly, the stench wasn't what I expected. I'd done my share of investigations in hotel alleys, and no matter how clean, they stank. Not here; like my native Vancouver, there was no real smell, unless you counted a light air of lavender and vanilla, the hotel's signature scent, distributed as hand lotion, soaps, shampoo, and conditioner. Only here in a place so uniquely itself that a receptacle for trash smelled like flowers, did this scene seem so incongruous. Disturbing anywhere, but even more so here.

Just one thing disrupted the relative peace and quiet in the depths of the four a.m. darkness. The thing that was the reason for all our lights, for a police photographer's flash snapping through the still night air, its strobe punctuating what I saw, the one thing that kept me there, even though every part of me wanted to be elsewhere.

One small hand, pale, fingers curled, clutching at a few leafy weeds poking through a tiny crack in the asphalt as if needing to hold on to the closest thing to earth it could reach in this sea of concrete and steel. Earth, living, growing things—the one avenue he could have had to safety. The tiny bedraggled weed hadn't been enough. Whatever had tracked him down and killed him had either known that, or taken its chances. Yeah, *its*. As in not human. Just like the most recent victim of what we were calling the Rentboy Ripper, though the MO had little resemblance to its predecessor. The only thing in common was the profession of the victims—children of the night, Licensed Professionals, once known as hookers, prostitutes. My victims were all of the profession older than human—all male, all fae, all in the Gaslamp. Which is why I was here.

Nothing like the hint of a serial fae killer to drop a spark in the very dry powder keg that was political relations between us and the human races. San Diego had always been a fairly easy, laid-back town. Tourists, convention-goers, Navy and civilian residents—all mingled with some semblance of polite disdain. I mean, for humans, the color of their skin or the weight of their bank accounts mattered very little nowadays. After all, until recently (as far as humans knew), every sentient being shared one thing: death. Or rather Death—the grim reaper who visited young, old, middle-aged alike, and no matter who you were, how much you were worth, eventually, the final score leveled everyone's playing field.

Not us. We didn't die like they did—do, would. Oh sure,

we could be killed, any living being can given enough effort, but we didn't just *die*. Old age? Yeah, well, my cousin had seen the turn of the millennium—the first one—and was still performing as a dancer at the Gaslamp Strip Club. Yeah, yeah, it used to be a steak joint, but a lot of things changed. Family restaurants became bars; steak joints with bars became stripper clubs—with a higher cover. And strip joints, well, let's just say that the Moral Majority didn't win this one. Can't say this happened all over the world, but it did in most of the sea and ocean ports and destination cities. Orlando? A heck of a new version of the Magic Kingdom. The one in Anaheim just got boarded up for lack of interest. I never really understood why. Maybe it's because I'm a halfling. Thanks to my promiscuous mother who, a whole lot of decades ago, had decided to relive her heyday, this time in Haight-Ashbury, I was the product of a Beltane ritual gone wonky. What Mama never knew was that she herself was a halfling. Wood nymph, most likely, I was never sure. She'd gotten herself killed in a nasty hit-and-run when I was twenty. I never learned which of the several men she'd banged on that particular Beltane had contributed his sperm to my making. He'd been full fae, no doubt about it. My own genetics proved that. But he could have been anyone. Never really worried me. Mama and her sister June raised me and I turned out okay. By the time humans knew of us, I'd been an adult for a lot of years and able to figure things out on my own . . . like why, when I touched certain objects, I knew their history. June was the only one who'd believed me when I was a kid. She'd died in a car accident just last year: drunk driver.

Some of us halflings were too human to make it in Faery; some too fae to make it in the human world. Me, I straddled the fence with the best of the undecideds. I could pass for either. Maybe that's why my nickname was Chameleon. When I'd joined the Bod Squad, a traveling investigative team made up of two humans, two fae, and two halflings, they named me right away—not Cam for Camilla (a name I'd been known to use), but Chameleon, since I could seem like exactly what was expected. In a difficult situation, I was a tough cop/dealer/criminal. In the middle of a ladies' church brunch, I looked like Mrs. Cleaver. Part and parcel of the package.

We operated outside the normal parameters of the law, but within the strict guidelines and treaties set down fifteen years ago. We were in charge of any suspicious deaths that might involve fae. Thus, being called in to work at three-bloody-a.m. on a night I was supposed to be off. Not that I'd been sleeping. I don't do much of that; it's part of my nature. What I had been doing is my partner—an extremely hot faery princess, who also happened to be assistant DA for the city of San Diego. Risa was nigh onto six feet, gorgeous, all golden skin, red hair, and green eyes. She'd been the subject of many a love letter, the golden child of the district attorney's office. Her conviction rate neared 90 percent, mostly because the crooks tended to fall in love with her at first site. Oh, it wasn't her fault, really. There was a touch of siren in her bloodline. They just couldn't help themselves: women, men, teenagers. I heard that she once got a marriage proposal from one of the sea kings. She never told me who. I was pretty sure it was Murrow, king of San Diego Bay and its surrounds.

"Fuck." I peered down at the boy's hand, the only thing not absolutely covered in blood and bits. "Damn, fuck, and shit." I loved cursing in modern-day English. It was so satisfying. I ran a hand over my hair, for a moment forgetting I'd cut it short and spiky. My persona tonight was that of tough woman detective. "Gloves," I snapped, holding a hand behind me as I squatted to get a better look.

"Problem?"

A hand slapped a pair of latex gloves into mine. I nodded as I pulled them on and leaned forward. "Jason, you got all this?"

"Got his head and shoulder, yep." The photographer kept snapping away as I tucked two fingers under the dead head, turning the face just enough to be sure. Damn it. I let his face down gently back onto the asphalt. "I know him," I said as I stood. "It's Donny." I pointed to the body's left. "Jason, make sure to get all angles on his hand, okay?"

"Why his hand?" Abe Abrams, detective with F unit and longtime acquaintance, bent over at the waist to get a closer look. I winced at his inability to squat. "Cam, the hand?"

For a moment, I wondered why he was asking, then I remembered. He was human. He didn't know.

"Donny just got licensed," I explained. "He should have a tat right there." I pointed with my pencil to the bare left wrist. "That blank spot shouldn't be blank."

"You sure about that?" Abe grunted, and with obvious effort, kneeled down. He played his flashlight beam over the dead boy's wrist. "There's no sign of the tat. Don't those last for the full ninety days?"

"Positive," I said. "I inspected his group not four days ago and verified the markings. Donny and his crew were supposed to be working here at the Leaf through the end of the month. Then they were supposed to rotate to the other Ivy Tree hotels through their probation."

Abe shrugged. "Maybe a john treated him to dinner . . . then—"

"What?" I spit out. "Then got his jollies in the alley behind the hotel before he killed Donny? Why bother? Have you been inside this hotel? They practically fall over themselves to give guests what they want, up to and including a blowjob if necessary. The Pros stationed here are the finest of the fine. Donny—Donal—was the best in his training group. Why would anyone want him dead? It's not as if prostitution is illegal."

"Money? What if it wasn't a john? He could've been mugged."

"A client," I corrected him. "Clients here spend more money in a day than any Pro could make in a month. That, plus Donny's tat wasn't removable by just anyone."

"Magic?"

"Yeah, fae magic and fae markings. Only removable by some-one with the appropriate training and with fae blood."

I flipped on my flashlight and pointed it down Donny's body, along the mangled back, the shattered leg bones, and then across the once pristine alley. "Blood trail's over there," I said. "Uphill." That could only mean one thing. Fae. Blood followed fae like rats followed garbage. Instead of flowing into the very convenient drain just south of what was left of Donny's once beautiful head, the boy's blood flowed up a slight incline, slightly north and west of his body. "Abe, I'm going to follow this," I muttered. "Blood's following fae here. Just another nail in someone's upcoming cof-fin." My stomach tightened at the thought of fae killing fae in this brutal way. Despite our abilities, our talents, there were so few of us. The days of the wars were long over. I wanted to catch this bastard, have whoever did this answer to fae justice.

Abe ignored me. He was a good guy, but just a smidge too close to retirement to want to be out here, working what could be a serial murder case—and worse, involving a fae Licensed Professional Worker, a protected class. Abe and I had both started in the department around the same time: him a fresh-faced de-tective out of the Central Division; me transferred in from fae relations up near the Mesa. I'd hated the PR gig—with a passion born of a million fiery suns and the anger of a true fae warrior. Making nice with human assholes, just because I was public af-fairs? Yeah, no. Not a job for me. I'd lasted all of a year before I nearly decapitated one annoying lout who'd had the balls to call me a whore. It didn't matter that our sexual practices weren't the same as human ones; since we most often tended to look like them, they wanted us to *be* like them. We were as similar as a goat is to a GTO. I'd barely restrained myself, packed up my things, and told my then supervisor I was leaving. Three weeks later, I found myself filling out the job application for a San Diego city cop. They hadn't accepted my application, but after negotiations I was brought on board as a special unit consultant and part of the Bod Squad, a.k.a. Risa threw a hissy and someone jumped.

I dropped to a crouch, peering down the flashlight beam. The blood trail faded, but a few drops were still evident. A low chime from my watch made me glance at the time. Damn. Soon, the early worker bees for the restaurants and hotels would begin to arrive. We were smack in the middle of tourist central, near the convention center, pretty much in the middle of the Gaslamp. I didn't know what ginormous gathering was in town this week—Comic-Con was over, but we were entering fall convention season. I hadn't paid attention to the info sheet at the station. We were supposed to have this data, but I figured anything I could look up on my phone was something that didn't need to clutter my memory. I stopped, sniffing the air as something pinged my awareness. Nothing on the ground. I turned my head and sniffed again. There, to the right. I pointed my light back behind a big gray trash barrel, this one marked with a stencil identifying itself as property of the Ivy Branch, a bar adjacent to the Leaf.

A small hole, no bigger than a rat, shone with a slick of blood on its edges. No rat caused that blood to end up there. Scent was pure fae. Pure Donny. Poor kid had been so excited about his placement too. The Leaf was so prestigious, its concierge known for excellent matches. Rarely did a Pro ask for reassignment from here. This was an amazing place for someone as new as Donny, but his beauty and abilities had catapulted him to the top of the list, so when the concierge asked to supplement their complement of Pros, Donal ap Dylan had been one of the lucky few. Now, he'd be just another stat, another murder. San Diego had just doubled last year's murder rate for the Gaslamp—only two last year. Now, with Donny's death, we were up to four. Three dead Workers added to a fairly standard drunk-and-disorderly-turned-knife-fight from earlier in the year and it wasn't even September.

Sure, humans didn't understand how anyone could want to

be a prostitute, a Licensed Professional Worker, but for those fae with enhanced sexual abilities, it was a way to earn a living legally and still keep their emotions and magic in balance. When we'd revealed ourselves, thanks to an accidental discovery in Roswell that led to one of those ridiculous alien autopsy videos, we'd weighed the odds. Thousands of us versus billions of humans. Our power, life spans, and sheer chutzpah won out. We didn't want to be caught up in another Area 51 debacle, nor run the risk of technology catching up to our abilities. It was time to make ourselves known, so we did. All at once, all over the world. Unlike stories of other supernatural species who've had to lay low and do this slowly, once all the fae clans were in agreement, it was as easy as putting the memories and knowledge into every human's head as they slept. Within twenty-four hours, it was as if we'd always been there. Because we had—that shadow in the barn that didn't belong; the scurrying feet in the attic; the face of the woman in the lake—not that I'd go so far as an arm in white samite, but still, a lot of those "edges of the eye," seeings were us. All of us, in all our various forms.

Sure, there were several years of bickering and politicking between the groups, but overall we'd just been granted citizenship for wherever we lived. A few countries weren't as simple, so many of those fae just applied for sanctuary and asylum status in more liberal lands. Canada got a great influx, as did the U.S. All either of those countries wanted to know was that we were able to gainfully support ourselves. Most of us could, in fact, most of us had been doing just that. After things settled, many of the fae leaders simply started taking over certain professions, such as prostitution. They cleaned it up, managed to get a bunch of laws passed, and now, in all states except Utah, prostitution was legal and limited to LPWs—who were all of fae blood. This sat a lot better with the various church groups; after all, we weren't *quite* like them. Unfortunately, now I was facing this case and someone who was tearing up young-looking male LPWs.

A flash of headlights signaled the arrival of the official crime scene techs. I nodded to the lead, a sprite who'd taken the unlikely name of Lavender Gray when he realized no human could pronounce his real name. "He's one of ours, Lav," I said.

A grunt was the only acknowledgment I got. The techs scurried through the alley in silence, placing markers, picking up near invisible bits and pieces, sealing up evidence bags. Abe and I watched just as silently. Jason trailed behind the team, snapping more photos whenever a technician pointed.

"You think we're going to—"

"Yes," I cut off Abe's words. "We're going to catch this killer." I had no intention of letting Abe voice my own unspoken doubts. So far, the trace evidence in each case had been so minuscule, so vague as to implicate pretty much anyone—with or without a motive. In the previous two cases, we'd interviewed the victims' clients, their team leaders, hotel managers, concierges. Abe had worked all his contacts at hotels, the navy, anyone who'd ever owed him a favor. Still nothing. So far, the only clues we had were that they were all males, all LPWs, and all looked very young. None of them were actually young, not in human terms—Donny had been at least a hundred—but young in fae terms. The other two victims had been in the middle of their second century. Two victims were blond, one a redhead. All had gray eyes. All had both human and fae clientele. Nothing in the victims' backgrounds indicated anything sleazy, drug-related, or any other criminal behavior. I was at a total loss. The usual motives didn't seem to apply. Jealousy? Perhaps, but there was no client common to the three of them. Money? Not a factor in Donny's case, he was only a beginner, making scale. The first victim had just completed his apprenticeship, but his new grade wasn't anywhere near the kind of money people usually killed for. The second victim's rate was average for a seasoned apprentice. Nothing seemed to fit. The only thing they had in common was their current choice of profession and their sex—traits shared by hundreds. (At last count, San Diego County licensed 210 male LPWs, 212 female, and just under 100 intersex.) Each had been beautiful, male, and perfectly turned out, skin soft with lotion, nails of feet and hands meticulously manicured. All three of them worked the Gaslamp, but so did many others.

What was so special, so unusual about these three that triggered their killer's attention?

"They're done," Abe's voice interrupted my thoughts.

The techs were climbing into their van and Jason was packing up his equipment. A coroner's representative loaded Donny, discreetly wrapped in a body bag and gurney, into his van. I blinked and yawned. "I'm going home." A quick cuddle with Risa followed by a few hours of sleep sounded perfect to me. "Lab at noon?" I asked Abe. "Then we can come back and talk to the staff." Beat cops had already handled the initial questions, but now it would be our turn.

"One," he replied. "I'm doing lunch with Leah."

I smiled. "Tell her hi for me." Abe's daughter was visiting from grad school.

"Yeah," he said. "Will do."

I watched as he trudged to his car, every month of his nearly twenty years of service evident in the weary posture. I knew he resented me sometimes. He'd aged, and not too gracefully, muscles losing tone, eyesight deteriorating. He'd never been a poster boy for *Sports Illustrated*, but Abe had kept fairly fit. Now, after two knee operations, he could barely make it around the block without pain. When we'd pull cases together, I saw the looks he gave me. How could I not? I appeared to be in my mid-twenties. My hair still as glossy brown (or black or red) as it had ever been, my eyes keener than his ever were. He thought we were around the same age, fifty-five going on fifty-six. I'd never told him he could be my grandson. It would have killed whatever was left of his self-esteem.

My stomach growled reminding me I hadn't eaten today.

I checked my watch again. Too early for breakfast at Richard Walker's, damnit. Sleep called, but hunger's voice outspoke it right now. Maybe I could cajole Risa into rising early and making me something to eat. For while she was a powerful fae, equally powerful at her job, at home she loved to play at domesticity. I knew it was a phase, but hell, right now it worked for me. I hated domestic activities. My nature lent itself more to fighting and physical strength. Risa was probably as good a fighter as I was, but she loved to cook. I took a deep breath, the lavender scent filling my nostrils. Damn, that stuff lingered. I looked around at the scene, no longer clean, but that would be handled by morning. The brownie city services would take care of that. Another yawn and a stretch. That was it. Time to go home.

No sooner than I'd made up my mind, I heard a squeak of door hinges. The green door creaked open, an eye peering out through the crack. I stared at it for a beat, then two.

"You coming out?" I asked.

Another beat and the door slowly opened to reveal a man of medium height, nattily attired in an expensive gray suit, perfectly complemented by a matching silk tie in varying shades of gray, a meticulously folded square of silk tucked into the breast pocket. I did a quick calculation. Newish suit, worn by someone who knows how to dress. Spent more on the suit than my monthly pay. A glance down confirmed the rest. Italian loafers, shined to perfection. Hotel manager, probably.

"Mister . . . ?" I ventured forward, my hand outstretched, senses poised to gather as much intel as I could with the incipient shake.

"Maggiano." The man offered me a brusque bow. "Forgive me," he said, remaining where he stood. "Ahem . . ." He motioned to the alleyway behind me, never closing the distance between us. "You are done here?"

I let my hand drop and stepped back, reassuming the mantle of officer of the law, even though, technically, I wasn't. "We're finished. You the manager?"

He nodded, an absent gesture. His attention was entirely taken up by the surroundings.

Humans, I thought. So nervous around death.

Maggiano finished his study of the alley and returned his attention to me. "Do you know what happened?"

"Other than the brutal death of a protected Licensed Worker?" I asked, giving the sarcasm free rein. "That's pretty much it."

He started, his surprise quickly masked by the standard obsequious hotel manager mien—bland, professional. He placed his right hand on his breast, again giving the short head bow. A flash of gold caught my eye. A Patek Philippe added another few thousand to the overall cost of his ensemble. I knew the Leaf must pay well, but if this was the kind of clothing and jewelry afforded by the manager, I was in the wrong business. Hell, all a person needed to manage a hotel like this was the ability to tolerate the vagaries of the wealthy, both human and fae, and be able to provide whatever amusement they required. That I had in spades. After all, I played PR flunky for nearly twenty years at Mesa division, this would be cake. It was a thought.

I realized I needed to question the man since he was already here. I'd hoped to freshen up a little before doing my bit, but what the hell? I never looked a gift opportunity in the mouth.

"Mr. Maggiano," I said, adopting my most pleasant PR-type voice. "If you could spare me a few moments?" I motioned toward the door, indicating we should step inside.

An hour later, I wished I'd just gone home when Abe did. It was as if I'd opened a dam.

"I've worked with them for years. And nothing like this . . ." He shuddered, a delicate move in harmony with his natty appearance. I suppressed the desire to roll my eyes and sigh. He'd been saying pretty much the same thing for the past sixty minutes. My instinct was to let him ramble, let him keep talking. Sometimes, we caught the bad guys by just letting them ramble. In this case, I was getting nowhere fast. Just talking in circles about how much

he respected the Pros, how the hotel business would suffer, etc.,
etc. Ad nauseum. With every gesture of his hand, the gold flash
of his watch reminded me how ridiculous it all seemed. This im-
peccably dressed man, smelling of the same signature scents as the
air around him, so rattled he'd lost all composure.

I slid a little forward in my seat, a comfortable leather armchair in an elegant cream color, the standard leaf image twining
up the wooden legs, stamped into the back. I needed to stop this
inane chatter and get the hell out of here. My nostrils were clogging up, the lavender permeated everything. I realized that it was
just my own reaction; humans and many fae would barely even
notice, but I'd been here so long, my sense of touch so sensitive,
that even the air molecules irritated me. I noticed that Maggiano
kept a bottle of the hand lotion on his desk.

A buzzing vibration at my hip interrupted my attempt to
stop Maggiano's overshare. Nonetheless, he stopped talking as
I pulled the phone from my pocket. The text was short. *Traces
of vanilla & lavender oils—skin, hair, lungs. Suffocated b4 wounds.*
The message came from one of my buddies at the crime lab. I
quickly sent my own text, this one to Abe.

Glad for the fae funds that had kick-started a supreme effort
to fund crime labs, I turned to Maggiano with a smile, now rec-
ognizing something my tired brain had overlooked.

"Apologies, Mr. Maggiano," I said. "Work."

He gave me a small smile. "I understand."

I returned his smile with one of my own, employing my best
trust me vibe. "I'm afraid the circumstances prevented me from
paying you a compliment, Mr. Maggiano."

He looked puzzled but didn't say anything.

"The hotel," I said, nodding toward the other part of the
lobby area. "So beautiful. A lovely setting."

Maggiano preened. "We do our best, detective. Our patrons
enjoy the finer things."

"Of course." I leaned forward a little, as if to invite his confidence. "That lovely scent," I said, and drew in a big breath, allowing a look of pleasure on my face.

"Yes?" Maggiano beamed. "It is delicious, is it not?"

"Indeed. Is it possible . . ." I dropped my voice to just above a whisper. "Would it be possible for you to share the secret of the scent?" I leaned closer, preparing myself.

He swallowed hard and began to shake a little.

"He was a good boy," Maggiano said in a quiet voice. "They all are. Such good boys to have such horrible—" His voice broke as he stifled a sob.

"You knew him?"

"All of them," he said. "This last one, Donal, had just begun here at the Leaf. Until last month, I was concierge at the Ivy Branch. When I got promoted to the Leaf as manager, I would see some of the other regulars on occasion at the bar."

"But you didn't see or hear anything out of the ordinary?"

He shook his head again. "Not a thing, detective. I wish I could've stopped . . ." He sighed and wiped his brow. "I'm sorry. This is just so terrible. If there's nothing else, might I return to the day's business?" Another flash of gold, the Patek Philippe shining in the light. "They were all good boys, if only . . ."

I nodded. "Sure, that's fine, Mr. Maggiano." I dug out a card and presented it to him. "If you think of anything, please don't hesitate to call."

He took the card and tucked it into his jacket pocket, the silver gray of the suit material soft in the dim lighting.

"Thank you, detective. I certainly hope you catch the man who did this."

I stood and offered my hand. "I will, Mr. Maggiano, I will."

"Why?" I asked. "They were good boys." I deliberately repeated his own words back to him. "They were legal."

He struggled, tried to pull his hand out of my grip. I simply waited until he eventually realized there was no way he'd win this. I was stronger.

He bowed his head and I let him go. All bravado left him, and he looked like used-up rag.

"How did you . . . ?"

"The oil in the lotion," I said. "The lavender scent is everywhere in the hotel, but the oil in that lotion is on your hands, and on Donny's body."

He seemed to accept my very simple explanation. Yes, it was that and then some.

"Did you get blood on your watch?" I asked, probing.

He glanced at his wrist then frowned. "How did you know that?"

"It's gold," I said. "Everything else you're wearing today is gray and shades of silver. Gold doesn't match and you look like the kind of man who would never be caught dead—"

He gasped, his eyes growing wide as I continued to explain. He'd given little away in his speech, but everything else pointed to him. The lotion, the watch, his nervousness. The fact that he'd been a concierge at the hotel where the other two men had worked. That he knew Donny's legal name—something that was only on his license paperwork.

"All I wanted to do was help them," he stated.

"Help them what?" I was genuinely confused.

"Get out of this life. This depravity. Selling their bodies to men and women old enough to be their fathers, their mothers."

"They were fae," I reminded him. "Donny was entering his second century. The others were older."

"They were boys," he insisted. "They bore the mark of Sodom on their wrists."

"You're part fae yourself. That's how you were able to remove the tattoo."

"My mother was half fae," Maggiano admitted. "She was once a licenser. She taught me the ritual to remove the marks."

"You drugged them?"

"With absinthe and sleeping pills." He sent me a pleading

look. "I didn't want them to suffer. After they were asleep, it was easy. A pillow on their faces, then I took them to the alley. Lay them gently down."

"Gently?" I slammed my hands against the polished wood of his desk. "Both Donny's legs were broken. His face and body were mutilated. That's brutality."

Maggiano shuddered and slumped into quiet sobs. "It was the only way," he managed to whisper. "The only way." He peered up at me again. "Don't you see? They would've just woken up."

Not trusting myself to do or say anything for fear I'd tear the man apart just like he had Donny and the others, I simply walked around behind the desk and with movements borne of long practice, cuffed Maggiano's wrist to his chair. "Detective Abrams is on his way," I explained. "You are under arrest for the murder of Donal ap Dylan, Bowen ap Calhoun, and Nolan ap Braden. You will be read your full rights upon processing." I shoved him into a corner and walked out of his office. I couldn't stand the cloying scent anymore, nor the sight of this man who'd killed so brutally, snuffed out three fae lives with little remorse.

I strolled out into the San Diego dawn, clearing my lungs of lavender and replacing it with the fresh seaborne air.

"He's inside," I said as a squad car pulled up and two officers sprang out, "cuffed to his chair." The officers pushed past me. I tucked my hands into my pockets and turned south. Six-fifteen. If I judged it right, I could make the three blocks to Richard Walker's just in time for pancakes.

ABOUT THE CONTRIBUTORS

Debra Ginsberg

GABRIEL R. BARILLAS grew up in Southern California. He began coming to San Diego on vacations, then on business, and finally stayed because of the girl. He divides his time between Los Angeles and one of the most beautiful places in the world, North San Diego County.

Greg Bear

ASTRID BEAR had a girlhood crush on Sherlock Holmes and Ellery Queen. She lived in San Diego from 1980 until 1987 and was married to San Diego native Greg Bear in the Jesse Shepard House, the setting for her story here.

Anne Fishbein

LISA BRACKMANN is a native San Diegan who worked her way through college thanks to a summer job at the world-famous San Diego Zoo. She currently lives in Venice, California, but is still a Padres and Chargers fan, though she's pretty sure that if either ever wins a championship, it is a sign of the coming Apocalypse. Her debut novel was 2009's *Rock Paper Tiger*, and "Don't Feed the Bums" is her first published short story.

Bill Kamenjarin

TAFFY CANNON has lived in a San Diego beach town for over twenty years and wrote all of her thirteen published mysteries within two miles of the Pacific Ocean. Her work has been nominated for Agatha and Macavity Best Novel awards, and *Blood Matters* won the San Diego Book Award for Best Mystery/Thriller.

David Clark

DIANE CLARK'S adopted hometown has been San Diego since 1977, and the military is a big part of it—from North Island in Coronado to Camp Pendleton. Her husband David is a second-generation San Diegan and she has drawn on deep family memories of World War II for this story. She has spent her entire working career as a writer or editor, and is a member of the Science Fiction Writers of America.

Ron Perry

DEBRA GINSBERG is the author of the novels *The Neighbors Are Watching*, *The Grift*, and *Blind Submission*, as well as three memoirs, including the best-selling *Waiting*. She has lived in San Diego for half her life, features it prominently in her fiction, and believes strongly that it lives up to its designation as America's Finest City.

David Mariotte

MARYELIZABETH HART is co-owner of Mysterious Galaxy, San Diego's genre bookstore for readers of stories of "martians, murder, magic, and mayhem." She works as the store's events coordinator and newsletter editor, and is also a reviewer for *Publishers Weekly*.

Ibarionex Perello

GAR ANTHONY HAYWOOD is the author of eleven crime novels, including six in the Aaron Gunner series, two in the Joe and Dottie Loudermilk series, and three stand-alone thrillers. His first Gunner short story, "And Pray Nobody Sees You," won both a Shamus and Anthony award for Best Short Story; the story is included in *Lyrics for the Blues*. His latest novel is the urban crime drama *Cemetery Road*.

Palmer Hughes

CAMERON PIERCE HUGHES is a native San Diegan who reviews books for *January Magazine*, *Crimespree Magazine*, the pop culture website CHUD.com, the *Philadelphia City Paper*, and other places. His first piece of fiction, "The War Zone," can be read in *Damn Near Dead 2* from Busted Flush Press. He has been an Internet journalist since 2006. And yes, he worships the sun and talks about the weather a lot. He hates rain.

Teri Dixon

MORGAN HUNT'S stint in the navy brought her to San Diego, where she lived for twenty-seven years, and where she set her Tess Camillo mystery series. She found work in the city as a technical writer, copywriter, video scriptwriter, instructional designer, and medical editor. Her poems have appeared in literary journals, and she's written for *Writer's Digest*. Now a resident of Ashland, Oregon, she is finishing a mystery screenplay.

KEN KUHLKEN'S novels have won the St. Martin's Press/PWA Best First P.I. Novel contest and been selected as finalists for a Hemingway Foundation/PEN Award and a Shamus Award for Best P.I. Novel. His California Century novels, featuring detective Tom Hickey and sons, are: *The Loud Adios*, *The Venus Deal*, *The Angel Gang*, *The Do-Re-Mi*, *The Vagabond Virgins*, and *The Biggest Liar in Los Angeles*.

MARTHA C. LAWRENCE grew up in a haunted house in Rancho Santa Fe, California. Inspired by her plentiful psychic experiences around San Diego County, she wrote the Elizabeth Chase mystery series, which earned nominations for the Edgar, Agatha, Anthony, Shamus, and Nero Wolfe awards. A former acquisitions editor for Simon & Schuster and Harcourt publishers, she is also the writing partner of best-selling business author Ken Blanchard.

MARIA LIMA is a writing geek with one foot in the real world and the other in the make-believe. Though her Blood Lines series is set in the Texas Hill Country, San Diego is also a city of her heart. She loves downtown and the crazy, awesome people who hang out there. If it weren't for that pesky thing called "needing to make a living," she'd be in San Diego every day.

JEFFREY J. MARIOTTE lived in San Diego for twenty-four years. During his time there, he managed one bookstore, opened independent specialty bookstore Mysterious Galaxy with his wife and another partner, helped build two publishing companies into industry powerhouses, fathered two children, and became a professional writer. He has published dozens of novels, even more comic books, and a double handful of short stories. For more information, visit jeffmariotte.com.

T. JEFFERSON PARKER'S eighteen novels include *Silent Joe* and *California Girl*, both winners of the Edgar Award for Best Novel. Parker is midway through a four-book Border Quartet that deals with how the drug wars in Mexico are impacting the United States. The first, *Iron River*, was published in 2010, and the second, *The Border Lords*, in early 2011. He has lived in San Diego County since January of 2000.

Nina Subin

LUIS ALBERTO URREA is the author of *The Queen of America*, a sequel to the best-selling *The Hummingbird's Daughter*. He is also the author of the best sellers *The Devil's Highway* and *Into the Beautiful North*. His story in *Phoenix Noir* won an Edgar Award. Urrea was born in Tijuana, Mexico, and moved to San Diego at the age of five. He spent much of his boyhood in National City and Shelltown.

Andy Andersen

DON WINSLOW is the author of fourteen novels, including *The Winter of Frankie Machine*, *The Dawn Patrol*, and *The Gentlemen's Hour*, all set in San Diego. When not writing, he likes driving up and down the Pacific Coast Highway on his quixotic yet noble search for the perfect fish taco. He lives on a small ranch in San Diego County.

Also available from Akashic Books

LOS ANGELES NOIR
edited by Denise Hamilton
360 pages, trade paperback original, $15.95
*Winner of Edgar and Southern California Independent Booksellers
Association awards; a *Los Angeles Times* best seller

Brand-new stories by: Michael Connelly, Janet Fitch, Susan Straight,
Héctor Tobar, Patt Morrison, Emory Holmes II, Robert Ferrigno, Gary
Phillips, Christopher Rice, Naomi Hirahara, Jim Pascoe, and others.

"These seventeen very different stories confirm just how many places
L.A. has become . . . Janet Fitch, as usual, operates at a scary level of
intensity. Her story, 'The Method,' opens with a string of zippy one-
liners that out-Chandler Chandler . . . I wanted to take my eyes off
the page and couldn't." —*Los Angeles Times Book Review*

LOS ANGELES NOIR 2: THE CLASSICS
edited by Denise Hamilton
336 pages, trade paperback, $15.95

Classic stories by: Raymond Chandler, James Ellroy, Leigh Brackett,
James M. Cain, Chester Himes, Walter Mosley, Naomi Hirahara,
Jervey Tervalon, Kate Braverman, Yxta Maya Murray, and others.

"In the 15 tales collected by Denise Hamilton for *Los Angeles Noir 2:
The Classics,* we enjoy a guided tour of urban crime in a city that some
would call 'ground zero' for pulp fiction . . . *Los Angeles Noir 2* offers
nothing short of great entertainment for lovers of crime fiction."
—*El Paso Times*

BOSTON NOIR
edited by Dennis Lehane
240 pages, trade paperback original, $15.95
*Finalist for Edgar, Anthony, Macavity, and Shamus awards

Brand-new stories by: Dennis Lehane, Stewart O'Nan, Patricia Powell,
John Dufresne, Lynne Heitman, Don Lee, Russ Aborn, J. Itabari
Njeri, Jim Fusilli, Brendan DuBois, and Dana Cameron.

"In the best of the eleven stories in this outstanding entry in Akashic's
noir series, characters, plot, and setting feed off each other like flames
and an arsonist's accelerant . . . [T]his anthology shows that noir can
thrive where Raymond Chandler has never set foot."
—*Publishers Weekly* (starred review)